Marilyn Bowering

is the author of one previous novel, *To All Appearances a Lady* (1989), as well as several books of poetry. She was born in Winnipeg and grew up in Victoria, British Columbia. She has lived and worked in Greece, Scotland, Spain and Canada, and now makes her home in Sooke, BC.

From the British reviews for *Visible Worlds*:

'Marilyn Bowering's second novel, *Visible Worlds*, is a *tour de force*, lavish in its scale, complication and information . . . Bowering unteases the epic story of three families over 30 years, across three continents and through two wars. With a fine balance of coolness and conviction, she pulls it off.

The narrator is Albrecht Storr, the son of German emigrés living in Canada. His story is a web of catastrophe, politics and romance from the start. It is 1934, and while Albrecht and his friend Nate Bone spy on a neighbour's séance, Nate's baby sister is scalded and dies . . . [meanwhile] Albrecht's twin, the inscrutable Gerhard, is sent back to Cologne to study music, is enlisted by the Nazis and ends up in a Soviet labour camp . . . Albrecht's account is interspersed with the story of Fika, the surviving member of the Soviet "First All Union Conference of Women" expedition to the North Pole. It is 1960, the height of the Cold War, and Fika heads for the West. Little by little, her memories knit her, too, into his story . . . The fast-action plot has a subtle backdrop, raising questions about the flimsiness of identity in the midst of political, economic and social forces. Characters casually lose their name, parents, nationality and home. Location becomes a matter of a dateline or a sighting of the sun. Horror and guilt are remembered in whispers, secrets and dreams, like an atmosphere which everyone is forced to continue to breathe. *Visible Worlds* is written with such panache and is so much fun to read that it seems churlish to resist its more fantastic moments. It is a wonderful piece of storytelling.'   LAVINIA GREENLAW, *Independent on Sunday*

'*Visible Worlds* is quite unlike anything I have ever read, and a fantastic antidote to the minimalism or fine-writing-without-events that can make some recent fiction so arid. Here we get a huge and richly detailed properly pageturning story, surprisingly knotted and plotted, magical and vivid. A vast and intricately wrought romance with its epic journeys into extremis and ice and its recurring themes of children lost and children found. A kind of alchemical intelligence illuminates the normally invisible filaments of friendship, love and truth – and their shadows of sibling rivalry, infidelity and secrets – as they thread through this indissolubly linked cast of close neighbours from the Canadian prairies in the mid thirties backwards and forwards in time and place – even space – from pre-war Central Europe to the Arctic in the Cold War.'   LIZ LOCHHEAD

'A masterful novel that grips from the very beginning . . . In recent years there has been a surge of successful Canadian writers whose diverse styles have often been linked by an incredible talent for storytelling. Marilyn Bowering is the latest author to join this prestigious rank . . . *Visible Worlds* is a fantastic and epic read that should carry Bowering to the top.'   *Leeds Guide*

From the American and Canadian reviews:

'A pan-generational journey that spans the northern reaches of the globe and the fire, ice and eccentricities of the lonely human heart. Set variously in Soviet Siberia, prewar Germany, wartorn Korea and Bowering's native Canada, this is a tale of interwoven families struggling to save themselves from the forces of history, raw accident and their own odd passions.'   *Wall Street Journal*

'The Canadian poet Marilyn Bowering's latest novel is a vast, sprawling feast of a book. You finish reading it glad of the experience, aware that some of the ingredients were fabulous, even astonishing.'
KATHARINE WEBER, *New York Times*

'I read Marilyn Bowering's second novel, *Visible Worlds*, during one of the hottest weeks I can remember in Seattle – and I couldn't get rid of my goosebumps . . . Freezing temperatures and vast snow fields convey numbing isolation; eerily beautiful meteor showers and the aurora borealis touch on themes of magnetism and connection to place . . . Bowering has an amazing ability to weave many stories and events together . . . *Visible Worlds* reminds us we are all connected to each other and to our histories – and that our lives should be viewed as much more than just the world we can see.'
Seattle Times

'Any one of the characters could fill up a novel; together, they form a powerful, sweet, sad chorus.'
Los Angeles Times

'A lyrical modern fable . . . The otherworldly, almost folkloric sweetness of Bowering's narrative casts a redemptive glow over this brooding tale of universal grief and suffering.'
Boston Globe

'Canadian writer Bowering's second novel memorably chronicles the toll taken by wars (the World Wars, Korea, and the Cold War) and random accidents upon three families . . . Like Pat Barker, Bowering is claiming territory that has long been a masculine preserve: martial battle and its long-term consequences . . . A narrative high-wire act, as well as a subtle meditation on chance, luck, and inevitability for all of which war offers the perfect if drastic laboratory.'
Kirkus Reviews

'Like her fellow Canadian Michael Ondaatje, Marilyn Bowering is primarily a poet, and her background shows: in the book's lovely imagery, in its striking economy of language . . . This lyric compression gives the novel an almost violent intensity. With its complex web of settings, time periods, and plots, often connected by the most tenuous of threads, *Visible Worlds* feels like a fever dream yanked straight from the collective 20th-century unconscious.'
Amazon.com

'A shimmering, powerful story about the intertwined lives of three Winnipeg families at mid-century, this novel by a noted Canadian poet evokes both great public pain and private human beauty during a time of profound world tension . . . Bowering writes with a poet's condensed, imagistic prose . . . Her language is dense and resonant, yet easily readable . . . A richly imagined, assured work of delicate beauty.'
Portland Oregonian

'Bowering maps the overlapping territory between science and spiritualism, love and madness . . . Bowering's characters prove so compelling that few would regard the overabundance of imagery or story lines as anything but a wealth of poetic reflection on tragedy and human endurance.'
Publishers Weekly

'A novel of profound imagination and stylish writing despite its many complications, this work belongs in most contemporary literature collections.'
Library Journal

'The reader reaches the end with the sense of having undertaken a long, complex, enthralling journey in the company of a throng of tragic, ordinary, brave human beings whom he has grown to love. It is astounding that Bowering has been able to chronicle so much in what is a relatively short book.'
ALBERTO MANGUEL, *Toronto Globe & Mail*

'*Visible Worlds* matters. It is darkly ambitious, somewhat compulsive and immediately complex. The tale is held together and moved forward by the passion of the voices telling the story – or rather by the desire of the story to reveal itself, to end uncertainty.'
Vancouver Sun

VISIBLE WORLDS

MARILYN
BOWERING

Flamingo
An Imprint of HarperCollinsPublishers

Flamingo
An Imprint of HarperCollins*Publishers*
77–85 Fulham Palace Road,
Hammersmith, London W6 8JB

Published by Flamingo 1999
9 8 7 6 5 4 3 2 1

First published in Great Britain by
Flamingo 1998

First published in Canada by
HarperCollins*Publishers* 1997

Author photograph by © Lincoln Clarkes

ISBN 0 00 655113 0

Set in Adobe Garamond

Printed and bound in Great Britain by
Clays Ltd, St Ives plc

For my father

Our lives are regulated by the heart, that fiery star palpitating in the dark of our bodies, suspended there in its cage of flesh and bone, as strong and mysterious as the stars above, and obeying laws more complicated than the laws we ourselves make.

Marguerite Yourcenar, *The Abyss*

If only we knew what was right, then, he argued, the problems of morality would be comparatively simple; and in quest of that knowledge he never ceased his constant examination of himself and others.

Plato, speaking of Socrates

I have a sort of faith in God, but I can't believe he came down and made wheelbarrows in a shop.

Alasdair Gray, *Lanark*

The problem is, of course, that the meaning of this strangeness is not manifest, it is hidden. . . . Miracles are not proof, they are not even evidence, and any attempt to see them in that simple light will always render them . . . ambiguous or disgusting.

But they may be signposts pointing out of the world of facts.

Bryan Appleyard,
writing on *Powers of Darkness, Powers of Light,*
by John Cornwell

It is only shallow people who do not judge by appearances. The mystery of the world is the visible, not the invisible.

Oscar Wilde

FIRES OF MAGNETISM

My father is an Odd Fellow. My brother, Gerhard, and I are—were—twins. I am Albrecht, named by my mother for her father. I am sitting in the stadium with my parents, on this early summer's night in 1960, watching the Shriners' annual charity football game. There are fifty Shriners, members of a parade band, seated in front of us. They wear red fezzes, harem trousers, and embroidered jackets. One of the Shriners has a black mamba coiled around his waist. In the breaks between plays, he rises to his feet, turns to face us, and doodles a few bars of "Little Egypt" on his flute. The tassel on his fez shakes, the snake lifts its head and looks around sleepily, making the orphans, who accompany my mother, giggle. My parents, resplendent in their respective Odd Fellow and Rebekah jewels, exchange conspiratorial, superior smiles. My father's mistress—my mother-in-law, Madame Pince-Jones—seated between my parents, frowns.

The Reds have just scored on the Blues, tying the game. The

Red quarterback, Acker, kicks off to Hoffberger, who runs the ball back to the Blue's thirty-yard line. Nathanial Bone, the Blue's quarterback, whom I've known all my life, steps back from the line of scrimmage and, under pressure from the Red line, yet appearing as if he has all the time in the world out there—they don't call him the Happy Wanderer for nothing—rears up, throws the ball, and hits Kimpchuk on the button. Kimpchuk, flying down the field from the Red forty-five, is in the clear, and he keeps on going all the way across the goal line. We leap to our feet, cheering. It takes some seconds for us to register that Nathanial Bone is now lying prone and unmoving at midfield. Nate's mother, Bella, who has flown back from Europe (where she has been collecting war orphans) especially for the game, inches closer to my mother. From her throat come the soft beginnings of a whinny. I put my arm around Mary, my wife.

The stadium falls silent. This is the prairie. Land and sky stretch away as if there were nothing but sharp edges to the world. If you tipped the plate northward, you'd slide into the Arctic. Southward, there's the Gulf of Mexico. I look up as I feel a chill wind. The stars stand out like individual snowflakes showing through a black cloth. It is then, without warning, that one of the stars tears free and plummets downward, scattering firefly yellow sparks, looming larger and larger until it resolves itself into a brilliant, spinning white sphere. The sphere slowly descends to the field and covers the body of Nathanial Bone; it stays a few moments while the universe seems to pulse in and out, and we all hold our breath, too frightened and stunned to do anything. After a few more moments, the sphere lifts, flicks itself into the pool of the sky, and disappears. We breathe a long sigh, left blinking through the after-image of light, staring up through its black and white and the raw yolk-yellow searchlights that have sprung up in pursuit. A lone Civil Defense siren howls its solitary grief. Few of the fifteen thousand spectators notice Sweets Christmas, a Blue's tackle and one of Nate's only close friends, take Nate's body in his arms and carry it to the sidelines. But I notice, and I run down to help Sweets remove Nate's helmet, touch the damp skin beneath the number 27 jersey, and feel fruitlessly for his heartbeat.

We remove Nate's boots, revealing his size fourteen long and slender feet. The boots are custom-made. Only those of us who have known him since childhood know how much he suffered with those feet. They have given him trouble all through his career; and after he came out of the labor camp, his toes swollen from repeated frostbite, I thought he'd never play again. I check and, as I expect, inside one of the boots is a good luck telegram from Nate's father, Bill Bone. I put the yellow paper in my pocket. But there is something else in the boot as well—a sheet of crinkled, folded onionskin, tucked well into the toe. I open it out. It is a map dated February 1951 and signed by my brother, Gerhard. *Gerhard.* I turn the map round, trying to make sense of it, reading the words penciled there. *Novo-Sibirsk. The River Yenesei. Lake Baikal. The Lena River.* It is a map of Siberia. A map drawn by Gerhard! I would know my brother's handiwork anywhere.

I put the map into my pocket and help Sweets move the body to the dressing room. I wait there, thinking over what I have seen, while Sweets runs for the team doctor. Gerhard has also sketched the North Pacific coastline, marking *Cape Deschnev* on the Bering Strait, and *St. Lawrence Island*, the stepping stone to Alaska. It is so near to the U.S. coastline that there are many defections there, men jumping overboard from Soviet fishing boats and swimming ashore. Most of them are unlucky. Nobody wants an international incident; nobody wants to trigger the Bomb. The American soldiers grill the defectors, then call the Russians to take them back.

I had been there once myself, in 1956, a messenger for Mary's bosses, flying right over Esquimaux in skin boats chasing after whales. I was supposed to pick up Nate the day they brought him out. They'd said they wanted him to see a familiar face. They'd said there would be two of them—two of the Korean POWs who'd stayed behind in North Korea and crossed over to the Soviets— but when I arrived there was only Nate, waving a white handkerchief from the deck of the trawler. I landed the Goose, and watched as the Americans filmed his departure. From the air, I'd seen the boat's litter of equipment, and too many men, wearing jackets with too many pockets, stretched out smoking cigarettes.

"What about the other one?" I asked Nate when he climbed aboard. I wanted to get out of there as quickly as possible. It hadn't been my idea to come.

"You know the Russians, Albrecht. They changed their minds." That was all he said. He scarcely looked at me; I don't think he was too happy to see me, and there wasn't a word about when we'd last met.

I shrugged. I didn't much care. If I'd needed anything to cement my feelings about Nate at that point, I had found it in the film of the POW confessions. It—and he—had turned my stomach, whatever people said afterward about brainwashing. I guess, for Nate, the workers' paradise just hadn't turned out.

Nate was thin and pale and looked like the last candle end had burned down inside him. We didn't talk much. We'd had our chance to say everything on our minds in that cave in Korea, and even after five years, as far as I was concerned, there wasn't anything new to add. I would never forgive him, although I had made my peace with what had to be. I had made the trip only to please Mary, who could, it seemed, forgive anything.

We flew back toward Alaska. A whale surfaced near an iceberg. It dived in front of the Eskimo boats, and when it came up again, it spouted red. It dived once more, making a turn for the frontier. For a border between the two most powerful countries in the world, there wasn't much to it.

I look at the map again. Who was the man who hadn't turned up? Could it possibly have been my brother?

Over the past few months, Nate and I had managed, at last, to talk. Maybe he'd seen his death coming, maybe we both needed to try to understand what had happened and why, if only to go on, if only to make better use of the time we had left. We'd spoken to the others who were part of our story—my mother and father, Madame Pince-Jones and Pru and Mary, and Nate's parents, Bella and Bill. They'd all had something to add. I'd thought I knew all I needed to know. But I hadn't considered Gerhard, not with any idea that he might have survived. Gerhard was a closed book. He'd been gone so long, I'd believed I was the only one who even really remembered him.

Gerhard, you should have seen how the ice looked from the plane that day. As if somebody had squeezed drops of color onto it and let them melt. It made me think of the music you played—how it could spread right through you and make you know that somewhere things were better, that the world was, in fact, a marvelous place. I never told you how proud I was of you, or that I loved you.

On the back of the map, there is a sketch of our Winnipeg neigborhood. Our address. The names of our neighbors. What am I to do with it? Gerhard disappeared in 1945, at the end of the war. Where did the map come from? Who was it made for? How did Nate get it? Why did he say nothing?

I look at Nate's face. It is closed over, smug with unanswered questions. Questions I didn't know I could have asked.

I close my eyes and try to remember the details: somewhere in the past, there must be an answer. Nate has tracked his long boots through all our lives. All I have to do is start with him.

1

THE DRIFT
OF LIFE

Let him at least note,
That my heart was bloody young,
That strong, like fear, was my will to live,
Strong and crazed,
Like my final day.

"Day Grows Darker," Leyb Kvitko

APRIL 25, 1960

The ice was shining a thousand notes of blue and green in the
brilliant sunshine, and the sun warmed her back as Fika (she'd
been named Elektrifikatsiya—Fika—in the labor camp) worked

quickly to pack her gear. Tent, sleeping bag, clothing, food, medical and navigational supplies were put away expertly. The pack weighed thirty-five kilograms, but she had carried forty kilograms on the longer part of the journey with no difficulty. She was not concerned about her physical condition: she had gained weight and was fully acclimatized, she had suffered no serious frostbite or other injury or illness, and, most important, she now had fifty-five days of polar experience to her credit. Although, according to conventional wisdom, her chances of survival had diminished because she was now alone, she knew that her motivation had increased tremendously: perhaps that counted for more. It would take her about a month, all being well, to ski the rest of the way over the icecap to Canada.

Yesterday, there had been the three of them: herself, Marina Pavlovna Cherskaia, and Ekaterina Ivanovna Pronchishcheva, close friends as well as members of the First All Union Conference of Women polar expedition. They had put in a difficult day, plagued by fog because of the warm temperatures, and making long detours around polynias, or ocean lakes, that had opened in the icecap. But when they had erected their tent on a clear stretch of windswept ice, they had been elated. Fika's sun sights showed that the change in the sun's angle was constant, indicating they were at the North Pole. It only remained to have their position confirmed.

They had warmed the radio batteries in hot water, looking for extra power to reach their base at the meteorological station on Severnaya Zemlya, now over a hundred kilometers away. Then Marina and Ekaterina had gone outside with the radio, while Fika had stayed behind in the tent to cook their meal. Fika had heard their laughter, suddenly freed after the days of strain, as they moved away to stretch out the antenna wires. Then there was silence, or as much silence as there could be within the perpetual moan of the shifting ice. But this sound, to which they were all accustomed, was broken by something new—several sudden, sharp bangs, and a roar that went on and on, louder and louder, in an eerie screech and wail that seemed to howl up through the floor of the tent itself. Fika had covered her ears, waiting for it to stop, wondering if she were about to die, for she knew that it was luck, as much as careful siting of the camps, that had kept them safe on the tide-, current-, and wind-driven icecap so far.

When the noise and shaking had stopped, she put on her boots and went outside, searching the thin white line of the horizon for any sign of her companions. She found a few boot tracks in the dry granular snow, but these only led to a broken antenna and to Marina's fox-fur gloves, dropped on the ice, it appeared, when Marina had lunged for the radio as it pitched into a suddenly opened lead. Why, or how Ekaterina had followed, or whether she had fallen first, was impossible to say. Now there was only the mute testimony of a new ridge of pressure ice, raised ten meters high as the separating pans had slammed shut over the gap into which the women had fallen, ton after ton of ice smashing and rearing with raw force.

Fika walked the length of the ridge to open water. Wafer-thin ice was already forming. Salt flowers, delicately crystalline, began to appear as she looked, but nowhere here, or wherever she turned, were her friends.

She lay in her sleeping bag in the tent, her senses completely numb, until the drone of a passing plane roused her. She wondered for a moment if it could be looking for them, but quickly dismissed the idea . The recovery plane would not put in an appearance until after the women's successful arrival at the pole had been confirmed. Then the whole world would know of their achievement. There would be photographers and television cameras—a victory here, now, at the North Pole, they'd been told, would be as significant as the victories already achieved in space. Her friends, both seconded from the Soyuz space program— Ekaterina, a biologist, and Marina, an astrophysicist—had commented that women had died for *those* achievements. And now, on the eve of success for this expedition, so had they. And for what? To show the world the "triumph" of Soviet woman-hood? Fika hoped the plane, likely Canadian or American on a regular defense patrol, had not seen her or the commas of Marina's gloves that she had left where they lay, as if Marina might come back to claim them. She was grateful for the cautious thinking that had supplied the team with camouflage gear—a white double-nylon tent and white cotton outer clothing, both reversible to orange—so that the surprise of their achievement might be complete. For if she were picked up by the Westerners now, it was more than likely she would be returned to the Soviet Union. Unless she was worth something to them. Which she would be only if she became the first woman, the first person, to cross the icecap to the New World alone.

There was a time for mourning, and it would come, but it wasn't now, she thought—not now when the door for which she'd prayed had swung wide open in front of her. She just had to step through, and go on.

As she ate the dinner that she had prepared, determined to waste nothing, she thought about the time she had spent with her two companions. They had wintered-over together at Severnaya Zemlya, training in expedition techniques, and building stamina until their scheduled departure at the beginning of March. They had experimented with food and tents and clothing, learning about each other's abilities and limits, until they had found which combinations worked best for them as a team. They had spent days and nights in the ice and snow desert, with no other living companions than the ivory gulls that drew parabolas on the pale sky; and they had lived with the fear and elation brought by surviving in a world bounded by treacherous frozen seas, and ranged by the polar bear.

The other women, both from Moscow, southwesterners, had only seen the Arctic in winter, but they had listened carefully as Fika spoke about the teeming seabird colonies, established on the great high sea cliffs in the spring, full of auks, kittiwakes, guillemots, and razorbills; the ice breeding grounds of the walruses, thousands upon thousands living among ice floes in the shallow waters off the coasts, and giving birth on the ice; and the tundra, spread with white, pink, and yellow flowering plants and shrubs. Later, in summer, the reindeer came, feeding on grasses, lichens, and sedges prior to their massive southward migration to winter in the taiga. During breaks from her medical studies, Fika had worked on a reindeer farm at Oymyakon, about nine hundred and fifty kilometers east of her home city of Yakutsk. She had traveled by sledge and on skis, living in a tent heated only by a small portable stove, even as they were to do during the expedition. At Oymyakon, she explained, the reindeer supplied milk and food and skins for clothing, and also hauled freight and people as they journeyed from one feeding ground to another. It was a partnership, a companionship as old as humankind. Marina and Ekaterina had teased Fika about preferring the tent to the multi-story buildings, piped-in gas, hot and cold running water of civilization; and about liking the reindeer more than her friends. But they, too, had come to love Siberia, and had found in it a space that mirrored not only loneliness, but freedom.

Even Yakutsk, where, until recently, Fika had practiced medicine, with its sawmills, tanneries, and metal-working shops, its deadening ugliness, was transformed in Fika's account. She had recounted her life there, spent in the town and along the shores of the Lena River, after her release from the labor camp in 1956. It was a life of extremes: a climate with temperatures that differed over seventy degrees between winter and summer; a landscape that included snowy plateaus tracked by white foxes and hares, and, littering the shores of the Lena River, even in summer, giant blocks of ice, fifteen to thirty meters high, that Fika climbed for pleasure.

Fika could only hope that her friends would understand what had pushed her to do what she was doing now, saying good-bye to her country.

After dinner, she sorted efficiently through all the belongings, taking a dry spare sleeping bag, dry clothing, and the lightest, most compact food supplies.

She was short of fuel, but with the warmer temperatures, if they held, she would need the stove only for cooking. All the spare gear she dragged to the lead and dumped, saving for last the notes and diaries that each woman had kept, and that were to be surrendered for examination on their return from the expedition. She resisted the urge to read them—there would be few truths in documents written for official eyes—but hugged them close for a moment as if they, by some magic, still retained the spirits of the dead. Then she consigned her own writings to the small pile and threw away the lot.

Back in the tent, she braced her mind against self-pity, and readied herself for sleep. She was twenty-five years old. She had left no unfinished business. Time would take care of her, one way or another.

Now, squinting in the morning brightness, Fika shouldered her pack. Gloves and socks, still damp from the day before when she had slipped on a stepping stone of ice in open water, were drying out tied to the pack. Her fox-fur hood and her goggles were within close reach. She slid her sealskin boots, stiff until warmed, into the bindings of the birchwood skis. The skis were made of carefully crafted thin strips and were tough and flexible, with the points bent upward and held by lengths of catgut. They were of a type she had always used.

The frozen sea mirrored the sky's orange and blue as a few clouds drifted along the horizon. In the distance, a skirl of wind shifted snow along the ice. She would have to keep a close eye on the sastrugi, the patterns of drifts: they were the best navigational tool she had. The sun, the sextant, the stars, and her trail sense were others. Now, to begin. Fifty minutes of skiing, then a rest. Lifting and sliding the skis along the ice, and praying that the ice would hold.

2

HUMAN
MAGNETISM

1 9 3 4

Nathanial's father, Bill Bone, who is almost never at home, is a wild animal trainer for the circus. Nate's mother, Bella, had been a bareback rider. Bella is not a handsome woman now, but you can tell that she must have been good-looking in her youth. You know this partly because she shows you photographs of herself in tights and spangles and talks about her many admirers, and partly because she looks as if she's lost something she never expected to lose. "She is in mourning for her beauty," says my brother, Gerhard, who is a musician and reads German poetry. I don't know, but she and Bill must have made a striking couple at one time. Bill is still impressive, when he turns up, although he is a drinker and is beginning to show a drinker's nose.

Neither Nate, nor his small sister, Lily, takes closely after their parents. Nate has his father's black hair and eyes, his father's tawny Cree Indian coloring, but where Bill is tall and bulky, his head like a hassock with bones showing through, Nate is finely built, with long slim arms and legs, and with a round, punched-in, elfish face almost without cheekbones. Lily is dark-skinned, too, her color the exact deep shade of the cedar chest, polished to burning, that my father made for my mother before they married. Bella has pale skin the hue of yellowed curtains. She broke her back in a fall from a horse, and walks with a limp. Maybe it is pain that makes her seem old and marks out black circles beneath her eyes. Lily's eyes are green like her mother's, but her hair is blond, not brown, and it stands up in a circle around her head so that she looks like an angel in one of my mother's German books.

The Bone house is situated next to ours to the west; the Fergusson house is on the other side, to the east. They are wooden houses like all the others on the street, narrow fronted and with two storys. The lots are long and thin. When Gerhard and I come home from school, we enter from the back lane, unless it is winter and the snow is deep; then we have to walk down the shoveled tunnel to the front door.

Gerhard, as always, is a little ahead of me as we go inside. I can never quite catch up to him: he has my mother's long legs, and her energy; things come easily to him. Today, my mother is emptying her kitchen shelves of china. She has crates of it, left behind by her family at the time they left, in a rush, for Germany at the outbreak of the Great War.

"Is Nathanial with you?" she asks. "Bella has been in and out looking for him all afternoon. She is like a drawer that doesn't know if it is open or shut." My mother's German accent is emphasized by her peculiar short tongue. It is a delicate, ladylike tongue that we often beg her to show. Sometimes, if she's in a good mood, she obliges. Its lozenge of pink candy is tied nearly the whole length to the floor of her mouth. It gives her an occasional lisp.

"No, we haven't seen him," says Gerhard. I look at my brother in surprise. He has just told a lie—and Gerhard always tells the truth. Gerhard is a clear melody moving inexorably forward in time. But the truth is that Nate had walked with us nearly all the way home, then had stopped to talk to Shadow Barnes, whose pet rabbit was ill. Nate had a way with animals. Shadow was asking his advice. I guessed "animals" ran in Nate's family.

"If you do see him, tell him to go straight home." My mother finishes clearing the shelf and wipes its surface down with lye. Today, her hands are as red as her hair, her one vanity. She keeps it long, against the current fashion, coiled in braids on top of her head. She says she is the "last leaf on the tree." We go through to the hall, Gerhard shoving me from behind, and upstairs to our room.

"What did you say that for?"

"Say what?" Gerhard flops down on his bed, the movement of air sending my model airplanes, suspended from the ceiling, into a spin. Above Gerhard's bed is a set of wings and claws, belonging to some large bird he found out on the prairie. He lies back with his head at the foot of the bed and his feet on the wall, his sock-covered toes stroking the feathers. He pokes his tongue in and out of his cheek, rooting for debris. He is afraid of tooth decay. He brushes his teeth six times a day.

I put my hand up to still the trembling planes. "About Nate. Why did you say that about Nate?" I look down at him. Although we are twins, we are very different. I am shorter and brown-haired, like my father. My mother calls us "trolls from the Bavarian forest." I know, and my father knows, this isn't a compliment, but we pretend to like it. We play it up, hunching our shoulders to our ears and stretching out rubbery lips. Gerhard is tall and straight, all Prussian: his appearance is a combination of snow, ice, and sun. He lifts a pale eyebrow.

"Think, Albrecht," he says. "Even you can think." He begins to hum a tune. He always does this when he doesn't want to speak to me. It is irritating. He hums, and strokes his elegant curved nose. There are plans for Gerhard to study music in Germany and to live with my mother's family there. As far as I know, there are no plans for me.

I rev up my brain. But all I can think of are the crisscrossing shadows of the airplanes and how much I want to learn to fly. Hard on that dream tail the rest of my fantasies. These have to do with the Fergusson sisters next door. I am going to marry one of them.

"What day is it, dolt?" Gerhard has stopped humming.

"Tuesday."

"What day of the month, stupid?"

"If I'm so stupid why ask me? . . . Oh! . . . Ah! . . ." Now I understand. Once a month, like clockwork, so regular that you'd think the letters had been written in advance, there comes a letter from Bill Bone to Bella from wherever he is. On these days, the dark circles beneath her eyes are darker, her green eyes grow red with weeping. On these days, Bella comes to sit in my mother's kitchen. The two of them put their heads close together and talk for hours.

But Bella can only do this if Nate looks after Lily, his little sister. Lily is too small to be left alone or to hear what her mother says about her father.

"I don't want to miss my lesson," says Gerhard. He plays staccato with his tongue on the roof of his mouth. I nod. The language lessons are important. My mother and Gerhard have begun to work on German every day before supper. Gerhard is to leave for Cologne in the summertime. "I don't want to sound like an idiot when I get there. They won't think I belong." I know what he means. "To understand is to equal" is one of my mother's favorite sayings.

I put my hand on my heart, mimicking our mother quoting poetry. "*Oh, how many times have I, striding through South German cities, / All of a sudden felt inside out, had to stand still; / Been here before. In some primordial age, my being with the same spirit. . . .*" I think it's funny, and I laugh until my stomach aches and I can't stand, and I can't get my breath. But Gerhard isn't amused. He sits up, frowns, his face all chipped angles. He puts his finger to his lips.

"Listen!" he commands. I follow as he bends to the airvent, beside the dresser, that connects our room to the kitchen vent above the stove.

"But I love him! I love him!" issues forth a thin, weepy voice. The sound is wet, like a strip of seaweed.

"Enough is enough, Bella. You can't go on like this. Think of the children! You wield the founding hand of motherhood!"

"But Friedl, what will I do?" We can hear Bella snuffling into her handkerchief.

"She's found Nate," says Gerhard crossly, sitting back on his heels. "He didn't spend much time with that rabbit."

"He doesn't mind watching Lily. He likes it." I don't mind it either. Lily is different. Being with Lily makes me feel good. I wish she were my sister.

"Bella'll be here forever," says Gerhard. We lean forward again, ears to the grate.

"But Friedl, he has always loved me!" wails Bella. "He can't have stopped!" Gerhard and I exchange grimaces. We are in for a long haul. She'll tell for the hundredth time how Bill Bone fell in love with her when she, Bella, was standing on her white pony, Poodles, barefoot, as Poodles cantered around the ring. She shot a popgun rifle at a cage of pigeons held by a dwarf. The pigeons flew to Bella's shoulders and perched there. The dwarf caught the horse's tail and swung up behind, scattering the pigeons in a cloud, as Bella balanced on one leg. Why this had impressed Bill Bone enough to make him suspend all judgment and fall in love was something I had never pretended to understand.

"I know, I know," murmurs my mother, comfortingly. Adding, to preempt the expected flow, "It was a long time ago, though, Bella."

"Oh no," says Gerhard, as the weeping breaks forth afresh. He can see his lesson floating away on Bella's tears. As, I suppose, can our mother. She sighs. We can hear her pouring water into a pan and moving dishes around.

"It's because of my limp," laments Bella.

"No, Bella, certainly not. You mustn't say that. It is not your fault. You have done nothing wrong. Bill Bone is a drifter." There is a pause. "He will never settle down. He is a womanizer. He is no good. You'd be better off without him."

This is new. Normally my mother takes pains to reassure Bella that it is only a matter of time before Bill sees the light and returns to his natural duties as a husband and father.

"How can you say that, Friedl?" cries Bella. "You don't know him the way I do. He is a good man, kind, sensitive, he is the father of my children. I love him!"

"You live in fairyland, Bella, you think the fairies will come to save you," says my mother brutally. "He is not coming back, not this time. You can wait for him as long as you like, until cows don't eat grass. You should divorce him and be done with it." We hear Bella's sharp intake of breath. Divorce! People don't divorce. Movie stars divorce. Our kind of people stick with, they stand by.

"I thought you were my friend!" cries Bella, shocked. "Nobody knows what I have suffered behind closed doors."

"I am your friend," says my mother. "That is why I am saying this. We will always stick by you and your family." A chair scrapes harshly across the floor.

"I am going next door," says Bella, with dignity. "I'm sure Madame Pince-Jones, *my friend, who has a warm heart*, will find some way to help me."

Gerhard taps my shoulder and points to the window. We see a pair of boots and a set of thin legs dangling. This occurrence is not as strange as it may sound. The houses are so close to each other that you can walk the roofs with one foot on each of the neighboring gutters. Directly below our window is the porch roof. From there, it is a short way to the ground. There is a thunk and a thud as the feet and legs—followed by the rest of Nathanial Bone—drop and land safely first on the porch roof and then on the earth below. There is a roof vent next to the chimney. Nate has been listening, too. This is both normal and essential since adults never tell us anything, although I wonder where Lily is while Nate is here, and what she is doing all by herself.

The front door slams and we hear our father come in. We return to our listening post.

"What did you say to Bella?" he asks. "She ran by me like a scalded cat." We hear him taking off his work clothes—shirt and pants, hopping as he removes his socks—and dropping them all into the copper boiler on top of the stove. Our father works in the St. Boniface slaughterhouse. Our mother won't let him have supper unless he first gets rid of the smell.

"I said she should get a divorce."

"You *what*?" We freeze at the vent, worried about what might happen next. Not that our father is a violent man—he is no Bill Bone—but he does have strong beliefs. He is a Lutheran and an Odd Fellow and, most important, a practitioner of Personal Magnetism. His standards are unusual but high. We hear a peculiar noise, a kind of growl, not, as we first think, of outrage, but of something even more rare in our house at this time. Our father is laughing. The sound rumbles up from below, catching us by surprise. It is so contagious that Gerhard and I have to smother our helpless faces in pillows.

"Gerhard! Your lesson!" Our mother is back to normal. I can see her face at the bottom of the stairs as I peer round the corner of our room. It looms, masklike, in the dimness. Bands of steel polish her tones. I sometimes wonder what she was like when younger, if she was more like us, less as I sometimes think of her now, a mountaineer constantly assaulting the unclimbable. On her way to the Matterhorn. Or the Eiger. Somewhere few women have ever been. My brother is gathering his books from the desk in the room behind me. Gerhard is her main project. If he is the peak, then I am the valley. "Albrecht, you come, too. Your father needs you."

"Coming." I think more about my mother as I descend. Her red hair glows in the lamplight, and her face falls almost in soft lines. Does she love my father? Does she love me? I watch as she puts her arm around Gerhard and guides him into the kitchen. Now that her expression has loosened, Gerhard's has taken on remoteness and coldness. Push and pull. That is the game they play. Giving and withholding affection. I envy Gerhard this: he knows how to be grown-up, how not to show what he feels all the time. Not like me: my face is a mirror. Clouds and sun stroll across it for everyone to see, getting me in trouble. He will have no problems with women—he can even manage my mother. He will get to exactly where he wants to go.

A few minutes later, I am in the parlor with my father. He sits on the sofa, dressed only in his underwear, reading the newspaper. It is my job, as the cold weather worsens, to massage away the pain of his rheumatism with pine oil. The bottle floats in a pan of hot water that is set, with a towel, on the side table. I do not mind this task as I am aware of how important his health is to all of us. He is one of the few men in the neighborhood still in work. The unemployed play volleyball in the back lane in warm weather, and skate with the kids on the hockey rinks in winter. There is something disturbing to me about seeing grown men acting like children. At least, unlike most of them, we will never have to go on relief, even if my father were to lose his job. We belong to the Odd Fellowship, which practices Friendship, Love, and Truth. Odd Fellows and Rebekahs take care of each other. We are commanded, among other things, to relieve the distressed. We have another advantage in our father's knowledge of Personal

Magnetism, although I do not understand exactly how it works. Personal Magnetism, my father says, is the mental equipment that can get you safely through your life.

The newspaper my father is reading is the *Volkischer Beobachter*. It is a Nazi Party paper sent by my mother's brother, my uncle Fritz, to assist Gerhard with his language studies. Hitler came to power in Germany a year ago. His biological principles, on which the map of the world is to be redrawn on racial lines, are much discussed in our house. My father likes to read aloud to me, translating what I do not understand, as I work on his muscles. He is a meat cutter, and is in and out of the freezer all day long. Some evenings, he is so crippled with pain that it can take half an hour of massage before he can straighten his legs. I am supposed to pay attention and make sensible comments on the politics of the day, but sometimes, as I rub the sweet, pungent oil first in my palms to make it go further (my mother keeps an eye on the bottle to see how quickly it goes down), the fragrance takes me to the woods at West Hawk Lake where we camp in summer. I like to climb the cliff west of the bathing beach and sit, overlooking the lake, imagining that I'm in a glider, riding high on the updrafts, peering down on splendid ancient forests and mysterious craters, my wings making flickering stampmarks on the landscape. Tonight, as I work the skin that is like an elastic band stretched and snapped back too many times within its fur matting, the strength of my hands begins an act of transformation, and before I quite know how it has happened, I am kneading the firm, resilient flesh of my neighbor, sixteen-year-old Prudence Fergusson.

"Albrecht!"

"Yes, sir!"

"Were you listening?"

"No, sir. I was solving my arithmetic." He looks at me as if I am both a puzzle and a disappointment.

"You must listen, Albrecht. It is your generation that will have to fight this war, when it comes."

"Yes, sir." He sighs and rattles the pages. He had joined the Canadian Army in the Great War. He still fought the Battle of the Somme at nighttime. I doubt he will ever be free of his dreams. I try to pay attention.

There was some strain between my parents that I didn't fully understand, but I thought it had something to do with the fact that my father and my mother's brothers were on opposite sides during the war. Her youngest brother, a promising musician, had been killed at Passchendaele. It had something to do, as well, with the articles my father read out not only to me, but to all of us at the kitchen table after supper, from this same Nazi newspaper.

"Where would you start, Friedl?" he asked my mother one evening when she agreed with a writer that it was best to send people back to their countries of origin. She opined that people were better off with what they knew, where things were familiar, and everyone spoke the same language and had the same customs. It was better for the *children*, she said. "Let's take our street," my father went on. "We have many choices. Who shall be first? The Ukes? The Poles? The Spics? "

"The Krauts!" I piped up. Gerhard snorted. My mother's look was sharp as an ice pick, but I ignored it. "Why not us? We're Krauts. I wouldn't mind." Sometimes, I could be reckless. I had a yen to travel, and I figured this might be the only way it would happen. I wanted to see the country of my ancestors and feel "inside out" like my mother. It didn't take the powers of an Einstein to see that my future, as far as my parents were concerned, extended no further than our neighborhood.

She ignored me. "Wilhelm. This is my home. I have no plans to leave it."

"That is not what we are talking about, as you know. We are discussing Europe."

"I'm simply saying that those who don't respect the law should go."

"Ah! So it's only law-breakers now!" said my father, striking the table hard with the edge of his hand. "What laws are we talking about? Freedom of speech? Freedom of assembly?"

"Wilhelm, there can be no truce upon moral issues."

I could almost hear my father grinding his teeth. My mother's reply skirted the edges of a larger conflict. In 1919, the year before Gerhard and I were born, my parents held opposing views on the Winnipeg Strike. It wasn't that my father was a socialist or a striker—as a Lutheran and Odd Fellow, he couldn't be—but he was a returned soldier, like many of the workers and unemployed who were demonstrating, and he sent down scraps of meat from the slaughterhouse to the strikers' families. For this reason, while other strikebreakers were beaten in their homes, he was left alone. My mother, on the other hand, served coffee and sandwiches to the wardens who "disciplined" the strikers with baseball bats. Unlike Clara Rivers, Charlie Rivers's mother, who didn't give a flying banana about the opinions of whomever she fed, so long as they were hungry, my mother did this out of strong political feeling.

"They had already proclaimed a Soviet Republic in Munich," she told me once when I asked her about it. "What did you expect

me to do? Stand by and watch my own city go to ruin in front of
me? There can be no peace between good and evil."

My city. Gerhard and I had mirrored each other's raised
eyebrows.

My father has thick eyebrows that meet in the middle. He draws
them together and they form a well for his small pale blue eyes.
"They're none of them angels, Albrecht, not Stalin or Dollfuss or
Roosevelt." He shakes his head. He believes in Vitality and says
that the mind "stalled in the deep woods" shows in the poor skin
of these men.

"What about Mr. Bennett?" I ask him. By referring to the
prime minister, I'm endeavoring to show how closely I'm listening. He takes a deep breath, but before he has time to answer,
there is a knock at the front door. I glance at my father. He nods,
and I put down the oil, and wipe my hands on a cloth. I have to
open the inside door, step onto the verandah, and unlock the
outside door. My breath makes steamy puffs as I stand gazing at
a flushed and excited Bella Bone.

"Albrecht, please tell your mother that a *certain person* has
arrived next door. Ask her to come at once." Before I can say
anything in reply, she has turned her back and is limping at a boiling rate down the walk. My father, who has pulled on his trousers,
appears beside me.

"What's that about?"

"I don't know. She wants Mother to go with her next door."
I'm wondering what he will say. Neither of us would choose to
risk my mother's temper by disturbing her in the middle of a
lesson, but the request is unusual enough that he'll have to think

it over seriously. My father rubs his hand over his chin and then searches behind his ears where he keeps matchsticks. He pops one into his mouth and chews it, shifting it back and forth, tick tock.

"Put on your jacket and see if you can find out what it's about. If it's important, we'll tell your mother."

Snow is lightly falling from the dark sky. I like it like this, in early winter, when the world is cleaned up by a coating of white dust. I wish it could stay like this forever.

I get ready and go back out, down the walkway, looking behind to see my footprints chasing me, and my father still watching from the porch. I duck low to sneak past Pince-Jones's front window, and around the side where there is a narrow passageway between the neighboring houses. As at our place, the window here gives onto the parlor, which in Pince-Jones's house is used as a consulting room. She had opened up business as a fortune-teller and clairvoyant shortly after the death of her husband, Mr. Fergusson, in the encephalitis epidemic. We'd thrown stones at him once, when, during his illness, he'd been put out on the front steps for airing. I am ashamed of this now, but his frozen face and body, arrested in the midst of a movement, his mouth ajar as if about to voice a thought, had both frightened and angered me. We'd been caught, too, and were in well-known fertilizer up to our eyeballs. Mary, Prudence's younger sister, has told me that her father had returned after death to help her mother. He is her principal spirit guide. Whatever that means to Pince-Jones, it means to us that we are not allowed inside the Pince-Jones's house: my mother has forbidden it, although she would receive Pince-Jones at home if she presented herself as Mrs. Fergusson and left her turban behind. My father refers to the clairvoyant as the Witch of Endor and will have nothing to do with her. Catholics make him nervous anyway, and he goes out of his way to avoid their churches, saying that the incense makes him sneeze. So it is with some interest and excitement that I approach the window. But there is someone there ahead of me. He draws his pinched face into the shadows.

"Oh, it's you," I say. "Move over." Nate moves aside and we both lean forward, crushed close to each other, our breath in synchronous rhythm as we peer between the half-open curtains into the room.

We see a red carpet bordered with pink roses, and in the middle of it the round consulting table at which Pince-Jones sits. She is draped in shawls embroidered with moons and stars. She wears a pink turban on her head and a white veil over her face. Mary and Prudence, both in white dresses, stand beside her, Mary scowling and scratching her legs, and Prudence gazing dreamily off into the distance. The client, a small blond woman with a handsome wide face, sits opposite Pince-Jones. "I've seen her before," I whisper. "I'm sure of it."

Both women gaze attentively at an upside-down water glass that is moving, apparently unassisted, back and forth across the table, stopping briefly at letters of the alphabet that decorate the table's edge. Mary records the letters on a slate in breaks between scratches.

"What's it say?" hisses Nate in my ear.

"I can't see."

Now Pince-Jones speaks, which is better, because we can hear her through the glass. Her voice is low-pitched, but as penetrating as a steam jackhammer. "How's she do that?" I ask.

Nate shrugs his shoulders and picks out a bit of putty from the pane.

"Do you have a message for anyone here?" she asks.

"Y-E-S." Now that Pince-Jones is speaking, Mary spells the letters aloud.

I'm not sure why, but I have the impression that she knows we are at the window, listening.

"Who is the message for?" The pavement-shattering voice tingles my ear.

I rub it. If I keep my ear too long on the glass, it sweats and sticks and loses all feeling. Nate nudges me and hands me a small water glass. He has two, one in each pocket. Maybe he knew I would come. We each wedge a glass against the window and listen.

"F-O-R M-I-L-D-R-E-D L-A-R-K," says Mary in a bored tone. Nate's elbow jabs my ribs. We know this name. It appears on posters all over the city. Now I know why the face seems so familiar. This is *the* Mildred Lark, the famous tiger trainer with the circus. It is said that there is no one better, even if she is a woman. She has trained with the best in Europe. She looks different, though, without her red jacket, trousers, high leather boots, and whip. The Tiger Queen!

"Who is the message from?" The window pane rattles.

"E-D-D-I-E," spells out Mary.

"That's Eddie Reece! He was my husband," cries Mildred Lark delightedly. She grasps Pince-Jones's arm. "He was my best friend."

"What is the message for Miss Lark?" asks Pince-Jones. She slides her arm away. Mary rolls her eyes, but this is serious. Pince-Jones's head tips back, her mouth makes a wet dark shadow behind the white veil. She has slipped into a trance, which is why, I suppose, she doesn't react when my mother creeps forward to sit on a little settee beside another bundle of dark tones in the background that I recognize, for the first time, as Bella Bone. So Bella has been here all along. But my mother! My father must have grown tired of waiting for me and have given her Bella's message. At least now I can stay where I am and see what happens. My mother, a Rebekah, in the Witch of Endor's salon!

"T-E-L-L H-E-R S-H-E M-U-S-T B-E-W-A-R-E S-U-L-T-A-N," intones Mary.

"Sultan's one of my tigers," explains Mildred Lark to her audience. She is used to crowds. She breaks a stick of gum and puts half in her mouth. "Sultan wouldn't hurt a mouse."

"Don't worry, Eddie," she says, leaning close to Pince-Jones's veil. "I can take care of myself." The glass is still spelling rapidly as Mildred Lark goes on. "Sultan's a wire-walker." She shoots a glance at Mary, who is showing some interest, to explain. "It's a real hard skill to teach. They have to cross their feet like this"— she puts her wrists one on top of the other, back and forth—"and they hate it! It takes *some* patience."

"B-L-O-O-D!" spells Mary. "D-A-N-G-E-R!" She is beginning to enjoy herself. She hasn't scratched her legs for half a minute.

"For Pete's sake, Eddie, don't worry," says Mildred Lark crossly. "What do you think I do? It's not knitting! You didn't use to be like this." She is irritated and restless. She chews the gum, hard. Suddenly, the glass is still. Prudence rouses from her dream, reaches over, and turns up a lamp. Pince-Jones flips up her veil.

"There. That is all I can do. Coming events cast their shadows. I am exhausted." She leans back in her chair, allowing Prudence to unpin the veil and Mary to pick up a small silver tray covered with a blue velvet cloth. This she holds out to Miss Lark. Mildred

Lark digs in her handbag and pulls out several dollar bills.

"It was worth it just to hear from Eddie, the dumb cluck," she says, laying the money on the tray. "He should've been a mother, he'd've been a happier man. Better luck next time, eh?" She winks at Mary, removes the gum from her mouth, and wraps it in a hanky. She smiles, and I can see why tigers obey her. There's a light inside her that sends waves through the room. It is just then, as both Bella and my mother rise from their observers' seats and step forward as if to speak to Miss Lark, that the screaming starts.

I know, at once, it is Lily. I don't think I have heard anything like that sound since, not even in Korea, when I watched officers of Syngman Rhee's army shoot their own men as nonchalantly as if they were popping off gophers. We all know it is Lily, and are paralyzed for several long seconds because of it.

Nate moves first, bolting from the window, down the passageway, across the snowy front yards, and into his house. I follow a second after. The screaming never stops or wavers in its intensity. I hold my hands over my ears even as I run toward it, meeting my father and Gerhard at the Bone front door. Gerhard takes one look in the kitchen and then runs away for the doctor.

We are in time to see Nate go to his sister where she lies on the kitchen floor, water from the pan of boiling water she has pulled on top of herself pooled all around her and stained rose-colored from the blood and fluids of her body. Nate is on his knees, tearing at the wall of noise with his voice. "Lily! Lily!"

"Don't touch her!" shouts Mildred Lark, who is next into the room. Nate backs away an inch, whimpering. "You!" Lark cries to me. "Bring cold water." I hand her the pail that stands at the back door and run home to fetch another. I hope it will be enough, because the pump is away down the street. By the time I return, Lark is gently ladling cold water over the child and trying to lift clothing away from her skin. It is no use. The skin comes too, lifting like a sheet that has been wrapped closely around her.

"She'll be all right," Mildred is saying as she works to Bella Bone, who kneels opposite, groaning. "I've seen it with animals a hundred times, it's just a bad burn." Although Lily's eyes are closed, the torrent of sound keeps tearing from her mouth. I don't think there's an inch of her small body that hasn't been scalded. Nate is crouched like an animal near her head.

"Please, God, let her die," I pray. I am weeping. My father, beside me, swears nonstop, a recital I've heard before only in short bursts during his nightmares. Pince-Jones and my mother hold hands like children.

The doctor and Gerhard enter. Gerhard comes to me. The doctor, red-faced from running, opens his bag, takes out a bottle, and pours liquid onto gauze. He presses the material over Lily's nose and mouth. In the silence that follows her drop into unconsciousness, and while the doctor labors to get a large dose of opium into her before she comes to, Pince-Jones tries to comfort Bella. "Oh, my dear!" she says, reaching out to her.

"Don't touch me!" Bella's hair hangs in two loose loops either side of her head. Her yellow face is hollow-eyed. She clambers to her feet awkwardly, as if she has grown very heavy or her limbs have lost feeling. "You knew!" she accuses. "You could have stopped it!" Every face but Bella's wears the veneer of shock. Madame Pince-Jones is on the brink of a faint.

"Bella, dear!" says my mother. "We know you don't mean it. You are terribly distressed." But Bella isn't finished. She turns her rage on Mildred Lark, who has backed off a few feet to make room for the doctor.

"Get out of my house, whore!" she hisses. "You've taken my husband and now you've killed my child. Get out, you bitch! Viper! Murderer!" I watch, stunned, as Bella hauls back and then slaps the Tiger Queen's face. Mildred Lark takes the blow and blinks. It is clear to me, if not to Bella, that Mildred Lark doesn't know what Bella is talking about.

"I'm awful sorry about your little girl," she says calmly. "I hate to see suffering. I don't have children myself, but I can guess how you feel." Bella works up a mouthful of saliva and spits. Mildred Lark wipes the spittle from her cheek with a handkerchief, the expression on her face still one of puzzlement. She looks around her for help, but we are as mystified as she is. Except for my mother, who has come to stand beside Bella.

"The moving finger writes. This is no time or place for Bill Bone's mistress," my mother says fiercely. Mistress? What's this? Even Nate pays attention, shifting on the floor so as to hear better. "You'd better go. This is Bill Bone's house."

"Bill's house?" repeats Mildred Lark in astonishment. Her eyebrows rocket upward. She points to Lily. "That's his little girl?" My mother nods, and Bella begins to wail, her face losing, all at once, the remaining vestiges of youth. Mildred Lark looks around the room once more, taking us in, her eyes returning to rest several times on Nate, still beside Lily on the floor. She shakes her head, and I know she is thinking that the world of animals makes more sense than this one, and we should all be put out of our misery.

———————

I awaken to hear the full chiming of the parlor clock—an antique, carved with grapes and hops, left behind by my mother's family. It is midnight. There is a scrape of feet along the roof, and the next moment the knock of a hand at the window. Gerhard is sitting up in bed, too. He rubs his eyes with the back of his hand. We have only just got to sleep. We both inspect the crouched figure and condensed face at the window.

"Hurry up!" breathes Nate through the narrow opening. I jump out of bed and raise the sash. Nate squirms through and drops onto the floor. There is ice on his eyelashes. He wears no hat or gloves. We wait for him to speak.

"It's quiet," says Gerhard, listening, after a minute of Nate's ragged breathing. It is. A silence you can hold in both hands and put in a sack. Silence you want to silence by drowning. Lily had awakened less than an hour after the doctor gave her the opium. We had had to put pillows over our heads to get to sleep. Now she has stopped screaming, and I'm afraid to ask what it means. A full sock of wind hits the bell in the Catholic church steeple at the corner. It thrums, sending cold metal scales up my spine.

"I can't stay here, you have to help me," says Nate. He seems smaller than ever. His ears stick out from a faded face. "I need your dad's car," he says. My mouth opens in surprise.

"What?" Our father has the only car in the neighborhood, a Model T Ford. He doesn't use it much in winter, but he keeps it ready for emergencies.

"Why? What do you want it for?"

Gerhard catches my eye and lifts one pale eyebrow. Now I notice that what I'd thought were shadows on Nate's face are bruises. He has been struck, not once, but a number of times, with considerable force.

"I want the car," Nate repeats stubbornly. Gerhard hums. He sits on the bed clasping his knees, his pajama-clad body like a thin, closed blade. I try to canvass him.

"What do you think? Should we?" But Gerhard is leaving the decision up to me. I can feel the heat rising from Nate's shaking body. He smells. He is so deeply frightened that he stinks. Nate thinks he's going to die. Gerhard and I don't have to speak to know this, and we also know why. Bill Bone is back and he's beaten Nate up. I hear a noise outside in the snow and go to the window to investigate. It is a brilliantly clear night. I see the houses across the road as if through a magnifying glass, the smooth ice of the road itself, our front fence with dark lines spiking from it in the moonlight. I hear the sound again. In the shadows of the Bone house, there is some movement. A figure emerges, a hunchback. Oh Jesus!

"Give me the car." Nate shivers and sweats on the floor of our bedroom. Gerhard stops humming, opens the bedroom door, and tiptoes down the stairs. I hear him go to the cabinet where the key to the shed is kept. He comes back up.

"The crank is inside the car," he says. "I'll help."

I watch the figure outside tripping up and down the road, bouncing the load on its back like a horse with an inexperienced rider. The load slumps to one side as the figure canters and wheels. It is Bella Bone, but what is she doing? My mind clamps shut on the answer and I continue to watch. She must be frozen. She is wearing only a nightgown. I hear the creak of the garage doors in the lane, then the crunch of tires on snow as the car is pushed out. Finally, a cough like a cat's when, after several efforts, the engine starts. Good for Gerhard. And good for our father. He treats that car well. Oiling and polishing it, cleaning the plugs regularly. He starts it up at least twice a week. Bella falls to her knees as the load on her back slips. She paws at the snow. I feel sick to my stomach.

"Mum! Dad! You'd better come!"

"What is it?" My father's room is smaller even than ours and is jammed with materials from his hobby. Old batteries, metal rods and chains, maps, varieties of lightning rods. The bedside lamp is another relic of my mother's family—two gold cherubs entwined with a lyre. It has been left burning low. My mother sits up and reaches over to turn it higher. I am surprised to find her here. Normally, she sleeps in her own room, an alcove off the porch. Unlike my father's room, it is kept spotlessly clean. She yawns, her long unbound hair falling over her shoulders.

"Albrecht, what has happened?"

"Please," I beg them, "just come and look."

"I'll go," says my father. He pulls on trousers and braces over his nightshirt. "I thought I heard the car," he says. I open the curtains and my mother edges out of bed to look.

"I don't see—There isn't anything. Oh!" Her face crumbles inside its bone scaffolding.

We all go outside. My mother wraps Bella in the blanket she has brought, my father unties the bundle from Bella's back. I don't want to ask, but I have to.

"Is she dead?"

"Yes." He holds Lily in his arms. "It's better this way. She was in so much pain."

"Is it? Is it better?" my mother asks angrily. She is crying. She leads Bella, using the tie of her dressing gown, toward our house. It is the only way that Bella will come.

Gerhard appears beside me. "Look!" I think, at first, he is pointing to the porch where Pince-Jones and her two daughters are standing and gaping, then I see that he is aiming above and beyond the houses, over the rooftops. In the sky are what I think are sparks from a chimney, except that they don't fly up, but move all together, along one path, growing brighter, until I am gazing, it seems, into the heart of a celestial furnace.

"It's a meteor!" Now we can see the tail streaming away from the body, and the body itself still on a magnificent straight course.

"Shouldn't it fall?"

"Quiet. Listen," he commands. I listen. But all I hear is the ice cracking beneath my father's feet as he climbs the steps with Lily. I know I don't hear what Gerhard hears, although I can almost see the music pass through his features. His face is alight, illuminated, completely strange to me. There are more fiery bodies, in groups of twos and threes, following the first. They form a procession covering what must be a hundred miles of sky, heading eastward.

"Albrecht, you'd better go after Nathanial." My father has come up behind me, his hand, strong from years of cutting meat, grips my shoulder. Gerhard has slipped away.

"I don't know where he is," I say, turning to find Bill Bone, huge and smelling of drink, next to my father.

"I'll kill the little bastard," Bill says. Tears, dark as blood, flow down his face. "It was his fault, he killed my baby girl."

"You'd better go," emphasizes my father, giving me a shove, sending me on my way, out of Bill Bone's reach. I turn to check behind me once before I round the corner of the house on my way to the lane. Something metallic glitters in Bill Bone's hand.

"You were with him, you son-of-a-bitch! The two of you! Fucking voy-yeurs! It's your fault, too! You left her alone! I'll fucking kill you both with my bare hands!"

I run as fast as I can, slipping in the skin of snow, oily with the red and green light of the meteor stream, and follow the narrow tracks of the Ford, praying to God that I can find Nate and the car so we can both get away. I lose the tracks on Pacific Avenue, pass a horse pulling the first of the morning's milk carts, then find the car, at last, stalled on the Redwood bridge. Nate is frantically trying to push it. I join him, both of us shoving the car until it starts, then I leap onto the running board, grab the steering wheel through the window and ease myself inside. Nate jumps in the other door.

"Where're we going?"

"I don't know. I don't care. Anywhere away from your dad." Nate's bruises pick up deeper color from the light of the meteorites.

"Lily's dead, isn't she," he says.

"You didn't know?"

"I wasn't sure. It's not as easy as you'd think to tell." We are almost clear of the city now, passing a Ukrainian settlement of white-washed houses, neat plumes of smoke rising from every chimney.

"It was my fault," he says. "I should never have left her." I don't know what to say. He's right. Lily *was* his responsibility. We drive on in silence, grateful for the two buffalo robes we have found in the car and wrapped around ourselves. Grateful for the frequent driving lessons I've had from my father when my mother is out with the Rebekahs.

I drive north, then east to Beauséjour, not thinking really, but half following the steady stream of light in the sky. "If we had an airplane, we'd be hundreds of miles away by now."

"Turn here!" Nate says suddenly. His face is tight with concentration.

"Why?" But I obey. He says nothing more, except to give further instructions. I just keep on driving. The farther away we go, the better, in my opinion.

After Whitemouth, the landscape changes. As we climb from the flat prairie into the muskeg, small pine trees appear and straggle beside the road like dazed soldiers. I know exactly where we are. My mother seeds these roadsides with wildflowers when we go on our summer camping trips.

It is hillier now. The car labors as it climbs, and backfires as we coast downhill to save gas. We are still following the meteors, which are lower in the sky now, but continue to defy the laws of physics, as I know them, by traveling straight eastward. There is more frost than snow here; it glitters along the edges of trees, and outlines the small stones of the dirt and gravel road. We pass Brereton Lake, then Falcon Lake, and then we are there, driving down the frozen dust track to the beach at West Hawk Lake and stopping beneath the bare, overhanging trees. They drip the black lines of their shadows onto the sand. Nate gets out and walks to the end of the dock to watch the display, and I go to the path that climbs the cliff from behind the picnic tables. From the cliff top, I can see a thick collar of ice at the beach shoreline. It gives way, in the deeper water, to a fragile film of ice so crystal clear that the light is both reflected back to the sky and falls all the way through to the shiny stones on the bottom. It is both mirror and window, a sensation, as I gaze downward, that makes me feel dizzy. I feel a strange prickling on my skin, and glance up at the instant there is a tremendous bang and all the light goes out. A fraction of a second later, the cliff gives a shake, as if a carpet has just been tugged straight beneath it. I wait a minute to get my bearings, then stumble back down in the dark to find Nate.

He looks cold and disgruntled more than scared or sad. "I wonder where they went?" he says looking up at the sky. "I thought we'd get closer."

"I don't know." I shrug. "Come on, let's go." I have no particular destination in mind—I just don't like the thick darkness here. I'd rather be back in the car. But Nate isn't listening. He is only paying attention—just like Gerhard does—to whatever he hears in his mind. He leaves the dock and walks along the beach, kicking ahead of him until his foot strikes an overturned canoe. He struggles to right it and then eases it onto the ice. He scrounges around beneath the thwarts until he finds paddles.

"What are you doing?" I ask, as he shoves the canoe out, its keel scraping across the ice. He slides it another few feet, and the nose drops and shreds the thinner ice. Another big shove, and the canoe plunges completely through and is floating; little crackling wrinkles spread out from its bulk. He keeps hold of the rope.

"Come on, get in."

"You're not going out in that, are you? It'll sink!"

"Come on. We have to."

"Says who?"

"Please, Albrecht!"

"There'll be holes in it. We'll freeze to death. We'll drown." He turns his back to me and hauls the canoe back to the edge of the heavier ice, so that he can reach it with his foot. He gives a quick light jump, and lands spot in the middle with his hands braced against the sides. The canoe rocks perilously.

"It's dark, Nate. You could die!"

"Please." It is not like him to plead. All I can see of his face, as he turns to look at me, is the whiteness of the raised planes of his cheeks and nose and chin. Somewhere, light is beginning to show once more, but I can't see from where. I hear it, though: it hisses through the air like a fine stream of steam.

"No." I'm shivering in a wind that scratches at the surface of ice and water.

"Then I'll go by myself." He turns resolutely, settles himself, and raises the paddle.

"All right, I'll come. Just wait a second." He knows I can't let him go alone: I'm older than he is, and he's my friend. I creep gingerly off the ice and back to the car to take out the empty oil can I've seen there. When I return to the canoe, the sky has found a veil of green. The aurora borealis. It drifts above us, gossamer and grassy. The hiss in the air changes to a whisper, and the veil starts shifting color—yellow, red, green. I push away from the ice with the other paddle, and then I start bailing.

I'd spent a week like this, in the summer, with my father, while Gerhard was with my mother in Brandon getting special music instruction. I had fished for the deepwater sculpin that lurk in these cold waters, not catching any, but content to trail the line as my father took magnetic measurements. In his hand, he'd hold an iron bar from which swung a chain. He'd measure the breadth of its swing, take a compass reading, and record the results on a map. We must have crisscrossed the lake north–south and east–west five or six times.

"How deep is it?" I remember asking. My father shook his head.

"I don't think anyone knows. The interesting thing is that it's highly magnetic." He surveyed me as if I should think this meant something.

"Is that important?"

"Oh, yes! It means all plants, animals, and humans born in this region possess special properties. They have certain characteristics."

"Such as what?"

He adjusted his arm bands so that his shirt sleeves were pulled back from his wrists. His arms are a little shorter than most men's; or else his muscles take up more space. "The magnetic rocks here come from outer space. The lake was formed by a meteorite crashing into the planet. Personal Magnetism teaches that all magnetic beings—including ourselves—are oriented to their places of origin." I must have looked particularly blank. Gerhard and I have shown little interest in his hobby aside from practicing certain exercises he has shown us. Eye exercises that will come in handy for when I'm flying, and for Gerhard when he is watching hawks. Memory exercises so that we can memorize a page of text at a glance. We have both used these methods for reading our parents' letters.

My father sighed. I made an effort. "Is that why Mother wants to go back to Germany?"

"Does she?" He seemed surprised.

"Will I always want to live in Winnipeg?"

He thought this over. "Not necessarily. It depends. It probably means you'll always feel a pull—just like all these rocks around the lake. They're drawn toward wherever they came from—out there, in space, the universe. I can measure the strength of that pull. We can learn something, maybe, about where all of us have come from."

As he said this, although I tried not to show it, I felt a tingle, a kind of vibration, and despite myself looked up. Out, toward space. There was nothing there but the sunshine. But this tingle is what I feel now, in the boat with Nathanial Bone, as he paddles us toward an island.

We scrape ashore with a final hard push that snaps the shore ice. Nate jumps out and we drag the canoe up the beach. We are beneath an umbrella of light, like the explosion of skyrockets at the fairground. There are curls of color like rivers of molten lava, and monstrous verticle rays sifted through with a sandstorm of color; color that ripples and undulates and whistles loudly at us. I cover my ears. My father says that no one really knows what this phenomenon is—they talk about ice crystals and reflected sunlight, but he believes it has something to do with magnetism. Someday, we will know the answer. The colors fade, and the veils are drawn away, as if by a magician, pulling pale silk scarves through a narrow ring. When the noise stops completely, the sky is empty except for the usual stars, cold and distant.

"We'll go up here," Nate says. He must have eyes like a cat. I can see little in this dark, but he climbs ahead of me, surefooted and confident, along a deer trail through thick scrub. There are birches, too, their bark like a leprous skin giving off a colorless glow. I keep looking down at the lake and wondering if the meteors have shed into its depths, wondering what this will do to my father's careful measurements, whether he will have to start over, and whether there really is something to learn from them. How could there be?

"Nate?" He turns around.

"What?"

"Nothing." But it isn't nothing. I'm afraid. Not of Bill Bone and his fists, now, but of how we've got here, what we're doing on an island in a lake in the middle of nowhere in winter. And I'm trying not to think about those meteors. Their strange behavior. And the appearance of the aurora borealis, like some coda to a symphony. Rocks skitter beneath my feet. I slip, and burn my hands in the frost, catch myself and pull myself, just behind Nate, over the lip of the hilltop. There, in front of us, is a squat cone of rock about a yard high and two yards across at its widest. It has half buried itself in the earth, breaking branches in its fall, and sending out a wave of earth that lies stilled—like Mr. Fergusson in the midst of a movement—in a perfect circle around it. We go over to it, and I touch it. It is still quite hot.

"I knew it! I just knew it!" Nate cries. He sits down and leans against the meteorite, heating himself up.

"Nate, what are we doing here? What's going on?" I slump beside him. I am shivering full bore now, despite the fever of the stone. I know I'll never get warm, never see home again, never eat cinnamon toast in the kitchen ever again with my brother and parents.

"Can you keep a secret?"

"Sure, I guess. I've come all this way with you, I suppose I can do that."

"You have to promise not to tell."

"I told you, I swear, I won't say anything." Nate examines my face for its trustworthiness, or lack of it.

"Okay. But don't say anything. Just listen."

I shrug. What have I got to lose? "Fine with me."

"You know what happened? When my sister stopped bawling?"

I shake my head. I examine the sky where the stars are picked out in white lead. Someday I will be up there, flying.

"My dad was with us. He said it was all my fault."

I nod. He doesn't have to tell me about the beating. What Bill Bone had done was obvious. Nate will wear the marks of it for weeks.

"I don't blame him," Nate goes on. "He was right, you know, it was my fault. I should have been there with her. I shouldn't have left."

We just sit there, me still shivering, and trying not to think how it might have been partly my fault, too—when I saw Nate at the Fergusson house, I knew that Lily was by herself. Nate has the most peculiar expression on his face. What is it? If I didn't know better, I'd think it was happiness.

"The thing is, Albrecht, Lily doesn't believe it was my fault, and that's what counts. She knows how much I love her, that I would never do anything on purpose to hurt her."

I look at my hands. They are blue and stiff. I put them in my pockets.

"When she stopped her crying, she stepped right into my mind." He scans my face, but I keep it blank. "She said to me that she would help me from now on, she'd always be with me so I wouldn't be so lonely. It would be better this way, she said, better than before." He peers at me again. "When we were in the car, it happened again. She was right there. She spoke to me. That's how I knew where to go. She gave me directions." He looks round, reminding me of how my father does his thinking, examining the world for evidence that it supports his system. "You see, Albrecht, now I know why I had to come here. It was to find the meteor."

I nod, carefully offering neither encouragement nor discouragement. But I am hearing in his words an echo of a story I've heard Bill Bone tell about his Cree ancestors. Bill has told it to us at least a dozen times. He tells it when he's drinking, but before he's drunk, after he talks about his mother's people, who were Creek Indians transplanted from Florida to Oklahoma, and who had acquired great wealth from oil wells. He tells it after he says that his mother's family decorated the oil derricks on their land with semi-precious stones, so that they shot light and color into the air for miles around. And he tells it after the story of how his mother joined the circus and met his father, a Cree, in Canada, and when he is trying to explain to Nate and Lily what happened to everybody, why there is no money now, why he's a drunk.

An iron meteorite once sat on a hill at Iron Creek, Alberta, close to where Bill Bone was born. Bill said it looked like a face, and that as long as it was left in place, the Cree and Blackfoot nations prospered. For countless generations, it was venerated. Hunters brought it offerings of beads and knives before setting out, and shamans brought patients to it to benefit from its powerful healing properties. It had come down from heaven to the earth. It did not belong to the earth. It was a gift. Old men remembered having heard old men say that they had once lifted it easily, but year by year it increased in weight until no single person could move it. About fifty years ago, it was removed by missionaries to the farmyard of a mission house. From that time onward, exactly as had been prophesied, the Cree and Blackfoot peoples suffered war, disease, the disappearance of the buffalo, and the loss of their lands. It was said that one day, when a new iron stone was found, the flow of misfortune would be reversed. There would be no more disease, no more war and death.

"Who's going to find the stone, Mr. Bone?" Gerhard always asked the question. We waited to hear the answer.

"Any of us could find it. At anytime. You just have to keep looking up." Then he'd stop talking and get down to serious drinking, and we'd slip away.

I clear my throat. I decide to risk saying something. "So you think that Lily told you to come here?"

"Of course I do." He smiles at me. It is a lovely smile, his bruised face smoothed of worry. It gives me the creeps. "But she's not called Lily anymore," he adds. He takes out his pocketknife and chips off a flake of the stone. "She has a new name."

"Oh?" There are no stars left. They have faded into the pre-dawn light.

"She's called Explanata." He yawns, curls up against the meteorite, and falls immediately asleep. I wish I could do that, but when I shut my eyes I see Lily lying on the kitchen floor of the Bone house.

"Could we have done something?" I'd asked Gerhard when we were at home. We'd shut the windows against the noise, but you could still hear it, like a cat yowling, like fingernails scratching your eardrum.

"Probably." He'd been cleaning between his teeth with a tooth-pick. "But we'd have to have been different people and known different things, wouldn't we?"

I have to work hard to rouse Nate enough to make it down the trail. I roll him into the canoe, and he falls asleep again at once. There is no wind, and once we are through the thicker ice I have no trouble paddling. It is a dream, the paddle dipping in and out of crackling ice-water, licking itself clean. I can forget what has happened. It is as unreal as my father's nightmares of the trenches, or my mother's stories about her childhood in Germany. All I have to do is get us home, put the car in the garage, get Nate into bed and myself to my room, where my brother is peacefully sleeping. I don't care anymore about Bill Bone. He doesn't exist. Nothing has happened. There is nothing to explain to anyone.

3

LIFE IS
MAGNETISM

All the while, as she was skiing through the *belli meglaw*, the dense snow cloud that obscured all distinguishing features of the terrain, Fika sensed the overall drift of the ice to the south. The ice pans were fragmented and moving as spring break-up began, the plates of ice shifting slowly, exposing more and more seams of open water. But the ocean currents, which kept the polar cap in motion, now ran in her favor, westward. What she could not tell, without a series of sun sights (which in the circumstances was impossible), was the *rate* of drift west. A mistake about her position could cost her hours, even days. A continued mistake would cost her her life.

The sun stayed hidden behind the snow, the frozen crystals falling but refusing to settle, the cloud with each moment thickening. Her breathing grew labored. She was adrift on thirteen million square kilometers of sea ice, but was confined to a space scarcely larger than her body. At any moment, she could ski straight into an open lead, not sensing it until it was too late. With no one to help her, she would drown, or die of exposure. A line of poetry beat, with the pulse of her blood, through her brain: *You will never be alive again, / Never rise from the snow* . . . Her ski tip caught in a pocket of slush. She fell and got up, then fell again, the mercilessly flat light giving no clues as to her position. Until finally, she got up and stood still, consciously easing her rate of respiration. The tempo of blood slowed to two words, *Marina, Ekaterina,* repeating themselves so that at length she listened and heard, knew that she was grieving for her friends, and was desperately lonely.

From her pack, Fika took a small twist of sugar. She poured the granules into her dry mouth, tasting cold dust before saliva sprang forth, moistening the sugar and releasing its sweetness. In the stillness, and with the sugar sending its strength through her veins, she could hear the snow, its sharp crystals colliding and making a kind of music, half real, half imaginary. She had heard it before when she was with the reindeer. It was the sound the jangling frozen air made around their bodies in the herd. She had heard it last night, too, when she had stumbled from the tent to urinate, and had seen a flash of light in the clear sky, bluish white, long and twisting like a snake. Slowly, it had faded, taking the metallic music with it, leaving the sky luminous for five or six minutes. A meteorite. There were hundreds of them each year, most of them, especially here in the far north, passing unnoticed.

She, Ekaterina, and Marina had found one on the sea ice near their training camp months earlier. It was black, part mineral, part metal, and weighed about half a kilo. From the age of the ice on which they had found it, they judged it to be from a recent fall. They'd surrendered it to the authorities, of course, but Marina had chipped off a flake, which she had kept for luck. Fika had found it among the things left behind in the tent at the time of the accident. When she'd picked it up, a memory had stirred, so deep that she could not quite catch it, and for an instant she'd felt herself observed. She closed her eyes now, wondering if she would see those dark eyes again and remember whose they were. Nothing . . . but the continuing rattle of snow, and the hum of her body as it cycled through its rhythms. She felt herself expand outward, joining with the jumbling air, moving farther and farther into the vastness, not losing her way, as she'd feared, but scoring a path across the vastness, mapping her way. She let out her breath in a sigh. It had been a near thing: she had trembled on the cliff edge of panic. She would have to find a way to deal with it—she couldn't afford to let it happen again.

As she rested, thinking back on her progress, calculating how far she had traveled from the last camp, the cloud thinned. Quickly, Fika brought out her sextant, leveled it, and took a sighting. A glance at the compass gave her a bearing. She consulted a map of magnetic declination, and the table of declination for each degree of latitude and longitude, and marked her position on the map. She was still on course. The path of dots reached back to the starting point at Cape Arkticheskiy, and described an Arctic searoad that would bridge two continents. She had only to complete it, step by careful step, testing it all the way.

It was not as if she were not prepared. She'd lived with snow and ice all her life. That last winter of the war, the last winter of her childhood, they'd used snow for insulation, and for water; and she'd made tunnels—hiding places, escape routes—all through the forest, waiting, and surviving, until Gerhard came for her. It was winter again when they'd arrived in the camp, the Russians letting them stay together because of his blindness. She had carried ice from nearby rivers, lakes, and swamps to the machine where the women worked, shoveling the materials beneath compacting rollers. Snow and ice were engineering mediums: you laid the ice track in the center, the snow in tracks on both sides. The rollers cemented the substances to the ground. Then the tractors came along the ice-road to take logs from the woodlot to the collecting point. Gerhard drove a tractor back and forth over the same route: he didn't need to see, he could "hear," he said, exactly where to go. When they found out he could fix machinery, they took him off the tractors and gave him tools. She remembered his hands, blunt from frostbite, work-worn, discolored, moving deftly, making repairs as he spoke to her, teaching her English so that he could talk to her secretly in the language of his childhood.

He spoke to her of places as unreal to her then as the lands of Sannilove and Andree, said to have left traces in the bottom morphology of the Laptev Sea and on the marine erosion of the coasts. Islands that had sheltered snow geese and sandpipers, walruses and polar bears; musk-oxen, too, which had crossed from other nearby islands to eat the thick, waxy leaves of the Arctic desert plants that grew everywhere, even on fossil ice. It was all gone—ancient islands destroyed, except for the traces on the sea beds, by the action of sea and wind; just as Gerhard's and her past had been destroyed by the war. He'd tried to give her the traces, filling in the emptiness of the missing years.

Fika wiped her goggles clear, then looked ahead into the white sky. The cloud was lifting once more. She could see ridges ahead. She wiped the blood from her nose. It had begun to bleed for the second time that day. When the bleeding stopped, she pushed forward on her skis.

Fika is in Yakutsk. It is seven degrees below zero celsius, but only the day before the sun had melted snow on the roofs of the houses. She is going with friends for a day in the forest. They have plenty of food—bread and black sausage, cheese, vodka. They are dressed warmly. The earth is frozen hard to a great depth below, but there is only a thin layer of snow. Their skis sing as they glide between the scattered trees. In the clear, dry air, you can hear the sound of a sledge, or the cracking of ice, carried for miles.

Now they are nearing the Lena River, which runs north through Eastern Siberia, emptying into the Arctic Ocean at the Laptev Sea. They pass into a forest of larch on its banks. Her friends want to stop here to build a fire for their picnic. But Fika, in the dream in which she skis and remembers, knows that she has to go on. She sees an old man in the distance. He is her great-grandfather, Otto, who, after the mass trials of 1877, was sentenced to hard labor in the salt mines at Ust-Kutsk. She believes that if she can reach him, all will be well.

While Fika blinks her eyes, attempting to bring Otto into focus, four distinct parhelia, or sun dogs, shimmer: one in each quadrant around the sun. They are connected by a rainbowlike ring of color. The temperature has dropped, the sky has cleared.

There is a lead of open water ahead meandering to the southwest. She follows it, searching for a place to cross.

In many ways, Gerhard had told her, the survival of Otto was a miracle. He had contracted dysentery, but had cured himself by eating charcoal. He also made friends with a doctor, a prisoner as well, who had come, originally, from the same area of Saxony as had Otto. Gerhard knows Otto's story because of Clara, Otto's daughter, who had told the story to Gerhard when he was a child.

The doctor secured better food and a straw mattress for Otto; he obtained permission for Otto to go to the surface of the shaft once each day to collect snow for washing. While the other prisoners lay down at night in the filth from their work in the mines, Otto took his piece of tent canvas, left the cave, and stood squinting in the pale Siberian sun. He piled snow onto the fabric, inspected the earth for signs of spring, and dreamed of escape, rubbing the clean snow over his limbs.

One day, the doctor came to examine a prisoner who was suspected of having typhus. The guards, terrified of the disease, stood well back while the examination took place. The doctor whispered to Otto, who was attending the patient, that he must learn all he could of botany and geology. Otto, who was already studying mapmaking with another prisoner, a gifted cartographer, added these new subjects to his syllabus. The school was conducted, after the exhausting labors of the day, in the lantern light of the cave. The teachers instructed in whispers. The prisoners joined together in the task of educating Otto, recalling childhood lessons or long-abandoned professions. When the call to the surface came, Otto was ready.

A party of the nobility was on an excursion from Talun, on the Trans-Siberian railroad, to Ust-Kutsk—a distance of two hundred and twenty-five kilometers—and from there through the reaches of the upper Lena River to Yakutsk. They required (since German was their first language) a German-speaking guide, as well as enlightenment on the features of the countryside through which they would be traveling. Otto was (at the doctor's recommendation) their choice. He was clean. He had kept not only his bowels, but his teeth, intact through the use of charcoal. His hair and beard were trimmed. He was given new clothes, and in a short while he embarked, with the group, on a mail steamer, the *Rabotnik,* a serviceable flat-bottomed craft with paddle wheels, and with its after part provided with a cabin for the comfort of the passengers.

There was still ice in the Lena River, although it was June. They left the village of Ust-Kutsk behind, passing gigantic blocks of ice strewn on the river shore. In some places, there were steep walls, as much as three hundred meters high, rising straight from the cold waters. At the top of the wall, visible as an undulating green line, was a plateau of forest. In other places, the river widened, enclosing numerous islands. They passed Kirensk, with its transport prison and cathedral; they churned by Vitim, a depot for the goldfields to which many ex-prisoners were exiled. They passed smaller villages, and columns of larch trees and Siberian pines, and then the slowly opened-out view of cliffs in regular layers of green slate and porphyry. As the river widened to several kilometers across, there were, as before, many small islands: on these grazed the little shaggy cattle that belonged to the Yakuts. Then came the Pillars of the Lena, an unbroken chain of spectacularly shaped limestone cliffs, extending for forty kilometers along the eastern shore. The passengers grew silent. More and more, they looked to Otto to provide reassurance, for they did not feel at home here. They felt their lives shrink in the shadow of the great cliffs; they sensed, here more than anywhere else, the approaching cataclysm. Although they did not know everything, they understood that Otto, in this new world, this borderland, was a lucky man. He was a survivor. In the privacy of their state-rooms, when the shoes and stays came off and they were, after all, only human, they prayed that some of his luck and skill would rub off on them. In their nightmares, they were cold, and a fire scoured clean the land; they dreamed that they were swept away and scattered, like ash, to the four quarters.

When they arrived at Olekminsk, the depot of the goldfields, where the great tributary, the Olekma, flowed into the Lena, they sent a messenger back to the labor camp; and when at last the steamer arrived at Yakutsk, and they viewed the Mother of Yakutsk, the fortress erected by the Cossacks two centuries earlier as protection against the barbarian hordes, they gave thanks for their safe arrival. An escort of soldiers had arrived to return them to the railroad. They embraced Otto and said farewell. They asked him to remember them. In order to support his memory, they gave him, as a parting gift, his freedom.

Fika leaned over her poles, breathing slowly through the mask she had put on when the wind had picked up, blowing ice particles into her eyes and skin. Gerhard's voice was in her ear, his arm warmed her as he told her Otto's story, for the hundredth time, on the wooden platform that served them for a bed. They had been given extra food: two hundred grams of bread each. The prisoners were being rewarded for completion of the ice-road.

Tomorrow, they would begin building a copper factory, but tonight there was bread, and soup thick enough in which to stand a spoon.

A thin film of ice had formed over the lead, and there were large solid portions that she thought she could use as stepping stones to reach the opposite side. She shuffled her skis onto the ice. She felt it sink behind her. She could have tried to fill in some of the gaps with lumps of ice and snow, but it was too late now. Only a few more feet to go. She felt the tails of her skis rip through the surface. With a sudden surge of energy, a sense of a push from behind, the tips touched safety.

4

THE
VENEER

1 9 3 5

With Bella Bone in the Assiniboine Asylum undergoing a cold-water treatment to shock her mind and body back to health, and Bill Bone touring the world with the Tiger Queen, Mildred Lark, it is only natural that Nathanial Bone should come to live with us. He has a cot on the floor in my and Gerhard's room. It is crowded, but we don't mind because we feel sorry for him, and sad about his sister who died. We have put Lily's picture on a shelf near his bed. We place flowers in front of it when we remember. Nate doesn't talk about his sister or about much of anything. Most of the time, he lies on the bed as stationary as a doormat.

When he is most unhappy, he brings out the piece of meteorite he brought back with him from West Hawk Lake. He keeps the stone under his pillow or in his pocket. Sometimes, in the dark, I hear him talking to Explanata. I tell my mother about this. She says it is normal for some children to have imaginary friends. She says Nate and I and Gerhard are almost brothers because we share a common scarlet thread of continuity through Odd Fellowship. (Bill Bone is an Odd Fellow! I hadn't known this.) I don't say that Nate's imaginary friend is really Lily.

My mother takes Nate to visit his mother in the asylum. The only gift Bella likes is sugar. She isn't supposed to have it, but Nate puts some in a packet in his pocket for her. He is always quiet after he returns and lies down, making patterns of falling stars—from air to blanket—with his hands. Each has a steeply descending trajectory. I overheard my mother say that Bella's is a difficult case, and that the cold-water cure isn't working. All Bella does is cry and say she wants to go home. Nate receives letters from his father from time to time. He lets me and Gerhard read them. We only need to look at them once to remember them.

Bill has written from the circus headquarters in Calgary and in Bangor, Maine, and also from Germany where he has recently gone to train bears. The best place to learn about wild animals, he writes, is in Cologne. Gerhard is very interested in this as it is in Cologne that he will be studying music. They pay Bill seventy-five dollars a week plus all the bear feed he needs. He writes that he is a hit, he is a skunk let loose in a nunnery, because they like to see a real Red Indian handling wild creatures over there. He says he can do whatever he likes. He even performs in private houses for Nazi bigwigs. Mildred Lark is in Cologne, too, with two leopards and one puma as well as her tigers. She and Bill have a new act, a *gemischte Tiergruppe*, as the Germans say. It includes the leopards and puma, the tigers, bears, and some baboons and dogs. Bill's bear, Nadia, a Russian brown bear, can ride a bicycle. My mother reports to us, as well, that Nate's father is "doing very well for himself, thank you," and she writes back to him that Nate is "happy enough" here; although Gerhard and I know better. He is not happy at all. He wants to live with his father and Mildred Lark. Ours is not a very interesting house when you compare it to a circus, but I don't understand how Nate can forgive his father for the things he has said and done. However, Bill Bone is Nate's father, not mine.

So many things have changed that my father has been through the house half a dozen times with his testing rods trying to account for them all. He has discovered major differences in the magnetic field. There are "soft spots" and uneven patches. I wonder if the variations may be because of the meteorite, which only Nate and I and Gerhard know exists. Things are bound to be different when you have a rock from outer space in the house. Gerhard, though, thinks there is more to it, and that the changes have to do with our mother. I am not sure, although I know that she is restless, especially after she receives letters from Bill Bone. I haven't read any of these yet. Unlike other letters, which she puts in the desk drawer, she keeps these ones in her apron pocket. After one arrives, she goes straight over to Madame Pince-Jones's house. This is new, too. She spends a great deal of time over there, and my father doesn't like it.

My father works longer hours for less money at the slaughterhouse, but in this way we are no different from other families whose fathers are still in work. All the men work longer hours for less. We count ourselves lucky to have money coming in and not to be on relief, although our father is always tired, and he complains constantly. Nothing we do is good enough. When I massage his legs, I do it too hard or not hard enough, or not long enough, or I wear him out. He doesn't like my mother's cooking. He says she puts stale bread in his lunch. He won't listen to Gerhard play the violin anymore because it affects his nerves. He is always reading and rereading his German newspapers, but he has stopped reading them out loud to me. He goes on long walks at night and comes home late. He and my mother never share a room. So we live within a shadow of unhappiness and we don't know exactly why. When I ask what is wrong, I'm always told, "It's the Depression. It's the same for everyone." But I know that it isn't. I can hear, sometimes, from next door, the sound of laughter.

I follow my mother to Madame Pince-Jones's house, staying out of sight until she is indoors, then I run round to the passageway between the two houses. It is evening. The lamps and candles are lit. My mother and Pince-Jones sit at the séance table, their hands joined, their faces like running watercolors in the smoky atmosphere. I'm not sure what they're doing. They could be praying. Suddenly, though, Pince-Jones puffs up, emits a shriek, and collapses in her chair. I can see the whites of her eyes, like rounds of watery meringue, as her eyes roll upward in their sockets. The veil over her mouth bubbles as she begins to speak, her voice gruff and too low for me to make out the words. Mary, her younger daughter, showing every sign of boredom, wipes her mother's forehead with a damp cloth. For a second, she stares right at me where I peer in, my chin resting on the outside sill.

"What are you doin' here, dog's breakfast?" I spin around to face Charlie Rivers, Prudence Fergusson's boyfriend. He is seventeen years old and outweighs me by thirty pounds. My eyes saturate with stinging tears of pain as he grips my shoulder. Before I can think of a reply, Prudence pushes between the two of us.

"Leave him alone, you big oaf," she whispers. "He's half your size. He's a baby! He's not hurting anything." Charlie releases me, but not before administering a final squeeze that leaves me faint. I smile in as friendly a manner as possible and point to the window, indicating silently that I am there for no other reason than to watch over my mother. Charlie's arm comes to rest on Prudence's shoulders.

"You're a peeping Tom," he says calmly.

"I am not! My dad asked me to see what's going on. He's worried about my mum." That was true. He wanted to know "what the two of them got up to together." I didn't really know why he couldn't find out for himself, although I had noticed that Pince-Jones made him nervous: he never knew where to look when he had to look at her, which wasn't that often, mainly in the street if they met. Charlie, who keeps matches behind his ears like the men, takes one and puts it in his mouth. There is a long silence as he twitches it back and forth in his teeth. I can't take my eyes from it.

"You're a liar, Storr," he says. "I know exactly why you're here. You're a peeping Tom and a pee-vert. You keep away from my girlfriend's little sister or I'll shove my fist right down your throat."

"That's not true!" I protest, aggrieved, my voice squeaking in my struggle to keep it low. The babbling flows unchecked from the room inside. "My dad sent me, I told you."

"Leave him alone, Charlie," intervenes Prudence. She bends so that she can see, like me, into the room through the gap in the curtains. Her body, next to mine, is warm. I can smell her perfume. Jasmine. Or gardenia. Something womanly. Charlie pulls her back.

"Come on, let's go," he says. "Use your loaf." I look at them curiously. Where are they going? Pince-Jones keeps her girls locked up tight, like all Catholic mothers. Whatever they have to do, they won't have much time for it.

"Pru? Why does my mum come here so much?"

Prudence scans my face at low beam, her interest clearly elsewhere. Even next to Charlie, she appears tall. Her body, in the wool dress, is a sculpture. Her hair, an auburn so dark it is black in this light, is piled on top of her head.

"My mother," I repeat, "what does she want?"

Prudence, who is a kind person, focuses. "I don't know. I'm not supposed to say." She peers down at her shoes, open-toed sandals that house two sets of pink-nailed toes. I wonder if she knows she is beautiful. Charlie knows. He makes a noise like a growl.

"Come on, let's go!"

Pru says shyly, "I wish I could help."

"What do you mean?"

"She's lonely. There's nothing unusual in that. You should hear some people."

"But she's always over here. We don't like it. She should be at home, with us," I say. Charlie spits out the match and starts to pull her away. Prudence gazes into my eyes. I feel myself falling. Her eyes are gray, mine are blue. My father says that the color of eyes is important. Ours, mine and Prudence's, are complementary colors. Charlie's, which are brown, aren't.

"I'll tell you this much," she says to me, bending to put her lips so close to my ear that I can hear the breath pass between her teeth. "She's deciding her future, and it has something to do with her family in Germany." She and Charlie slip away into the darkness.

I crouch to peek once more into the parlor. Now the two women are examining a large crystal bowl of water. This is Pince-Jones's "magic-mirror." Within it, she views portents of the future. What does my mother need to know? I have no idea what to tell my father. Mary, who has given up all pretense of interest in the proceedings, sits crumpled, snoring slightly, on a settee. Her thin legs stick out in front of her like a boy's. She has told me many times how much she hates helping her mother. She would rather be drenched in boiling oil or, if given the choice, conducting experiments with ants. She likes to redirect their pathways with running water; she saves crumbs from her toast for them. Last summer, she charged us a nickel for her guided tour of an anthill.

"Albrecht!" I leap up, smashing my head on the windowsill. I have been sitting on the ground, leaning against the side of the house. My heart is battering my ribs.

"Mary! What are you doing here?" I peer around distractedly, trying to solve the mystery of how she could be in the house and out here at the same time.

"Poor Albrecht. You've been asleep. Never mind, you haven't missed anything." I am blushing. These days, when I'm around her, she makes me feel like a fool. This is annoying because I've known Mary and her sister forever. Gerhard and I used to play with Mary when Pru and Charlie and the older kids ran away from us, leaving us behind. I didn't mind her then. She didn't cry when we hit her, like most girls; she'd just hit back. Now, though, I'm not sure what to think except that she's gotten too big for her britches. Sometimes, when I see her in the street and she's with a friend, she turns her head away, pretending not to see me, and the two of them laugh together, making me feel like an idiot. So I ignore her, too. This time, though, she gives me her cat's smile and shakes the short dark hair away from her face. "Our mothers have gone over to your house. They'll be there a while, but we'd still better be quiet."

"To my house? You're joking! They'd never go there, my father wouldn't allow it." I am astonished. The day that Pince-Jones crosses our threshold is the day hell freezes over. My father has said so a hundred times. She dabbles with spirits, she's a Catholic and a widow, she is not to be trusted.

"Well," says Mary, "there is no forever. Your father is in for a big surprise, I'd say. Come with me. I want to show you something." She pulls me up by the hands and draws me along behind her to the backyard. Her hand is hot, thin, and bony. When we are standing beneath the apple tree, she turns to face me.

"Do you think I'm pretty?" I swear she bats her eyelashes. "Do you want to kiss me?" I don't know what to say. She is only thirteen. Mary is just a friend. I gaze away into the milky softness of the sky as if overcome.

"Well?"

"I can't say I've thought about it," I say diplomatically. I am searching for a way to change the conversation. I don't want to hurt her feelings.

"Oh." She is disappointed. "You're not at all like your brother, are you? He likes me. He told me so. Gerhard's better-looking than you, and he's not afraid to say what he thinks."

"We're twins! We're just the same." Somehow, she has touched a nerve.

"No, you're not. You're not at all the same. He's much more mature."

I tilt my face forward and place my lips on hers. They are soft, and kiss back. "Is that mature enough for you?"

"No. Your brother's a better kisser. But he's had more practice. Let me show you. Just to be fair." She kisses me again, demonstrating improvements. Funnily enough, I don't want her to stop.

"We'd better go in," she whispers after a few minutes.

"We can't," I whisper back. "Your mother will be back any second."

"She'll be hours yet."

"No. I told you. My father's a scientist and an Odd Fellow, he doesn't believe in Catholics. He'll kick her right out."

"He doesn't believe . . . ?"

"I can't explain it. Your mother makes him upset." I am nuzzling her neck, I can't help it. I feel warm all over. I don't care what she says about anything, I just want to keep kissing, being blind in her mouth, against her skin, making connections. Electricity. I think I see lights.

"Don't worry, she'll be hours and hours," murmurs Mary again.

"Why should she be?" I murmur back.

"Because of what they're telling him, silly. Your mother is going to go to Germany with Gerhard. When the war starts, she wants to be there, not here."

"What! She can't do that!" I pull away, startled. "She has to stay here."

Mary steps back and regards me coolly. Her eyes float specks of ice.

"Why shouldn't she do what she wants, Albrecht? Is she supposed to just stay around the house with you?"

"You don't understand, Mary. This is her home. She's a mother, a Rebekah, she can't just go off and do what she wants. I don't get it." I sit down, slumped against the apple tree, not caring that the grass is wet. Mary stands over me.

"Look at it this way," she says reasonably. "There's a war coming. She'll have to take sides sooner or later, won't she? We'll all have to. That's what war means—two sides." Her eyes, filled with ice now, though blue like mine, are not kind.

"How do you know what will happen? How do you know there'll be a war? Who says so? Madame Pince-Jones and her spirit helper, Mr. Fergusson, from beyond?" The sarcasm, overdone the instant it leaves my mouth, shames me. My mouth feels pinched, my spirit small.

"Mary," I say at once, "I'm sorry, I didn't mean it, that was a stupid thing to say." I reach for her, but she doesn't shift. The damage is done.

"You're absolutely right, Albrecht. My family, dead and living, are lunatics. I agree with you. Don't expect me to argue. It's something I know all too well. But that doesn't make what I said wrong. Your mother *is* going away. She prefers Germany and everything about it. She prefers Gerhard to you. I don't blame her for that. I do, too. He's nicer, he has feelings." My heart contracts. I have lost whatever it was that I was about to find. There is a rustling of shrubbery behind us.

"Who's there?" Startled, I grab Mary's hand, feeling its pulse and its coldness. What she said about liking Gerhard better hurts. I can see why she would, though. Gerhard's not a bastard like me. I bow my head, as my father has taught me to do in time of crisis, to avoid mixing my heart's magnetic rhythm with that of the respiratory system. It's supposed to help, but I still feel terrible. The swishing from the bushes stops.

"Let's go inside," Mary hisses into my ear as we listen, now, to our watcher retreat. Whoever he is, he's not nimble on his feet. A bull elk in a china shop would make less noise. I follow her in through the kitchen door. "Your hand is cold," she says, and she puts it to her lips. Her mouth makes butterfly wings on my palm. My heart is still beating its half-stopped rhythm. When she raises her head, she says, "I'm sorry, I was trying to get back at you for what you said. I do like you. I'm sorry. I really don't care about your brother."

I put my arms around her and we stand in the dark, hoping to find each other once more behind the words.

She takes my hand again and leads me down the hallway, glancing back once or twice with her fingers to her lips. "Shh!" The floorboards creak. I hear a distant moan. We stop, alarmed. Then start again when all is quiet. Mary opens the door to the parlor, her mother's consulting room. I have not been in here before, despite having seen it from outside so many times. It reeks of incense, sweat, and perfume, of oppressive, unbreathable suffering.

"Should we be here? I don't like it."

"Don't be silly." She guides me with the pressure of her hand so that I don't bump into furniture. We navigate to the far end of the room, to the left of the window, and open—with a key Mary takes from inside a lampshade—what appears to be a small locked cupboard door. Inside is a phonograph on a shelf, with a number of recordings beside it. Mary reaches up and undoes a latch. The shelf is attached to a panel, which swings forward and becomes a door into an alcove.

"I found it a few weeks ago by accident," she whispers. "I don't think anybody but my mother knows it exists." We enter, and Mary fumbles in the dark until she finds a candle. She strikes a match and lights it. We are in a room not much bigger than a large closet. There is a stool set near what looks to be a round table covered with a cloth. A wide metal tube rises up from above the table through the ceiling.

"It's a lens and mirror, look." She lifts off the cloth, and I see, to my shock, a design of a naked man and woman on the concave white table. The design moves. I gasp as I recognize Charlie and Prudence.

"Where are they?"

"Be quiet," cautions Mary. "I'm sure they can't hear us, but it's best to be careful. They're in the sitting room. You can see everything that goes on in there!" Her voice is gleeful and excited. The couple on the sitting room divan shift places. Now Prudence rides Charlie. Her head is lifted, her hair has come undone and shakes down her back. Her eyes are closed, her mouth open. I can see her full heavy breasts, almost feel them under my fingers as I watch Charlie's hands on them. My groin aches.

I am enthralled, embarrassed, excited, ashamed.

"You can touch me," whispers Mary. She has unbuttoned her shirt. She places my hands on her small breasts inside her slip as we watch her sister and Charlie. Then she undoes my flies and takes my penis in her hand. She helps me to find her inside her panties, and we touch each other, lost in ignorance and ecstasy until I feel her shudder under my hand and then I come, too. I feel dizzy and empty.

Mary tucks her clothing into place, then, deftly patting with her handkerchief, helps me with mine. I can't let go of her. I don't want to leave here. I don't ever want to go back. We watch the scene in the glass in front of us. Charlie and Prudence rest in each other's arms, looking like an arrangement of sculpture. I think they are sleeping.

"How can they do that, after doing that?" I could no more sleep than I could, at the moment, fly an airplane.

"Look!" says Mary. There is movement in the sitting room, and it isn't on the divan. Somebody has been crouched, hiding, in the corner behind the curtains. "Nathanial Bone!" He crawls slowly across the floor on hands and knees, opens the door inch by inch, edges out.

"He watched!" I cry, aggrieved. I am angry that Nate has intruded, once more, into my life . He's always there, everywhere I go. I don't want him around anymore. We aren't brothers, despite what my mother says. I wish he would go home.

"We watched, too, Albrecht."

"If I were Charlie, I would kill him."

"If I were Prudence, I would die!" Mary stuffs her hand in her mouth to stifle her laughter. I feel a surge of desire once more and put my arms around her.

"We shouldn't do it again," I say to her.

"No, we shouldn't," she whispers back. I am holding her tight, and I still can't take my eyes off Prudence or bear not to touch Mary.

"If you come here again, I'll kill you!" shouts my father without a vestige of poise. The Magnetic Temperament has deserted him. All his special training gone down the drain. Pince-Jones flees along the path, her turban unwinding. There's a light in every house on the street. A face at each window. My father grips my mother by the arm. She is crying.

"Dad, stop it! Leave her alone!" I pull at my mother's other arm and we tug her back and forth. Gerhard, who is returning from a music lesson, comes running. Behind him is Nathanial Bone. I see them all, frozen in mid-step as they catch sight of us, like Mary's father with encephalitis. Frozen in time. My brain won't let go. I don't want what is going to happen next.

"Did *you* know?" demands my father roughly, abruptly releasing my mother and grabbing me. "Did you know and not tell me?"

"You're hurting me!" He blinks at me, dazed. I'm not sure whether he sees me. "Dad, Dad, it's me, Albrecht." He drops my arm, and passes a hand in front of his eyes as if pushing away fog.

"I'm sorry," he says at last. "I'm just so surprised. Everybody else seems to know. That woman told me." He waves his hand in the direction of Pince-Jones's house.

I sit on the front steps with my father. Gerhard has taken my mother, sobbing, indoors. The faces at the windows are withdrawing. I wonder where Mary is, and if Charlie and Prudence woke up in time, before Pince-Jones returned. I hope so. I want them to be happy.

"She's going away," says my father, turning a bewildered face toward me. "She says she doesn't know if she'll come back. I asked her why, but she wouldn't say. A man needs a woman he can count on." If ever a man's mind were stalled in deep woods, it is his. It certainly isn't present here, on our street, with the air cool and smelling of spring. He puts his head in his hands.

"Dad, it's okay." I can hear the voices of my mother and Gerhard from inside my mother's bedroom. They are speaking in German.

"I don't understand. I have good brain power, I don't congest my stomach, my magnetic powers are increasing."

"I think I understand," I say. He lifts his head and pays attention. I wonder how to begin. All I know, I know from Mary. When we left the cupboard with its viewing system—Mary tells me that it's called a camera obscura, that she'd found a note about it in her mother's papers— we went outdoors to sit once more beneath the apple tree. There, she told me what she'd learned in her mother's consulting room about our family. "Bill Bone's been writing Mother letters."

"Bill? Old Bill? What's he got to do with it?" I watch as my father tries to sort through the strange drift of life. I will never understand my parents, and I don't want to be like them. I like things to be clear and straightforward, as they are between me and Mary. I hate these secrets and complexities, all the hidden corners of grown-up lives.

"Never mind, Albrecht. It is all right," says my mother tiredly, sitting down next to me. "It is my job to say why I'm going, not yours. Go back inside with Gerhard." I rise, pausing to confirm that my father has calmed down, that he won't hurt her. Not that he ever has; but I am unsure of my father's capacities. After all, he did fight in the war.

Gerhard and I stand at the window in our room. Nate kneels nearby on the cot. The window is open and we are silent, listening to my mother's story.

"Long before I met you, Wilhelm," she says, "I had a lover. We planned to marry, but he disappeared. He was in the Luftwaffe in the war."

"Why didn't you tell me, Friedl? I'm not a hermit or a prude, no normal human being is, I would have understood." We hear the slide of cloth on cloth, as he takes her in his arms.

"Wait," she continues, "that is not all." More rustles as she settles herself a short distance away on the step. "I *would* have told you except that I bore a child by him. When I returned to Canada after the war, and my family stayed behind, I left my daughter with them. I wanted a new start. I didn't tell you about her because I did not believe you would accept a child out of wedlock. You are always saying it is the little seed from which the great plant grows." There is silence now, so burdened with restrained emotion that I can scarcely breathe through it.

"My parents told me that the child had died. I grieved for her. It is only recently I learned, after some hints from my brother Fritz, that she is truly still alive." I am thinking furiously. Is it grief, then, that explains my mother's strangeness?

"Still, Friedl," says my father eventually, with a sigh, "you could have told me."

"You wouldn't have married me, Wilhelm. I know you. You are too proud." A further silence. Even the frogs, which sing every night without fail, have closed their throats.

"Perhaps you are right," he sighs. "I do not sign my name to any blank sheet of paper. I might have worried about what people would say."

"And now?" she asks him. "Is it so different now?" We are all thinking about the Odd Fellows, I'm sure. What would they say? And the Rebekahs!

"What does a daughter born long ago have to do with you wanting to go away now? Surely she is grown up and on her own. She may not want to see you."

"Bill Bone has met her. He has talked to her. He has met and talked with my Charlotte!"

"Albrecht said there have been letters from Bill," my father murmurs darkly.

"He says she is in danger. She needs me."

"How did he know to find her, Friedl? You must have told him about her. Told him—and not me!" My father is angry once again, and I don't blame him. He is the last to know everything, it seems. I try to imagine how I would feel if Mary kept something important from me. I can't. It isn't possible.

"Bill has seen Fritz. Fritz must have told him. Bill was inquiring after Gerhard. I asked him to."

"You asked him?"

"Wilhelm! Why don't you trust me?"

"After what you've just told me? Give me one good reason to trust *a woman like you!*"

"I knew it!" she cries. "You are not a person who can understand. You are a man without a heart!"

Gerhard is shaking his head. "I don't like it, she's not telling everything."

"What do you mean?" I ask. I feel sorry for my mother. I think that I am beginning to know her for the first time.

"Gerhard's right," agrees Nate. His elbows are propped on the windowsill. He is massaging the meteor stone between his palms.

"How would *you* know? Getting messages from 'out there,' are we?"

Gerhard frowns, stopping me from saying more. We have a pact never to make fun of Explanata. I don't know why: it's just something we've agreed on. But Nate has annoyed me.

"I know how you know things, Nate. You're a sneak, that's how."

"What do you mean?" His head, too big for his body, swings my way. He throws me a troubled look.

"*You* don't know anything, Albrecht," says Gerhard.

"I know more than you do." They turn away in disgust, but I have nothing to add. I hold tightly to the memory of the camera obscura. My secret with Mary. This is knowledge I don't plan to share. Especially now that the two of them are ganging up on me: they're like a wire scratching at a crystal.

My parents make it up. My father even apologizes to Madame Pince-Jones and invites her to dinner, although she finds a series of plausible reasons not to accept. It is decided that my mother will visit Gerhard in Germany after he has been there a while and has had a chance to settle into his new life. I ask if I will be able to go then, too, but am told there won't be enough money. As it is, even though Uncle Fritz has said he will help to pay for her visit, my mother must save every penny she can. She is looking after Bella Bone's chickens and selling the eggs, and everyone knows how much my mother dislikes chickens.

When, at last, we wave good-bye to Gerhard at the train station, it is with a sense of frustration. Mine that he is getting away and I am staying home; and my mother's that she must wait for the passage of time.

It is just over a year since my brother left, but it feels like forever. Nothing goes well these days. I dread getting up in the morning.

By the time Nate and I go downstairs for breakfast, my parents will be fighting, or not speaking to each other. I think I hate the silence more than the shouting.

It is my mother's fault that today begins badly. She greets my father with the news, in the kitchen, that today is the Feast of the Virgin and she plans, therefore, to take it easy. She deserves a bit of a holiday. Besides, she adds, when she sees my father's face, it is going to be too hot to bake bread.

"The Feast of the Virgin?" he cries, instantly affronted. "The Feast of the Virgin is for Catholics. We're not Catholics, we're Protestants, and I'm protesting!"

"It is only an expression," says my mother severely. "You know very well that I am a good Protestant, too. You must show more tolerance, Wilhelm." She turns to me and Nate. "My family in Cologne marches every year for the twelve thousand Protestant martyrs. Just because I am a Lutheran and a Rebekah doesn't mean that I have to be narrow-minded and ignorant like some people." My mother takes burned toast out of the oven and scrapes it into a pail. She starts over.

"Why are you talking about martyrs? You said the Feast of the Virgin. The Feast of the Virgin is a Catholic holiday. I know where it comes from, too. From that nest of the Knights of Columbus next door."

"Nest? They are not animals. You have Catholic friends, too, Wilhelm."

"Your friend Pee-Jones," he says rudely. "A hundred years ago, she would have been burned alive. You've said so yourself."

"I have the capacity to learn, Wilhelm. I have changed my opinion. Madame Pince-Jones is not a witch, as you so rudely imply. She has a special gift. She gives me helpful advice. I believe that God works through her. And if we are getting into that sort of conversation," she continues fiercely, "about people with peculiar beliefs, what about your metal rods and chains, your stupid exercises in Personal Magnetism? That is truly medieval!"

Nate and I avoid each other's eyes. These arguments are all too familiar. I think my parents have lost their bearings. My mother spends more and more time with our clairvoyant neighbor, while my father stands helplessly peering out the window, as if by doing so he can penetrate all the secrets next door. When he's not doing that, he seems simply lost.

"My work is scientific!"

"It is not!"

"Yes, it is!"

My mother puts a rack of toast in front of him. I know what will come next. He will complain that the toast is cold. She will say that she is serving it properly. In small pieces. On silver. She will not compromise on decent manners. Neither of them will eat a scrap.

"So," says my father, slathering marmalade—to my surprise, but in the way my mother hates—onto the cold toast, "how do you plan to spend your day? Searching for bleeding statues?"

"Wilhelm, your language!"

"That's not language. That's Catholicism."

"I am so tired of your hurtful comments," my mother says, removing her apron. "If I can't have a friendship with a Catholic, who isn't that different from us, not like Jews or Negroes, some of whom are *your* friends, who can I be friends with? You want me to be locked up in this house alone, although I have no one. I have had enough of it. I am finished.

Don't worry," she adds dramatically, "soon I will be gone forever. You won't have to see or talk to me anymore." She folds the apron into a tiny square and places it neatly, but mistakenly, in the cutlery drawer.

"You can be friends with decent people," he says.

"Who isn't decent? If you say one word against my friend . . ."

"I'm not saying she isn't decent." There's a look on my father's face that puzzles me. I can't think what it reminds me of until I remember the dog I chased away from Bella Bone's chickens—a good dog, a well-trained dog, who knew I'd found it where it shouldn't be. "I just mean people should know how to bring up their children."

"I suppose," says my mother, turning to face him, a bread knife—forgotten, I think—in her hand, her cheeks as red as her hair, "you are referring to poor Prudence Fergusson. In case you don't remember, seeing it has been so long, it takes two to make a child, and one of them is a man."

"I am not a person with your breadth of experience, Friedl," says my father. My mother blanches. "But what I know about takes place between a man and wife."

"Wilhelm! The children!" Until then, Nate and I have been invisible presences, absorbing every word without appearing to be listening. I cut my toast into tinier pieces. Nate stirs milk into his porridge, round and round. No one speaks. I can hear my parents breathing, and I can hear—who could not?—everything my parents have left unsaid. Topics unmentioned for months, explosive subjects, too hot to handle, revealing too much pain. I know what they are. My grown-up half-sister, Charlotte, born out of wedlock. Her father, my mother's dead lover. My mother's upcoming trip to Germany and the letters from Bill Bone. The facts of life in their myriad forms, including Prudence Fergusson, who is as big in the belly as the side of a barn.

I finish with my toast and regard my parents. They are ignoring each other. My mother sifts flour, having forgotten her decision not to bake bread. Puffs of it defy gravity above her work counter. She has built up the fire for the oven, and it is already beaming heat into the hot morning. My father practices his eye exercises, oblivious to the sweat running into them. He will be late for work, but there is no point in telling him. He knows the time, and that we depend on him. He must be angrier than usual. I hope he won't get so angry that he will lose his job. We need him to keep working until I finish school and can train to be a pilot.

Back and forth, up and down, corner to corner, his eyes complete the routine. He enlarges the pupils to a startling blackness, then shrinks them. The effort is supposed to be mesmerizing, but to me it is only another oddity.

I hate depending on him. Something has happened to my parents: they are no longer solid. They are like ghosts of themselves, incomplete and partly absent, as if they, themselves, have forgotten who they are. I plan to go harvesting in a few weeks with Charlie Rivers, Prudence's boyfriend, who has a car and has said he will take me with him out to the farms. I can hardly wait to get away. Nate would like to come with us, but he is too young and not strong enough. He eats little, and he doesn't sleep. He spends his nights talking to Explanata about his father and the bears, or Mildred Lark and her tigers. I have tried to interest him in other things. I have taken him to the airfield to watch planes take off and land, but he isn't interested. He doesn't really care about them, not the way I do. Not even as much as my brother did, although Gerhard would get distracted and end up watching birds. Gerhard, who is living now far away in Germany.

Nate still stirs his porridge. He is more tired than usual. We were out late last night.

"Any mail from Gerhard?" I ask to break the deadlock.

"No," answers my mother.

"I don't think so," says my father. They exchange angry glares. It has been too long since we've had a letter. Months now. We know, from what Gerhard had written earlier, that he had passed his first exams and that his German had improved. He had made friends with other foreigners. ("Foreigners!" commented my mother, appalled. "He is no foreigner!") He was to begin lessons with a famous violin teacher. That was the last we heard. My brother is often reserved—he believes in concord without discord—but his letters were so restrained, and said so little about his daily life, that we were all worried. I felt that he was hiding something, even that he was afraid.

"You should write to Fritz again and find out what's going on," says my father.

"Of course I have written," snaps my mother, "but I can't make him answer."

"You could write again. We shouldn't have let Gerhard go. I told you so, but you wouldn't listen."

"Listen to you! Have you written even one letter to your son?" It was beginning all over again.

"Well, then," I say, getting to my feet and carrying my dishes to the sink. "Nate and I should be going."

"Going? Going where?" asks my father. This is one son who isn't getting away.

"Have you forgotten what day it is?" says my mother to him, spots of color still highlighting her face.

"How could I? You told me first thing. The bloody Feast of the Virgin." He still looks angry, but sad, too, as if he can't comprehend why they argue.

"No," says my mother. She plunges her hands into the dough and begins kneading. 'Nathanial's father has returned from Europe; he has sent us tickets to the circus."

"But that's tonight. I want to know where these boys are going now." He has pulled on his shirt over the singlet he wears winter and summer. Armbands snap the sleeves up neatly just below the elbows.

"We're going down to watch the circus set up," says Nate, his face all aglow with eagerness. "We watched the train come in last night."

"Last night? You were out last night?" says my mother.

"I thought the circus wasn't supposed to arrive until this morning. That's what I was told." My father shoots an accusing glance at my mother, but it is clear that my parents have joined forces.

"No," I say, grabbing my shoes and urging Nate ahead of me out the door, "the parade is this morning. The train came in last night."

We are outdoors, safe, away. Without having to explain how we left the house and got in again in the night without their knowing. It is easy to do once you get over your fear of heights. Ease out the bedroom window and along the eaves to the far side; then pass over onto the roof of the Bones' deserted house next door, and jump down onto their porch, where it doesn't matter if you make a little noise. The same process in reverse, but using the drainpipe to shimmy up, takes longer but still works.

My mother had done her best to keep news of the impending arrival of the circus from Nate for as long as possible. He is so excitable, and things can always go wrong. But there are circus posters all over town, and notices in the newspaper. The headline act is the Mildred Lark and Bill Bone Wild Animal Menagerie. The problem is that there has been no recent word from Bill. As I knew, because I'd managed to read the letter, the tickets were sent by Miss Lark. What did this mean? With Bill, you never knew. Nate still hoped to live with him, despite everything. He had no hope of his mother: of Bella, there was no good news. You could sense his need (his dark eyes were indicative, according to my father, of a Moral Temperament) to put his family back together.

We had found the circus the night before at the railyard. Rain sluiced out of the black August night as if the Red River itself had up-ended over us. Lightning flashed, and thunder boomed. The big cats screamed each time. The circus people, each one loaded with equipment, held gunny sacks or squares of canvas over their heads as they jumped from the coaches and set to work moving wagons off the flatcars, or manhandled cages from stock cars and placed them on tractors. We stood by as elephants were prodded down wooden ramps with bullhooks, and the cage boys swore at us for getting in the way. We tagged along, following the haul the whole two miles to the circus lot, asking everyone we saw if they knew where Bill Bone was. They didn't answer us; they didn't speak to towners. Finally, as we stood to the side, dripping wet, observing the elephants lower their heads and unroll the canvas of the big top, a young woman took pity on us. We must have looked pathetic.

"What'ya want with Bill?" she queried. She took a closer look at Nate, blinking through the rain. "Hey, you must be the kid! I've heard of you." She chewed gum thoughtfully and popped a few bubbles. A string of lights came on, outlining the gate where we stood and highlighting the youthfulness of her face. She wore a mask of make-up that didn't hide her plukes.

"Bill says he's not available," she told us at last.

"Bill says?" I swiveled my head ostentatiously. "I don't see Bill saying anything." I was cross. Nate had switched off his face. "Why are you saying that?"

"Beats me, kid." She examined her manicure. "Maybe he's not feelin' too well." She looked up and winked.

"Hey, Nora!" someone yelled at her, "Get over here."

"I gotta go." She took the gum from her mouth, wadded it in a scrap of paper, and put it in her coat pocket. "I'll make sure Bill knows you was here." She skipped away, then called back, "Don't take nothin' personal," and sprang into a tumbling sequence of forward flips and cartwheels, raindrops spitting from her clothes and hair. Her laugh, like untarnished silver, lasted long after we were able to see her.

Nate and I stop to splash our faces at the standpipe in the road. It is difficult on this hot, dusty morning to believe that last night's rainstorm ever happened. Dust pouches up from our feet and settles on our clothes.

We find Mildred Lark, the Tiger Queen, surveying the barred arena inside the big top. "They can't get the damn hoist right if I don't stand right here and make them do it," she fumes, giving us each a nod of recognition.

"Tie that rope up—no, over there!" she shouts at a cage boy. He fumbles the rope, letting it slip so that one end of the hoist tips. Lark stalks over and pulls the rope tight. I can't believe how strong she is. The boy's face is red with humiliation. "It's my damn life on the line," she says to him.

"Bill and I are different," she explains when she returns. "I have an instinct for safe distance. I like to stay out of paw range. Bill, he'll do anything. This is his idea." She points to a platform inside the arena. "We stand on that with Brutus, one of my lions, and the hoist lifts us way up top." We crane our necks and examine the far upper reaches of the tent. "People think we're crazy. We are! It's nuts." She points to the cage boys still struggling with ropes. "They set off firecrackers; the rubes love it. So far, it's worked, but it scares the pants off me."

"So, how are ya, kids?" She smiles that thousand-watt smile, and embraces us, giving our bones and muscles a good going-over with her hard hands. I know we've been rated, but she gives nothing away. Nate and I smile foolishly back, dazzled and breathless. She has white teeth and blond, almost white, hair. "Bill don't always understand these things, but I want to do right by his boy." Her eyes narrow and search out every inch of us. "Brutus has been around a long time, see. He knows the game. He's grown a little over-familiar with Bill, that's all, and I don't want anything else to happen. So make it nice. I don't want Bill upset."

I don't know what she's talking about, but I feel as if I've been X-rayed. She'll have found those small pieces of toast. "Well, you go on and find Bill now, I'm busy." She walks us outside. "He's with the bears. Don't put him in a bad mood, understand?" She turns on her heel, her blond ponytail flicking back and forth like a candle flame in the wind. She is the only woman I'm acquainted with who wears trousers.

As we stand, a little stunned by the noise and smell and light, a little bewildered as to where to start looking for Bill, she returns. "Look, kids." She pauses, and I know an apology is coming. "It's not your fault. Bill's just Bill. You gotta take him or leave him, understand? You coming to the show tonight?" We nod our heads. "Okay, see you then." She starts to go, stops, and turns to me. "Tell your ma, young fella, tell her to leave Bill Bone alone." Then she is gone for good, carrying vitamins, cod liver oil, and lime water to the tigers, and leaving Nate and me unsteady on our feet, our heads ringing with questions.

We drift over to where the elephants are being readied for the parade, the bullhands draping them in spangled blankets and strapping on tasseled head-gear and howdahs. Some of the men, unshaven and looking as if they haven't managed much sleep, have put on wide hats with tall white plumes, and sport lace ruffles around their necks, although they are shirtless. Biceps and chests are tattooed with hearts, flowers, crosses, or pink or blue nudes. On one man's chest, there is an eye with rays surrounding it, just like on the cover of one of my father's books. The eye rests between the nipples. Cage boys in purple trousers and shirts adorned with white lace wear a kind of Napoleonic hat. They scramble in and out of squads of horses, which are all plumed and beribboned and carry riders in spangled tights.

Behind the horses, the other animals line up. A tankwagon loaded with barking seals, and another with a gigantic bellowing sea lion, lead the brightly painted menagerie cages. They are crimson and gold, turquoise, magenta, and purple, each bearing crude portraits of the animals they enclose surrounded by curlicues and furbelows. The hippopotamus's den is sunset pink. Nate murmurs a running commentary to Explanata—something I haven't heard him do in a while, and which reveals his nerves.

On other wagons are larger-than-life-sized portraits of the sideshow freaks. The bearded lady, fat man, knotted man, sword swallower, snake charmer, and so on, although none of these performers is yet in evidence. I know, from Bill and Bella's stories, that the freaks tend to be shy. Almost everyone else is in place: only a few floats and wagons are still straggling in. Clowns lounge on tailgates, saving their feet for the long walk, while a troupe of young acrobats practice a few last handsprings on and off the steady horses. "My mother should be here," whispers Nate. "She'd love it." Tears come unexpectedly to my eyes, as I grasp for a moment the world that Bella has lost. We notice the young woman, Nora, now dressed in a satin leotard, leap onto a horse and stand on her hands on its back. She waggles her feet at us.

It takes me a few minutes to work out the theme of the spec-tacle. It is both biblical and Oriental. The camels are accompa-nied by some, if not all forty, of Ali Baba's thieves. The Queen of Sheba rides in a howdah along with Solomon, who in this version is also black-skinned. Then there is the gorilla in a glass-enclosed cage, and Mildred Lark, standing on a barred float with two of her tigers separated from her by a flimsy dividing panel. She holds her whip, and is resplendent in a gold and black Chinese jacket and a gold peaked cap.

The ringmaster takes up position at the front on his white horse, flags are unfurled, and with the drummers setting the pace, the parade sways, swaggers, rides, and staggers toward town. There has been no sign of Bill Bone or the bears.

"Come on, let's go look for him."

"No," I say, putting my hand on his arm, "we'd better wait till they're gone." Nate and I wait, hidden behind the elephants' quarters—a circus wagon from which two wings of canvas are stretched. Inside the shelter made by the wings are bales of hay, footlockers, metal suitcases, and a table set up on trestles. Beside the stake line are several large oil drums filled with water. We run from the enclosure to the drums and crouch behind them, peering around, waiting to see if we've been spotted; it's like playing cowboys and Indians. Still, there is no one in sight. So we stand up, reasoning that we are less conspicuous if we appear more honest, and stride through the lot with what we hope appears to be a sense of purpose. Most of the performers are, of course, gone, but we find the knife thrower, one hand wrapped in a bandage, perfecting his aim. His target is a board with the figure of a woman outlined on it in colored balloons. It is set against the big top canvas. As we pass by, nodding hello, the tightrope walker emerges from the tent, where he has been testing the wires, to complain that he was nearly skewered by a mis-thrown knife. We slip by as the argument heats up.

There are murmurings from inside some of the living quarters, and the odor of cooking bacon and eggs sits thick as smoke round doorways. Nearly everybody not required in the parade is either eating or napping. Where to find Bill Bone or the bears among all these caravans, we have no idea. It would do us no good to knock on a door and ask. If we woke someone up, we'd be lucky to get away without a beating.

It is then, as we are about to give up, Nate sadder by the moment, his shoulders drooping like bent shovels, we hear the bears. They snort, rumble, and blow inside their enclosure. We had seen the run earlier, but it had been locked up and quiet.

Now the sound—and the smell—is terrible. The animals grind their teeth and snap their jaws; they defecate where they stand in their cages. A one-armed man, unshaven and filthy, dressed in a torn green shirt with the left sleeve dangling loosely, is shambling up and down outside the bars, snorting like a gorilla, banging the bars with a stick, and stopping every few steps to drink from an amber bottle. As we look, he tilts his head back and gives a war-whoop.

"Let's go." I tug at Nate's arm.

"No." He pulls his arm out of my grasp and edges closer, color seeping from his face until he is as pale and empty of hue as my mother's bread flour.

"Dad?" he calls hesitantly to the drunk. The man halts, blinks a few times as if waking, then slowly turns to see the small, too-thin boy.

"I'm drunk as a skunk," he says. Almost insolently, keeping his eyes fixed on Nate, he raises the bottle to his lips and drinks. "What the fuck are you staring at?" He belches. "Haven't you seen a man with one arm before?"

"I wasn't staring. I didn't know," says Nate helplessly. "I didn't know you'd been hurt." He is trembling. "I'm here to see you. I got your letters."

"What letters? I never wrote you any fucking letters." Bill spots me shrinking backward and frowns. "Welcome to the show, geek. Welcome to the geek show." He smiles at his stupid joke.

"Dad," says Nate again, pleading. "I want to come and live with you. Please let me."

"Don't shoot till you see the whites of their eyes, son. Shoot the whites in the eyes." He smiles and blinks a few times. "Did I invite you? I don't remember inviting you. If you don't have a fucking invitation, you're not welcome." He falls to his knees. "I wish I had a gun. I'd squeeze the trigger on those lice." He lapses into silence except for intermittent hiccuping, while I wonder what lice he means.

"Nate, let's go." But Nate moves even closer to his father.

"Dad, I want to talk to you."

"Go ahead and talk," says Bill. "I can't stop you, but don't you goddamn well feel sorry for me." I jump as, without warning, Bill topples over, falling horribly on his stump. I close my eyes and open them, expecting to see blood. But there is none. Just Bill Bone lying there moaning, a little dirtier from the mud.

At least the bears have quieted down. They still stink. It isn't like Bill to let his animals stink. He takes good care of them, I've been told so a hundred times: if there's one good thing about Bill, it's that he looks after his animals. But then Bill stinks, too. I sniff. I smell the alcohol, but what else is there? The bear shit, and . . . garbage! As if Bill has rolled himself in garbage to torment the bears. Is that possible? Or to torment us?

"Goddamn bear did this to me," he whines piteously, his face still in the dust. Nate has worked his way round to his father's far side. Bill rolls over to look at me, and winks. It is a sober, wicked wink. Sober? No, that's not possible, but he's not as drunk as he's been making out. He sits up, lifts an imaginary rifle to his eye, sights along it, points it at Nate. "I'd like to plaster me a nice young buck." He lowers the gun. "How can I live like this?" He waggles the empty sleeve. "I'm not a good man, but I don't deserve this."

"Dad," says Nate. "I'm sorry. I don't care about anything else. I just want to be with you. I'll look after you, don't worry." He reaches to touch his father. In the scenario of his hopes, which is all too evident, Bill will embrace him with his one good arm, tell him he loves him, say he forgives him for his part in the death of Lily. "Dad, I'll do anything, please let me stay."

Bill shrugs away from the touch. He yawns, sits up, and kicks away the bottle, which has fallen to the ground. "You're a piece of crap, kid. You lie down for it. You're not worth the trouble." He yawns again and looks around, wondering what to do next for entertainment.

I feel sick to my stomach. Nate's complexion is green. He crawls and half stumbles backward in shock, then turns and runs.

"What'd you do that for? What'd he do to you? You're crazy, a crazy old man!"

"Stupid kid," says Bill, watching Nate disappear. He glares at me. "You got something to say, come here and say it." He steps toward me menacingly, then reaches over and rattles the bars of one of the bear cages.

"You're his father! You're supposed to look after him," I shout, although I'm scared. "He wants to be with you—what's wrong with that?" Bill is big, and even with one arm, he is a lot to be scared of. All that's in my favor is that I don't think he remembers me.

"He knows what I'm like. He's just forgotten. And I know what he's like, too. It's a tough world, kid, and you'd better get that one figured out right now. He'll get over it. If he doesn't, too bad. He'll turn out like his mother taking cold baths in a concrete tub." Bill spits into the dirt. "If he can pay his own way, he can do what he likes. There's no one stopping him."

"I'll tell him that," I say bitterly.

"You do that."

Suddenly, I remember something important I have to ask. It seems ridiculous now, but I have to try. "When you go back to

Germany, can you do something for me?"

"Germany? Do something for you? Now why would I do that?" he asks, surprised. He searches his mind to try to place me. "Well, you might as well ask."

"Will you go and see my brother, Gerhard? I'll give you the address. He's in Cologne. I know you go there. You've seen my sister, Charlotte. We haven't heard from him. We're worried. Just see if he's all right, that's all."

Bill's eyes are black, narrow slits, red-rimmed with lack of sleep, pain, drink, I don't know what else. Those eyes travel a great distance before they reach me. "I won't do it for you, you stuck-up brat. I know who you are. Don't think that I don't. Don't think that I don't remember. You're a child-murdering bastard, too." I begin to walk away, thinking I'm lucky to leave with my life, and that I probably have Mildred Lark's ameliorating influence to thank for it, too.

"I won't do it for you, but I'll do it for your mother," he says.

Years from now, Nate will tell me how he runs from the circus lot straight down the only road there is, smack dab into the tail of the Spectacular. He can't go past it, not with two dozen camels patrolling the fringes; not with knots of high-strung performing horses stretched through the length and breadth of it. And not with a crowd twenty feet deep that has gathered to gape at the half-dressed acrobats, the ferocious animals, the color, the danger. It is danger, after all, that keeps the crowds coming. A dim hope that someone will fall, a rope fail, that they will see Nature red in tooth and claw, Nature at the throat of its prey.

Nate tags along at the rear with the clowns, gradually elbowing his way by, and earning a few kicks in the shin in the process, until he is alongside the wagons. Mildred Lark, keeping one eye on the crowd and another on the thin barrier between her and the tigers, spots him. "Get the hell out of here, you'll hex us!" She is tense and worried. Sultan has taken a few swipes at the partition, and she knows it won't take much to make him have a real go at it. Nate ducks beneath the sea lion tank and comes up behind the elephants. They are gorgeous. Their plumed, bare-chested riders sway in the howdahs with the dignity imparted to them by the height, width, and breadth of the great beasts. These creatures, to which Nate finds himself drawn, are afraid of nothing they can see coming; but they are very much afraid of fire.

So it is, that as the parade nears Main street with Nate caught up in it—thinking he has nothing better to do with his life anyway than to dodge a hot mound of feces let loose by the elephant, Queenie—some fool lights a sparkler, and there is a sudden shower of sparks at the side of the road. Queenie rears on her hind legs, shakes off her driver like a flake of dandruff, drops down and charges the crowd. Most of them scatter, but a few, too frightened or innocent to run, freeze. One of these is a little boy. As Queenie bears down on him, Nate, who is running in fear of his own life, spots the child sitting like a flower in a flood, holding a yellow paper windmill. He tackles him as if he were playing football, and rolls him out of the range of Queenie's feet, even as the bullhands pull on the leg chains and get the hooks into Queenie to stop her. Nate has saved the child's life.

He spends the rest of the day on air, walking through the city, a hero revealed at last, wondering what he should do next to let the world know who he really is.

———————————

Prudence spends the day at home. She washes clothes, puts them through the wringer, hangs them to dry. She scrubs floors, bakes bread, cleans out the cutlery drawer, mends her stockings, irons her sister's blouses, and undertakes the other thousand and one tasks it has suddenly occurred to her she has to do. Now and then she straightens up to rub her aching back. By evening, when it is time to go to the circus—Mildred Lark has sent Pince-Jones and her girls tickets, too; Mildred Lark never forgets a friend—Prudence is too tired to go out.

"Lie down then, dearie," I hear Madame Pince-Jones say when I go next door to collect her and Mary. "Put your feet up. Are you sure you're all right alone?"

"I'm fine, Mama. You go and have a nice time." You don't have to see her face to know it is wearing a brave smile. I think she is very brave, both she and Charlie. They love each other and they don't care who knows it, even though Pince-Jones won't let Prudence get married: she's too young, she says, and Charlie isn't a Catholic. Clara Rivers and her son are God knows what. They're not Bolshies—otherwise Clara wouldn't be friends with my mother and wouldn't have been allowed, when we were younger, to look after us. But they certainly don't go to church. My mother says it's a shame: she doesn't know how Prudence, *in her condition and forever after*, will be able to hold up her head. When she says this, my father turns *his* head away, but I see the expression on his face, and he looks sick. "Are you sure, love?" croons Pince-Jones.

"I'm fine, Mama. Just let me rest."

Mary is waiting on the porch with me. My parents stand at the end of our walk, waiting, my father looking uncomfortable, shifting from foot to foot. Mary and I exchange glances. 'It's all right," says Mary. "The baby's not expected for a few weeks."

We know what the parents don't know: that Charlie and Prudence have a plan. That it is not a very good plan doesn't occur to us. The plan is that Charlie will deliver their baby in secret and afterward place it, lovingly wrapped, at the door of the parish church, where there are always ladies present cleaning and polishing brass, arranging dried flowers, starching surplices, and so on. Charlie will wait round the corner to see what happens. "Just like the baby Moses!" says Mary when they tell us. We have to be in on it, in case somebody has to run and find Charlie in a hurry. Right now, though, Charlie is out of town, scouting the countryside in his old touring car for harvesting work. He isn't expected back for some days.

It is summertime, so there is little danger to the child in its being outdoors for a few hours. Once the baby is found by the church ladies, it will be sent to the Catholic orphanage. In the meantime, Prudence will tell her mother she has suffered a miscarriage. Her mother will take pity on her: Prudence and Charlie will marry, and then Prudence, grieving for her lost child, will demand a replacement infant at once. They will proceed to the orphanage and pick out their own baby. It will be happy and well nourished, and probably recognize them as well. They will be able to hold their heads up in the street *forever after*, and the child will not suffer the stigma of having been born out of wedlock.

It is hardly surprising that everything goes wrong.

While we are on the streetcar, my father and Pince-Jones squabbling, through my mother, about whether or not to expect rain, Prudence's waters break.

She is a strong, healthy young woman. She looks after herself well. She believes, as she should, that a woman's health is the nation's health. Also, she and Charlie have been reading books from the library, and she knows what to do. Between the contractions, which are much stronger than she'd anticipated, she gathers essential equipment: blankets, cloths, scissors, cord, and so on. The applicable pages in the library book are held open with an elastic. She puts an oilcloth down on her bed and lies on top of it, keeping the book in her hands.

While we are gaping, openmouthed, at the aerialists flying into each other's arms, or catching each other by the heels, Prudence shakes like a tree in a storm as she enters the final stages of labor.

We've seen Bill Bone's brown bear, Nadia, circle the ring on a bicycle, and Mildred Lark's Sultan leap through three hoops of fire, and we've gazed in fear and amazement as Bill and Mildred rise on the hoist with Brutus to rapturous applause, fireworks blazing the climax. We're in a daze, exhausted, and take our time afterward, waiting until the band has packed up its instruments, to walk out back to the cages. Bill is there, in a white silk shirt with the loose sleeve pinned up. Neither now, nor during the show, does he bear any resemblance to the mean, unshaven wreck I'd talked to with Nate. His skin glows with health, his thick black hair is neatly brushed. His new teeth—almost as white as Gerhard's—shine brilliantly in a series of stunning smiles. Bill Bone smiling! He keeps his good arm around Mildred Lark, letting it drop only to pat her bottom in those bush trousers as we walk along beside the cages. My father asks questions about wild animal feeding arrangements, and murmurs regrets about not having brought along his magnetic measuring equipment. "We have much to learn from Nature, Bill," he says. "Nature speaks. We have only to be silent, and listen." I, like my mother, am silent. I walk behind the others with Mary, dropping behind when I can in order to hold her hand and massage the plump mound beneath her thumb, wishing we could find a place to be alone. My mother glances to and away from Bill's stump, her head rocking like a pendulum. Pince-Jones stops in front of every animal to stare into its eyes, declaring, finally, that they are all too stupid to be hypnotized.

We have tea with Bill and Mildred in their caravan. They do a kind of dance—Mildred with the china cups and Bill with boiling water and teapot—brushing past each other in the tiny kitchen, touching and not touching so that you can almost hear the electric crackle in the air between them. They are used to each other, they move in concert, they know about the sparks they generate. My father gradually grows weary. He looks discouraged, as if the sight of the two lovers saddens him. My mother is red in the face, more angry than anything, although I don't know why. Pince-Jones is never still: getting up to look at a knickknack, sitting down and turning over teacups to read the writing on the bottom. She narrows her eyes, scanning for auras. She touches cushions and blankets as she wanders through the room, and is in Mildred Lark's closet, fingering her costumes, before Mildred catches her eye and Pince-Jones says, "I don't know what it is, I'm so restless. Something isn't right." She proposes a séance, but we decline.

It is past midnight when we board the last streetcar home. We are each preoccupied with our thoughts, with our lives, or, more truthfully, with our thoughts about the lives of others.

In the immediate euphoria after the birth of her baby, Prudence has cut the umbilical cord and bound it with cotton. She has cleaned the child and wrapped her in a flannel. She has disposed of the afterbirth in a sack, dug into the soft earth beneath the apple tree. Now she is awake, or she thinks she is awake. She cannot sleep, although she is extremely tired. She is also hot. Her head burns, her entire body shivers and shakes with ague. She cries so often for Charlie that she is sure she sees him come and sit on the end of the bed. "Don't forget our plan," he says to her. He does this several times, but she falls asleep at least twice more before she is able to rouse herself enough to sit.

The child is a perfect bud. Her wide, translucent lids partly cover alert slate-coloured eyes. Fine light hair mists her skull. Her fingers are long and thin. The baby finger crooks. The nose and mouth, small and anonymous, give nothing away but an awareness of being *here*. Prudence continues the examination, touching the fold of fat at the chin, the inch-wide birthmark at the back of the neck, the long bumpy ribbon of spine, thin buttocks, bent legs, the impossibly small feet. Prudence catches her breath, and blinks away the sweat filming her eyes. A curtain of red washes through her vision, then recedes. *Come on, Pru, come on!* says Charlie. She slips her fingers between the tiny toes. They are so small: the skin between them is silk soft and nearly clear. She bends and kisses the delicate insteps.

It has taken hours, it seems, to get this far. Pru can hear the hens, restless in the heat and still not asleep, clacking in the

Bones' backyard. She has stopped to rest three times. First on the verandah, where she remembers how her father would stand there in arrested motion, during his illness; second at the side of the road, where she is sure she sees Bella Bone, in her white nightgown, pawing and bowing, carrying her heavy burden; and last here, on the steps of the Bones' deserted house. Except that she is certain that she has walked much farther. A fluttering, ringing sound troubles her ears. It is bells. Probably church bells. She knows she is to take the child all the way to the church, but she can go no farther. Perhaps she is already there? The child is so light in her dizzy arms that she can scarcely feel her. She might be a leaf, a leaf Prudence could let drop, but mustn't. Prudence lays her down, kisses her one last time, and makes her way, step by step, home.

When he steps onto the porch of his old house, ready to climb the drainpipe to the roof, and from there to cross to our house and to our bedroom, Nate finds the child. On this day of all days, this night of all nights, when he has had time to reflect on who and what he is meant to be— on his painful past and his capacity for greatness—he knows at once why the child is there. He turns back the flap of flannel and peers into the bright little face. He does not think of possible mothers: he is not interested in mothers. Bella has once and for all cured him of that. There are plenty of children and plenty of mothers in the world. But he, Nate, needs a child, and he knows who has sent her. *Explanata*. To heal him of his wounds.

He leaves her only long enough to gather up a few belongings, and to write a note to my mother, explaining that he has gone with Bill. He says nothing about a child. A child is a private matter. A child is family.

We are hurt by the way Nate has left us. I kick his belongings under the bed and never look at them again. My mother frets over the general ingratitude of children and says she has let Bella down. My father shakes his head and opines that we will all, eventually, receive our just mental deserts. We do not, nor does anyone, connect the two incidents: Nate's running away, and the tragic disappearance of the infant. My mother says that Prudence *has got what was coming.* My father says, "For Christ's sake, Friedl, have you no pity?" Prudence, buried in fever, had revealed nothing of sense until it was too late: a search of the orphanages turned up nothing. No trace of the missing baby came to light, despite notices in the newspapers and an offer of a reward for the child's return, generously made by the Odd Fellows. It doesn't occur to anybody that Nate might have taken the newborn. It is not a thing that a twelve-year-old boy would do.

5

MENTAL
MAGNITUDE

The world sat before her in shades of white and gray, blue, light blue, and turquoise. She tried to remember what she had been doing before she entered the ice cave. She could remember seeing the stalactites and stalagmites. They stretched toward each other, never quite meeting. They had made her dizzy with light, and she had turned round and round, lost in their colors. But before that? There'd been a blue, gray, and white sky. Gray and white snow. Hours of crossing leads, many of them small ones, sometimes over very thin ice. There was rough ice, too, piled by the blowing wind, the icecap thicker here, because of the drift, than on the Soviet side.

Fika reached for her goggles, and as she realized that she did not have them with her, she registered the absence of backpack, of her skis and other gear, and that she was sitting, completely disoriented, in the open. She looked at the sun, but it was no help, rolling as it did just above the horizon, day or night, like a fat red balloon. She could hear her heartbeat, its message as lost to the rest of the world as the fading human pulse of the cosmonauts, some of them women, who had been unable to return to earth. Marina had told her how she had listened to their final messages, the voices faint, on the radio, as nail scratches. She had listened until the voices and pulses were extinguished.

> Enough of living by the law
> Given by Adam and Eve.
> The jade of history we will ride to death.
> Left! Left! Left!

The Soviet song sprang into her brain and took Fika suddenly to her feet. Now she could see the tent! It was bright orange—for some reason she had erected it colored side out—dangerously visible on the ice to overflying planes, but a lifesaver to her now. What had lured her away from its safety? What had she been thinking of?

The little stove was melting snow for water, and she was opening a tin of meat, when it came to her. She'd felt herself disappearing, one more white dot in a white world of dots, throughout the day. Weighted with fear, fighting it as well as she could, but too frightened to do otherwise, she had put the tent up so that, if nothing else, it could be seen, a thumbprint in the nothingness. Then she'd gone to check the surrounding ice for thickness. At an open lead, a seal poked its head above the surface. It was the first living creature she had seen for days. She had climbed an ice ridge for a closer look, and it was then that she had discovered the small ice cave, bent to enter it, and been engulfed in its light.

When the swirling stopped, she was standing outside the two-story barracks at the new camp, close to the barbed wire. Although it was night, she could see for miles over the open land. She was wearing her winter clothing of wadded pants, wadded jacket, wadded winter cap with dogskin earflaps, heavy under-clothes, heavy canvas gloves, and a pair of *valenki* on her feet. When she breathed, she could feel frost enter her lungs, could hear the ribs below her heart crack with cold. She felt no pain, only a great weariness.

Gerhard's face was a wedge of bone. The better food of the new camp had made little difference to him. He coughed frequently, and his sightless eyes looked red and sore as the two of them stood facing the eastern sky where minutes before a line of meteors had passed, so white and bright that they had appeared to be only about fifteen meters above the horizon.

He told her, then, the story of Andrei, the Swedish airman, who with his two companions had left from Spitsbergen in their hot-air balloon, the *Eagle*, in July of 1897, hoping to reach the North Pole in less than a week. They had carried sledges, and a canvas boat, and other survival gear, including carrier pigeons and message buoys with which to communicate with the world. Floating above the polar sea in their hydrogen-filled balloon, unable to bear the idea of living and dying—forgotten within the ranks—the men wrote in their journals and sent out notices of their progress. One pigeon was picked up by a Norwegian sealer. In the tiny cylinder it carried was a bulletin giving the expedition's position. But of the thirty-six pigeons sent, this was the only one that succeeded in delivering its message.

While the world waited for news, there were reports of sightings from Norway, Winnipeg, and Sakhalin Island. The Esquimaux at Angmagssalik said they had seen a damaged balloon, and heard screams and gunshots. Other accounts came in from Yakovlevskaya and Krasnoyarsk, Siberia, from Tungus natives in Yenesei Province, and from northern British Columbia. Message buoys washed in on the north coast of Iceland, on the coast of Norway, and in King Charles Land, Spitsbergen, but no trace of the expedition was found.

Fika listened, her vision washed in after-images of light that made the darkness in front of her terrifyingly dense. From somewhere in that darkness came a snap like breaking wood, a noise, Gerhard whispered, that could only be made by striking a frozen limb with a stick. Someone had been made to dip his hands in a barrel of ice water before he—or she—was beaten. Someone nameless and lost.

Thirty years passed, said Gerhard, before Andrei and his men were found on an island. They had set up camp there and died very quickly afterward, no one knew why.

Now, safely in the tent, Fika heated and ate the meat, made tea, washed in the remaining hot water, and then went outside to relieve herself. When she had finished, she looked at her watch. It was time to sleep.

You cannot expect a life, any life, to run smoothly, especially not the life of a freed prisoner. Still, for a while, all goes well. In 1882, Otto, Fika's great-grandfather, obtains permission to marry the daughter of a Skoptsi baker who sells bread to the goldfields. Otto and his wife live in the village of Spaskoie for several years. She operates a bakery, and Otto guides parties of the nobility on their expeditions. Four children are born to them. The last child, Clara, will be Fika's grandmother.

After Clara's birth, the family moves to Yakutsk, where Otto hopes, through the influence of his powerful clients, to obtain his pardon. He wants to take his family out of Siberia, either back to Germany or to the New World. But these hopes are obliterated when, in 1889, when Clara is a year old, the family narrowly escapes death during the terrible massacre of the political exiles in Yakutsk. From then on, they live in hiding in the remotest regions of the Lena Delta.

It is a wild and desolate country. As they journey northward, first the spruce trees, then the larch, disappear. Finally, there is only the hardy Siberian larch remaining on the delta fringes. There is little to remind them of the outside world; and the only evidence of other human beings is the occasional fox trap and the tents and yurtas of the Tunguses, where they are fishing at the mouths of streams. Yet the family is more or less content, and Otto suppresses his desire for a different kind of life, letting it appear only in the stories he tells his children.

There are thousands of islands in the delta. Each is covered in moss and swamp, and separated from the others by channels that frequently shift their depth and direction, sometimes several times during the course of one summer. It is on one of these islands that the family is living, and fishing, at the end of June 1908. Early in the morning, there is the sound of a turbulent wind, and then the noise of a distant explosion. The earth trembles, there are more atmospheric blows, and an extraordinary roar, like that of a thousand wild animals, emanating from underground. Even before the first explosions are heard, the family sees a heavenly body cross the sky. As it touches the horizon, a giant flame cuts the sky in two. If they live, vows Otto on the spot, covering his eyes against the light, which is too bright for the naked eye, he will send one of his children away from this desperate place to the New World.

So it is that in the late summer of the following year, Otto and Clara travel by kayak, navigating with care so as to arrive safely at the island summer home of the Tungus chief, Vinokuroff. Otto has arranged for two guides to meet Clara there. One of these men is a Tungus who has been ill, and could not accompany the rest of the men on their hunt for wild reindeer. The other is Nicholas Hanner, an escapee from the goldfields who had turned himself into a moderately successful trapper. He had met Otto the year before at Bulun, where Otto had gone secretly to trade furs.

Here, after saying good-bye to her father, Clara waits for the weather to turn cold: the next stage of the journey that her father has planned for her—a journey that will take her out of Siberia forever—must be made by dog-sledge.

In October, Clara and the two men set off across the Arctic ice toward the mouth of the Olenek. They camp near a small group of yurtas, where the dogs are exchanged for reindeer, and continue on toward Anabar. They travel quickly over the land that rises from the valley of the Olenek, then turn southwesterly to cross the frozen tundra. They encounter dense fog, heavy with ice particles, that obscures everything in front of them but the horns of the nearest reindeer.

Day after day they travel, resting only where there is plenty of moss for the reindeer to eat, and making their meals from frozen fish cut in slices.

From Anabar to Katangskoie, from there along the northern edge of the Anabar Massif, a plateau broken by valleys . . . At length, having spent fifty-one days on the journey and having travelled a distance of about three thousand kilometers, they arrive at Dudinskoie on the lower Yenesei, where the Tungus guide leaves to return to his home.

Now Clara and Nicholas must travel the seven hundred and twenty-five kilometers upriver along the Yenesei to Turukhansk by reindeer sledge over treacherous river ice, where there are stretches of deep snow with water beneath. Once, a reindeer plunges through. Quickly, Nicholas cuts the harness, and then he and Clara pull the reindeer out by rope. They take shelter at a nearby station where the animals are fed and rested, and they are given old news by the few disheartened people who live there. There is nothing to see on this stage of the journey but poor trees. Nothing to do but travel, and talk to each other of their hopes for the end of the journey. They cross a stretch of taiga through forest and arrive, late one night, at Turukhansk.

It is here, at the house of the acting chief of police, that Clara and Nicholas are married. They use the false papers that Otto has obtained for them, and tell a story that they have prepared.

Nicholas is a surveyor on his way to rejoin his party at the railroad at Krasnoyarsk. Clara, a distant cousin, has been on a vist from Tomsk. The story is not questioned. The long winter night has fallen, and the Turukhansk settlers, busy with cards and vodka, and with their private quarrels, have other things on their minds than the two young people. It is a world of adventurers and exiles and nearby colonies of banished sectarians. Where Stundists and Skoptsi and Duchobortski hold fast to particular and inflexible points of view. Particular enough to justify the suffering that has been forced upon them.

It is a marriage of necessity, of course, not just because of the pregnancy, which is in evidence by the time Nicholas and Clara reach Krasnoyarsk, having traveled the long fourteen hundred kilometers with horses, braving snowstorms, but because in the whole wide white world of winter they have only each other.

Clara waits until after the baby is born. She works for Mrs. Shehegoliov in her feeding house and school for orphans, while Nicholas, with his false papers, toils with the surveyors. Then, one day in early 1912, while the baby is with Mrs. Shehegoliov, Clara boards the train to Ob. As Nicholas knows, when he is told this at the station where he has gone to make inquiries, the Ob train connects to the length of the West Siberian railroad, which joins with the Samara–Zlatoust railway; and then from Batraki on the Volga River to the Black Sea. He and Clara have discussed the route often, although she has never said when exactly she would go. He has no papers; he cannot leave, himself, to try for a better life. When she can, she will send for the child. And he will try to believe that there is a way for him to acquire the papers he needs. Better not to say good-bye. Better to plan to meet again. Somehow. Someday. Somewhere.

As for now, restless and cold in her sleeping bag, her mind still full of the music Gerhard sang to accompany the stories—music he had composed, as a boy, when he had first heard them—Fika brushed away leaves of frost that had formed around her nose and mouth, and gradually awakened in the dim ocher light of the tent to hear the hiss of wind outside. When it fell quiet, there was the tinkling sound of reindeer, the squeak of feet on snow.

Quickly she put on her boots and went outside. Of course, there was nothing there, certainly not the child she had imagined riding a reindeer, the child traveling north with Nicholas after Clara had gone. There was likely no one alive who knew what had happened to that child.

Fika returned to the tent. There were things she had to do, submitting to the discipline that had been her lot as long as she could remember, taking care of herself in the mechanical way she had come to rely on: cooking and eating, making sure she was properly dressed, plotting her position, dividing rations for the rest of the day, attending to her skis and other equipment, then breaking camp and packing. Anyone could have done it: Marina or Ekaterina, for instance, if they had lived . . .

6

THE
MAGNETIC
EYE

1937

It is a night of a thousand stars on the freighter *Native Star*, chartered to take the circus to Germany in September of 1937. She has sailed out of Los Angeles at San Pedro en route to Hamburg. On her deck is Mildred Lark, walking arm in arm with Bill Bone. Mildred has cut her blond hair short. It sticks out in points beneath her white sailor's cap. The cap's blue ribbons flip into Bill's eyes. "Fuck me," he growls, "you're like a mean kid with a hacksaw," but he loves the feel of her muscular body close at his waist. She has tucked a hand into his pants pocket below the flapping pinned-up sleeve of his stump. He also loves the cool slap of wind on his skin, and the nearness of the starry sky through which the ship seems to plow. The stars are like ice-chips thrown up in its wake.

They are almost twins, these two, Mildred and Bill, dressed as they are in sailor suits and each with a limp. Nadia, Bill's bear, had toppled from her bicycle onto him, breaking his ankle. Although the ankle has healed, the limp is a habit, perhaps partly in sympathy with Mildred, who was recently raked, hip to calf, at Mildred's Wild Animal World in California—their home in the circus off-season—by Sultan. "A love tap," she calls it, bearing no grudge toward the tiger. The scratches are clean. She expects, soon, to recover completely.

Behind them, at a constant distance, follows Bella Bone. You can almost see the magnetic lines that flow between her and Bill. Bill tenses a leg, raises it, puts it down; it is as if Bella's own long leg is on an attached string, rising and lowering at the same time. Nate thinks, as he watches them, his mother in the black she has worn ever since Lily's death, that they are so much in time they could be pedaling a bicycle; or they are like the head and tail of a comet, a linked ball and chain on the same trajectory. Where Bill goes, Bella goes: whatever the world has to say about it, whatever Mildred Lark or Bill himself says, the contract is unbreakable. Especially now that Bella is needed to raise the young child.

Nate worries about his mother's future, although he hopes Bill will never cut the final ties. How would Bella survive?

But what can be done for Bella has been done. Bill rescinded his agreement to her commitment in the Assiniboine Asylum and, at Nate's insistence, sent money so that she could come to

California with them and join the Bone ménage. "She would make a good nurse for Elizabeth," Nate had argued, and Bill and Mildred agreed. They loved the child—Nate's miracle child—but who could take enough time out of their own busy schedule to care for a two-year-old?

Bella is happy with the arrangement. She has given up her claim to Bill's bed and accepted Mildred Lark as her replacement with equanimity. She is not to be blamed for her change of heart. When you think of what Bella has been through, who would have the right? That white-tiled room with concrete floor, and lengths of steel pipe along the walls; those shining, dripping taps protruding at one end, and the bath itself, with its thick wooden lid, a hole cut in the top for the head and two smaller holes farther down, through which her hands were brought and strapped before the lid was locked on . . . the functional, brutal accoutrements of cold water therapy. What wouldn't be preferable to that? Why should it matter that her husband lives with two women? What can such a private matter weigh in the overall balance of good and evil? Of sickness and health?

"It weighs less than a feather, is less harmful than standing outside in a blizzard in your bathing suit," said my father, when the subject of Bella's arrangement was raised in our home. But then, we didn't know the whole story; we only knew what we were told, and we had troubles enough of our own to keep us busy.

Still, Nate watches Bella sometimes, with the horses in the hold, as she rubs against their flanks, nickers into their ears, whispers to them of her secret understanding, and he knows it isn't so easy to fix things. When asked how she is, though, Bella will say, "Fine, just fine." She writes to my mother, "Everything is fine, I'm fine, thank you, you're welcome. When the sun shines, I want to live," and my mother rages wordlessly over Bella's escape from the small world of Ross Street, biting her cheek and rapidly clicking her short tongue against the roof of her mouth . . .

Bella nurses and grooms and combs little Elizabeth as if she were her very own. For Elizabeth is a gift from heaven, a second chance. Elizabeth has made them into a family again. Elizabeth is the linchpin.

Native Star rolls and lurches down the Pacific coast. Nate stands in the bow with the child, watching phosphorescence trim the bow wave. A shoal of flying fish flashes, shining, through the water, racing the keel, leaping into the air, flipping over in mistimed aerobatics that land the fish upside down in the waves. Elizabeth crows with pleasure, and reaches out her arms as if she would catch them.

Nate, at fifteen, is as tall as his father, with shoulders as broad, too, although he is skinny—too thin, you would think, to wear with any authority the football uniform of numbered cotton jersey and canvas pants that he prefers. In California, though, he is a football star. He is the Big Gun who spiked a running attack for his high school team; he hoofs the ball effortlessly, always on target; he can go both ways, playing both offense and corner defense; he is a superb passer. Despite his youth, he has already been scouted by an agent from the Cleveland Rams. He has a great career ahead of him: he plays as if his life depends on it, even in practices. Other team members are a little afraid of him, for there is nothing he dislikes more than losing. "Once burned, twice shy," says Nate to those who question this attitude.

Even here, at sea, he works out on deck with his coach, Professor Clyde, putting himself through a regimen of calisthenics, and practicing passing and receiving. Clyde—who oversees the sideshow—is responsible for much of Nate's success. He was once a great football player himself, but he killed his wife and paid the price for it in jail. The sideshow freaks, and Nate, are his second chance.

Elizabeth wiggles free of Nate's hand to run after Bella, who has just passed by on her circuit of the deck. The child's fizzy blond hair traps sparks of light from the uncovered portholes of the salon as she whizzes along. Nate has drilled a small hole into his fragment of meteorite, and threaded a thong through it. The stone hangs around Elizabeth's neck, flipping and flapping as she runs. As long as she wears it, he knows he can find her. She speeds up to Bella, and trips over her feet, perilously close to the rail. Bella reaches out a long arm and scoops her to safety. "You're fine, Lizzie, just fine," she says, giving her a cuddle.

A thousand times, even on this night of a thousand million stars, when he can feel the prickle of starlight on his face, Nate has pictured the child escaping his care and plunging, forever lost, into the sea. To allow Elizabeth, even when she is with Bella—where else could she be as safe?—out of his sight while he attends to his work is a torment to him. But he cannot always have her with him. There is no way he can watch her every minute. He is responsible for the elephants, for one thing, and they cannot be trusted with her. Romeo, the twelve-foot-high African elephant, once picked her up in his trunk, raised her over his head, and dropped her. Elizabeth shouted with pleasure as she flew through the air and bounced in the hay. But Nate had seen the cruel gleam in Romeo's eye, and knew that the jealous elephant had wished her death. There were stories, told by the bullhands, that reinforced his fears. One beast had ripped a man who had struck it, years before, limb from limb and tossed the pieces of his body over its back. Another elephant, mad with jealousy of its handler's new bride, had crushed the young woman against a wall by the easy swing of its trunk. An elephant could wait forever for revenge. Nate knew he could not hide his love for Elizabeth from Romeo. Nate could take no chances.

Bella hugs Elizabeth. She lifts the child in her arms. "Up now, easy does it." Bella, always thin, has lost weight. Her hair is completely white. Her skin has paled, too, as if blood has been withdrawn from the entire system. Elizabeth, on the other hand, who has been decorated in sequins and ribbons by the acrobats, glitters brilliantly. These two—Bella and Lizzie—are jewel and setting, performer and stage. Nate can hardly bear to look at them: so many feelings jumble together in that darkness and brightness. And he can hardly wait for Elizabeth to be put to bed, to have seen her safely through another twenty-four hours.

On down the coast to the Panama Canal, with some of the animals suffering from seasickness and others from fevers; several carcasses are sadly consigned to Gatun Lake . . . sailing on to Cristobal, past Puerto Rico, through the Mona Passage, in sight of the Azores, and then on up to Le Havre, where they take on feed and continue to Hamburg. Arriving safely.

Bella Bone had gone in a spurt of dust, and now she was completely independent, out of my mother's reach. And on the verge of adventure. This is too much for my mother. "After all we've done! There's not an ounce of gratitude in that family! I knelt at the bedside, I held her hand, I cared for her child!" She has just received Bella's letter telling her about the forthcoming European trip and extolling the California orange trees in blossom—"Friedl, you would be just delighted"—and the excitements of the flood that had threatened to overflow the Los Angeles River and break its levee—"Many lost their lives!" My mother can't believe it. Bella Bone, of all people, slipping her collar and going abroad. And Mildred Lark, the circus hussy, appearing in films and making a name for herself with Wild Animal World. And Nate, playing outstanding football, breaking records and, what's more, turning out to be handy with the elephants. And not a word about Bill Bone, not a word about anything, or anyone, of real significance.

"The eye of the Lord is in every place," says my mother darkly, condemning her friend. Her jealousy and envy, her bitterness at her own lot in life, are dreadful to see. All at once, it seems, my mother ages. Her hair is less red, more brassy blond, her skin has the texture of fatty soap. The sun and moon, constant in their motions, cease to rise and set for her. Soundless birds, colorless flowers plague her world. Nothing pleases her. Not my father's offer to realign her to her birthplace through magnetic channeling ("You are such a fool, Wilhelm! There is no such thing as magnetism in Cologne."), nor my own invitation to take her to the airfield to watch the planes holds any interest or prospect of relief. "Oh, if only I could speak! Such things have happened, even in this very room." She shakes her head, heavy with its mysterious burden. It is useless to talk to her.

"There is only one place I wish to go, and it is forbidden to me," my mother intones gloomily. "Why must I suffer because I am married and have children? Why cannot I do what I want?" She sits at the kitchen table, day upon day, twisting a strand of dull hair round her finger. She rubs the knot smooth with her index finger, releases it, and begins over until her head is a bush—or like moss with tendrils. She frets over the lack of news from Gerhard and pens letters of complaint to the newspaper about the postal service: "Only a mother such as I will understand the pain of lost letters." She is found writing poems, in German, to her grown daughter, Charlotte. "Oh, if only I could see her one more time!" she groans, for Bill Bone has written that he has had several more opportunities to see Charlotte on his trips to Germany; and Uncle Fritz, at last, has reluctantly confirmed that Charlotte is indeed alive and well and living not far from him. He suggests that now the secret is out, my mother should come to see her. "It is time to put the past behind you, time to look ahead. You must think of your daughter's future." But through all this, my father has been adamant. It is too dangerous, Germany is in turmoil, he does not think it safe for my mother to go.

"What about your son?" says my mother. "What about Gerhard? Why have you abandoned him?" My father no longer bothers to answer; he just shakes his head in despair.

My mother will not eat. She drags her bony frame, sad braids drooping over her ears, to see Madame Pince-Jones and take what comfort she can in the medium's prognostications. Finally, at the end of his tether, finding no solace in any corner of his life, my father goes, too, and listens to what the next-door neighbor has to say.

———

"You won't be able to do a thing for Gerhard," my father warns. "You might even put him in danger." The battle has ended. My mother has won. She is going to Germany. It doesn't take a Pince-Jones to see that my mother's very health is at stake. The warning is only my father's last attempt to salvage his pride. We are standing together, helplessly, watching my mother pack.

"Don't be so silly, Wilhelm," answers my mother, opening a musty leather suitcase on the bed in her room. "These are my people. I know them, I know exactly how to deal with them. I've always been much closer to the Fatherland than you. You have no feeling for it."

"My feelings or lack of them aren't responsible for banning Jewish children from schools or putting Jewish composers, musicians, playwrights, and actors out of work," says my father drily. "Friedl, life is made of individual energies. These little energies don't die, they add up!" He reads newspapers. He listens to the news on the radio. Because of what he fears is going to happen, he has designed a magnetic survival kit. It is based on Napoleon's view of the voltaic cell as a replica of human life: *Voilà l'image de la vie: la colonne vertébrale est le pil; la vessie, le pôle positif; et le foie, le pôle négatif.* According to the Greeks, electricity is the soul residing in electron. We are slumbering dynamos. He needs funding to develop a prototype—the army is interested—and he has hopes for its endorsement by the Odd Fellows, whose organization extends round the world. Napoleon was an Odd Fellow, my father claims, or he would have been, given the opportunity. The sympathy was there, the *understanding*.

"Even Madame Pince-Jones knows a war is coming, Friedl," he pleads, hopelessly. "We have had many talks about it, she sees things as I do. I cannot understand why you refuse to look at

what is in front of your eyes!" I understand. A war would interfere with my mother's plans. My father, who has put on weight as
pounds have sloughed from my mother, stuffs a pastry into his
mouth. There are crumbs on his chin, on his clothes, even caught
in the thicket of his hair where he has run his fingers through it.

"I do see what is in front of my eyes!" comments my mother
acidly, surveying his figure. "Something is entering your mouth
all the live-long day, Wilhelm."

My father, that believer in good digestion, grimaces. She is
right; he does not know why he is treating himself so badly, but
he will not be deflected from his argument. "You have no idea
how painful this will be for you, Friedl," he says. "I'm afraid for
you." There is a long pause. "I love you." My mother looks up,
astonished. She has been blowing dust from the old suitcase.
Never, in all their discussions, has my father expressed these sentiments. "There is compulsory labor service for all young
Germans," he continues. "Gerhard might have been affected—he
has German citizenship. There could be dozens of reasons—even
worse ones than we've thought of—why we haven't heard from
him. Your brothers will be clicking their heels and snapping out
right arms to Hitler, Friedl. You won't like it." My mother's mind
snaps shut. I see this as it happens. Mention of her brothers is a
mistake. There is a sudden dark veil over those eyes which had,
for a moment, revealed clear blue depths, and such longing.

"I have listened to you from morning to night," she says,
sweeping a polishing cloth over the leather, then beginning to line
the suitcase with tissue paper. "You don't care about me, you don't
care about your own children. Only people and events that are far
away matter to you." My father's chin jerks as if she has struck
him. I know, and I suppose he knows, and she certainly knows

she can't possibly mean it. If anything, my father cares about us too much. He is all too aware of his helplessness and how little he can protect us. He has a tiny salary, no savings, and little influence; we totter, daily, on the brink of disaster. His job is all that saves us. The most ordinary thing—an accident to him, a house fire—could bring us to ruin. Moreover, my father has stayed with us when other men, as we have seen in our neighborhood, have found the world an easier place without family responsibilities. My stomach tightens with anxiety.

My mother straightens up to ease her back. Worry lines chase through the muscles of her face. "I'm sorry, Wilhelm," she says. "You know how nervous I am. I am a woman. My thoughts are always with my children. My brother, Fritz, understands my worries. That is why he has sent me the money for this trip. I know you do what you can, I know you would give me the money I need if you could." This is as near to an apology as I have ever heard her give. She brushes her lips over my father's cheek. Then she bends down, finishes placing the last of her neatly folded clothes inside the case, and straps it tight. "There." She turns to me as we hear a car drive up. "You can take this out now, Albrecht. The taxi is here." I glance at my father, and he looks at me. There is nothing more to do or say. I know that Gerhard's silence must terrify her. She has already had one child—Charlotte—taken from her, and for years she had thought her dead. The fear of losing another must be unbearable. When Mary and I marry and have children, as we plan to do, I will not let them out of my sight.

Once she is gone, my father sits in her chair at the kitchen table. He had wept when he read that the Italians used mustard gas on civilians in Abyssinia. It was the only time I'd seen him cry. He doesn't weep now. It is worse than that. He is silent, his eyes hard and shiny with unshed tears. I sit across from him and draw circles on the table with my finger. We both know that the trip is madness, but we do not imagine—how can we?—its consequences.

The circus and my mother arrive in Cologne at almost the same time. From Hamburg and the famous Thier Park of Karl Hagenback, the circus travels to Bremen and Münster. After Cologne—Bill Bone and Mildred Lark's old stamping ground, where they had trained animals at the zoo—the circus is heading to Frankfurt. In the meantime, they set up on the fringes of the market, within sight of the tips of the *Dom* spires.

My mother's ship docks in Bremen. She takes the train to Cologne, where she is met by her brother, Fritz, at the station. Fritz, a schoolteacher, is the only member of the family in Germany to have left the countryside for the city. He is a small, compact man who dresses in English tweeds. He spends his leisure hours hiking or skiing. He has no family of his own, and had been glad, so he says, to take Gerhard into his home and to oversee his schooling.

"But there is nothing to worry about, Friedl," he tells my mother when she airs her concerns as they climb the stairs from the Haufbann. "If that is why you have come, you have made your long journey for nothing." Fritz carries Friedl's bags. His flat is only a short walk away. "Gerhard is a fine boy. He is intelligent. He is making a place for himself here. You should be proud of him."

"I understand that," says my mother, trying to overcome her disappointment at Gerhard's not being there to meet her, "but he doesn't write as he promised. Where is he now? Did you tell him I was coming?"

"Of course, my dear!" says Fritz, setting the bags down and resting. It is a late afternoon in September, but the heat is that of a summer's day. He tugs a handkerchief from his pocket and pats the moisture from his face. An odor of eau de cologne bites the air. "Gerhard has another obligation, that is all. He is with his unit of the Hitlerjugend, in Nuremberg, for the annual Nazi Party Congress. He will return in a few days time and you will see him then. In the meantime, you are in my hands." He smiles at his sister, thinking how old she looks, how she has let herself go.

They are standing outside an eighth-century church, originally a convent, that was modeled on the Church of the Nativity in Bethlehem. As she examines its exterior, and remembers that inside there is a clover-leaf choir, the famous blue interior glass, the shrouded figure of the dead Christ at the entrance to the crypt, the fact that there is nothing remotely like it in Winnipeg, tears squeeze into my mother's eyes.

"It is so hard, Fritz," she says, clutching her brother's tweed-covered arm, "so hard, sometimes. I have been so lonely, and Wilhelm doesn't always understand."

"There, there, dear sister, you are home now," says Fritz, wondering what has happened to the pretty girl he used to know. For his part, in his opinion, he has kept in excellent shape. Perhaps the Canadian winters, which he scarcely remembers—he had been so young when the family had returned to the Fatherland—were to blame. He is lucky to have escaped them. He is hoping that the visit, and the opportunity to right old wrongs, will restore Friedl's vitality and looks.

"I feel badly about your situation," he says, as they resume walking. "I said to our parents, time and again, 'You must tell her the truth; you should not have told her a lie, only harm will come of it. Friedl needs to make a life with her daughter. To say Charlotte is dead only compounds the wound.' But they would never listen. They thought they knew best. Don't blame them, Friedl, they did what they believed was right."

"But they are dead, Fritz. Why didn't you say something to me then?"

Fritz looks uncomfortable. "There is a great deal to tell you, things you won't understand now. Maybe by the time you go . . ." But my mother is too distracted to listen. Now that she is here, the past is the past, and there is only the *now* that will write the true story of her life.

"The river, Fritz! There it is!" cries my mother. She peers all around, craning her neck so as not to miss a thing. Fritz sighs.

"Yes, the river. Look there." He points out a stain on the side of the building they are passing. "That is how high the water rose last winter. I thought my flat was done for, too, but the water receded just in time. We are here." Fritz opens a door and they climb the four steep flights of stairs to his apartment.

"But Fritz! It is wonderful!" she cries as they enter. She goes straight to the tall windows in the sitting room. "The views! You didn't tell me! I had no idea!" It is an attic flat with a view of the river and the bridges, and the great cathedral. Friedl basks in the golden light that spills over the city and radiates from its stonework, washing over the pastel-colored houses. When she can bring herself to turn away, she examines the rest of the room. Under the sloping roof are bookshelves. There is a coal fire burning in the grate despite the heat. Her eyes seek, and soon find, what else she searches for. She moves around the room, touching objects that have been taken from the family home. An old clock. Chinese vases and Dresden ornaments. A Bavarian hand-carved chess set.

"It makes me happy to see these things," she says softly. Fritz has lit his pipe. He stands, still smiling, watching her. "You are so lucky. Of course I have a few pieces, too, from the old days, and nice things of my own now, but it is the reminders of my childhood that I miss. I am *so written on by the roll of time*." He is afraid that she will start to blubber.

"I have put your bags in your room," he says. "Go and freshen up, then come back and have a drink with me. I have something to tell you."

"What is it?"

"Something you want to hear, but it is also a surprise." He gives her a little push, but she stands her ground.

"Please, Fritz, tell me now."

"Perhaps I shan't tell you after all," he says, with an edge of the malice with which he had tormented her when she was a girl. She makes a girlish grab for his pipe, but he holds it out of reach. "Yes, now I am certain of it. You will have to wait."

"Is it about Gerhard?"

"No, not exactly."

"About his music studies?"

"No, not that either," he replies with growing irritation. If she were to go on guessing, she would guess more than he wanted her to. The surprise, which he had planned so carefully, was in danger of being spoiled. "You will definitely have to wait now. I will not answer any more questions."

"Then you must be going to tell me about my Charlotte, who was taken from me, who I thought was dead, who I have thought of night and day since I learned she was alive," my mother says eagerly. Suddenly, the past has become urgent. The tears are there, ready to spill.

"But you have not followed my orders!" says Fritz with mock severity. He forces a laugh and relights his pipe, puffing heavily at it until it flames. "I have decided on your punishment. I will say nothing more until tonight. Then you shall know all."

"What is going to happen tonight?" she presses. But Fritz will not be budged. Whatever he has to tell, he will tell in his own good time.

"I have invited friends to meet you," is all he will reveal. He hopes she has some decent clothes to wear. "They wish to welcome you to the city. Now, go and tidy yourself, as I have already asked, then we will have a drink and we will talk, as you wish, about Gerhard."

"The boy loves it," says Fritz firmly when my mother complains about Gerhard's involvement in the Hitlerjugend. Fritz has told her that it takes up all Gerhard's weekends, as well as several nights during the week. "They march, they sing, the bands play. They go on outings together, healthy outdoor hikes. It is just the thing for a boy his age."

My mother sips her drink to steady herself. "My dear brother, I know you have done your best, but my son came here to study music, not to be a boy scout. He has a future, possibly a great one, ahead of him. He is not like other boys. His destiny isn't parading up and down playing soldier, it is with music. I thought you understood that. I was counting on you."

Fritz stands in front of the fire, stirring it with the poker. He has changed into a maroon English smoking jacket. He puts the poker down and goes to sit beside his sister. "I will speak frankly, Friedl. Things have changed. These are not the old days. There is not much call for a boy of Gerhard's age who does not want to play soldier. He is healthy, he is good-looking, he is just what Germany needs."

"Germany needs musicians!" she protests. "We have always produced the best! I sent him here to be the best! It is his chance! You don't know what it is like over there! There is nothing! No music to speak of!

"Fritz," she goes on, touching his hand, hoping to bridge the coolness between them, "this is my dream. Wilhelm and I have sacrificed in ways you cannot understand to send Gerhard here to be taught by great teachers. And what have you done?" she adds bitterly, as he removes his hand from hers. "He could have played at soldiers at home. At least I wouldn't have lost him." She is too angry to cry.

"You haven't lost him. Don't be absurd. I have done what I could for Gerhard," says Fritz stiffly. "You have no idea how things are. You come knowing nothing and you think you can judge me and tell me what to do." He takes a breath to control himself. "Friedl, Gerhard attends the gymnasium. If he continues to do as well as he is doing presently, he will go on to the university, or into any civilian job he puts his mind to."

"I have heard about jobs," says my mother. "There is the Arbeitsdienst, the labor service, and then the Army to come first. It will be too late. He will never catch up. He will have wasted his talent, and I will have wasted my life."

Now the tears burst forth, a river slopping over its banks. Fritz thinks of the Rhine and how it can overwhelm. My mother sets down the glass that had been in her mother's wedding service on the side table that had belonged to her grandmother, and sobs. There are pulses, waves, variegated tremors of weeping.

"I am simply telling you that the first duty of a German child is not to the family, not to his mother or father, and certainly not to his uncle, but to his nation," says Fritz, not unkindly. "If you didn't want him to be German, you should have kept him in Canada. Surely he could have continued his studies there."

"But it wouldn't have been the same!" objects my mother, lifting her face from her hands. "There isn't the same respect, the deep understanding." Her swollen, red-rimmed eyes appeal to him.

"Children don't belong to us any longer, Friedl," he says gently, awkwardly patting her shoulder. "There is a new world order. You should see my students. You should hear what I teach them in history. Did you know that Dante and Leonardo da Vinci had German ancestry?" He laughs coldly and then, as if in despair, stands up and begins knocking his pipe out into the fire.

"But I don't understand," says my mother. Her face is tear-smudged and pitiable. How childish she looks, despite the lines around her eyes and the dull brass and gray of her hair. Is this what happens when you live, as does my mother, in a dreamworld?

"I could not find a good music teacher, let alone one of the best, for Gerhard, even if I thought it was the right thing to do," says Fritz. "There is not one to be had in the whole city."

"But Gerhard wrote to us, just after he arrived, that he was going for an interview," she says. "Cologne is full of the best!"

"So he did and so it was," says Fritz. "He did very well, too." Fritz takes a pipe cleaner from his pocket and cleans the pipe stem.

"Well, what happened? Did the teacher turn him down? Did he think Gerhard was badly prepared?"

"No, I told you. There was nothing wrong with Gerhard's abilities. The teacher," says Fritz, as he reaches into a pouch for tobacco, "was sent to the KZ, the Konzentrationslager, where they send all the misfits, those who don't support the social scheme of things as I do. As Gerhard does. As you will, too, if you are bright enough, at least while you are here."

"But Fritz!" wails my mother. "There must be other teachers! Send him to one of them!" Her dreams, her sacrifices, her selection of one son over the other will be for nothing if she doesn't get her way. Her marriage. Her work for the Rebekahs. Even taking care of Bella Bone's chickens in order to give herself spending money. She dislikes chickens so much now that she can no longer eat eggs.

"Friedl, you are here for a visit. It is best if you do not concern yourself with these things."

"I want to know what happened!" she shouts. "It is my right!"

"If you insist," says Fritz with exact politeness. "After the interview, we had a visit from the SS. They searched the flat. They read all my letters—yours, too, Friedl. They talked to my friends. They went to the school. I nearly lost my job over it."

"But why?"

"The music teacher was a Jew and a Communist. They suggested that we—Gerhard and I—were sympathizers. I did not know at the time, or I would never have made the appointment. I was following your instructions, Friedl. That teacher was top of your list. As a schoolteacher myself, I must be above reproach or I am finished. I will end up in the KZ, too. If it hadn't been for the assistance of a person in a high place, I don't know what might have happened."

"There!" she says, with deliberate naïveté. "You do have influence. You have nothing to worry about."

"Please, Friedl," he says to her, dropping his eyes. "Don't think about your plans for Gerhard anymore. He is in good hands. He has powerful friends. He will go far if we leave him to do what he is best at."

"And what is that?" asks my mother icily. "Please tell me what it is you know about my son that I, his mother, do not."

"He does what he is told," says Fritz without a spark of irony. "He does it with good spirit and with all his heart. He remembers everything that is said to him, and everything that he reads. He thinks about things and inevitably chooses what is right."

"You will have to trust me," pleads my uncle. "It is not your business anymore. Gerhard will return in a few days, and you can see how well he is for yourself." Fritz attempts a smile. "You are still just young enough, surely, for the bedroom. You should mend your fences with your husband and have more children. It would take your mind off things." My mother looks away in embarrassment.

Fritz dusts shreds of tobacco from his hands. He sits in an armchair. He lights his pipe. My mother daubs at her face with a handkerchief, then powders her nose. "Now," says Fritz calmly, "I have to prepare for this evening. It will be easier for me if you are not here. I am used to doing things for myself. Why don't you go out for a nice walk, see a bit of the city, practice speaking German, remember what it is like to be a German again while I undertake my little tasks. I will expect you back here at eight o'clock."

"All right," says my mother, "I'll go. " She fetches her things. She even gives Fritz a kiss as she leaves. He may think the matter is concluded, but for her it has barely started. Territories have been sketched out, that is all. She will talk to Gerhard when he returns. Things can't have changed as much as Fritz says. Music is Gerhard's life—he wouldn't give it up without a fight. Fritz always exaggerates. He is a person who lacks insight.

My mother enters the street as the sun begins its descent over the far reaches of the river. She dawdles near the riverbank, watching the barges pass, speaking with the fishermen, old men, mostly, who have memories of better catches. She makes her way slowly to the *Dom*, hoping to make peace with its incense and candles and to overcome the Lutheran strictures of her upbringing, for she has need of consolation. But once at the cathedral, she cannot make up her mind to go in. There are too many people, there is too much activity. She stands irresolutely on the steps, then turns away in the direction of the market.

The day, with its warmth, is gone. With the fall in temperature come heavy clouds rolling down the valley and over the city. It is like a wall or a lid descending; she finds that she is taking deep breaths, as if the cloud has sucked up air. A few thick drops of rain fall onto the pavement. My mother pushes through the crowds around the foodstalls. They are eating sausages and drinking beer, vying with each other for the best cheeses and produce. Housewives with string bags, officers with their batmen, selecting, rejecting, sampling everything from breads woven into elaborate dough coiffures to thimblefuls of schnapps. She watches an officer stick a knife into a cheese so soft that it runs off the blade. He wipes it on the back of the dress of a woman who, when she turns around angrily to protest, and sees who it is, adjusts the outrage to a smile. The officer catches my mother's eye, and winks. She finds herself smiling, too. It is funny.

Pushing past a group of girls, no older than the Fergusson girls next door at home, all of whom wear too much make-up in her view, she comes to a clothing stall. She fingers woolen scarves and gloves, handmade in the country in beautiful colors and patterns, with Gerhard and Fritz in mind. But the thought of her brother and her son depresses her. She hears music, a high-pitched thread of sound that resolves into the puff and wheeze of a calliope. She follows it to a carousel, remembering a day when she had come here as a young woman with her Luftwaffe lover. They had stood, watching the children ride the painted horses, holding each other's hands. She had been pregnant with Charlotte. It could almost be the same children, she thinks, as then. Still dressed in too-heavy overcoats trimmed with velvet collars, hair flying in pigtails or cropped close to show off high foreheads and bony noses. They shout with ecstasy, or ride calmly, in trance, the scarlet, white, and pink horses, trimmed in gold and silver. She closes her eyes, letting crests of cries and laughter pass through her, leave her behind.

"Aren't they lovely!" remarks an elderly woman nearby.

My mother opens her eyes. "Yes, they are sweet," she agrees.

"My grandchildren," says the woman happily. She points to a blond child on a silver-maned horse. "Over there, that one, she is my youngest granddaughter." My mother nods. "Have you children and grandchildren, too?" asks the woman.

Charlotte. There is Charlotte, thinks my mother. Old enough now to produce children of her own. Grandchildren my mother may never see. An entire life in which she has played no part. Given up, so that she could have a respectable marriage with a respectable man. Wilhelm. She thinks of their estrangement from each other, the confusion as they listen to themselves say words they scarcely recognize. Hurtful words, delivered with impenetrable borders of ice. She does not know how this happened, what became of the young woman, full of life and hope, who had stood with her darling, mirroring the joy of the children's faces in her own. My mother peers around, as if through some quirk of time, or spliced magnetic loop, that younger self might reappear. The older woman examines her inquiringly. "Are you looking for someone?"

"Excuse me," says my mother. "I must go." In her misery, she scarcely notices where she is headed. A knot of youths, wrathful and sullen, block her path, but she walks right through them. Groups of women, too lightly dressed even for this weather, stand isolated, in shadows. Men in rags throw scraps of paper onto fires set in hollows; she smells the musk of animals, and fresh dung, and looks up at a wall of light stretched across the wasteground, shadows moving through it on the fringes like ghosts stepping in and out of a river. And there in front of her are the unmistakable tents of a circus.

She advances. The wind, summoned by the fall in temperature, the dead hand of cloud over the city, catches at her hair. She has to hold it back from her eyes with one hand to read the poster. Bill Bone and Mildred Lark. Animal Trainers Extraordinaire. The Tiger Queen and The Red Indian! They have painted a tiger mask on Mildred's face and given Bill a headdress of feathers. He holds a threatening tomahawk. Behind Mildred is Sultan, behind Bill is Nadia.

The show band is warming up; she can hear it, muted, at the entrance to the big top. My mother does not ask herself how it is that the circus has come to be here in Cologne, nor is she surprised that she has stumbled upon it. Doesn't she need comfort? Doesn't she deserve assistance, rescue . . . love? There is no doubt in her mind, shaped as it is by her long association with Pince-Jones, and by her disappointments and losses, that destiny is about to unfold. Her heart beats faster. Here is the straw she has prayed for.

She inquires at the admission gate for the animal trainers and is directed into a maze of "streets" delineated by colored lights. Trapeze Row, Clown Alley, Horse Blind. Deeper into the complex she goes, into the knots of wagons, cages, and tents that announce the relationships in which the circus people and animals live. The more beautiful young girls she sees in spangles and tights, the more handsome muscular men in ruffled shirts carrying whips, the more she feels her own muscles become lithe, breasts full against the cloth of her blouse, belly, thighs, bottom defined through the wrap of her skirt. Her hair swirls, her face reflects the opalescence of the raindrops that dampen just enough to make her sense the crackle of nerves in her skin. Electricity. A skittering thread of energy in eyes, tongue, fingernails, kneecaps.

And he is there, when she least expects it, when memory, long repressed, gives up a room in an empty house, a woman with red hair flowing down her shoulders, sitting in the kitchen. The twin babies are sleeping. He pauses only a moment in the doorway to note that the woman is crying, then his thumb is on her spine, pressing switches of feeling from the nape of her neck to her sacrum. He *takes* her standing up against the pantry door, threatening the shelves of china. She has never told anyone.

She holds her breath. He is bent over, emptying a water bucket into a barrel near a string of elephants staked out behind one of the larger tents. A flash of sheet lightning fixes the set of his wide shoulders, and the tensing of his naked back muscles, smooth as a shake of foil, in her brain. Another flash of lightning sets the elephants ablaze, their jeweled and plumed headdresses and sequined blankets spattering the air with color. There is no mistaking his tall frame, the heavy head of black hair, the silver of his skin. My mother holds her breath, not daring to speak. As she waits, an elephant reaches out with its trunk and nuzzles his pocket. It is an eerie, affecting sight, and it breaks the spell enough to propel her forward another few steps.

"Bill!" she whispers. He straightens, alert now, but keeps his back toward her. He is still, except for the flexing of a hand.

"Bill, I know I promised I would never try to see you like this, but I didn't plan it, I didn't know you were here. I was just walking in the market—I've come to visit my son—it's the merest chance." She doesn't know what to say next; she is unnerved by his silence. *Courage, Friedl,* she can hear Pince-Jones say. *When destiny knocks, you must answer.*

"I've tried to forget. You don't know how hard I've tried. I thought I had put you out of my mind, but I can't, not anymore. We can't just turn our backs on how we feel, or it will destroy us. It is destroying me. I can't go on like this, I need love. Please, Bill, please hold me, I am so unhappy."

My poor mother. Nate tells me himself that these are the words she uses. Too many years too late, and addressed to the wrong man. For it is he, and not his father, who is feeding the elephants. He who recognizes her voice and freezes, listens, then goes on mixing Queenie and Romeo their meal of sorghum molasses, sweet feed, and hay.

"Bill? Won't you at least look at me?" She steps nearer, puts out an arm, and turns him around. He jumps, as if startled at her touch, looks puzzled, lets recognition slowly dawn, reaches out to take cotton wadding from his ears, and shows it to her before stuffing it into his pocket.

"Mrs. Storr! You gave me a shock! I've sore ears. Been treating them. Can't hear a darn thing. What a surprise! What did you say?" He blinks, feels as if he has gambled on a third down but doesn't know if it's the right decision. Time running out.

"Oh!" she cries out, shrinking back. "I'm so sorry, I thought . . ." She takes in the performance. Assesses it. Chooses to let it stand. It is impossible to say who is most embarrassed. Oh, my mother, one who always treads alone some banquet hall deserted.

"Nathanial! What are you doing here?" She is so angry that she would like to slap his face. It is painfully evident, now that she has a close-up look, that he is scarcely more than a boy. "You ran away! You didn't let me know where you were! I was worried sick! Have you any idea how much trouble you caused? I treated you like a son!" There is more lightning. The big cats begin to yowl and then Queenie, followed by Romeo, trumpet in answer. Nate goes to them, whispers reassurances, strokes their trunks and legs. Rain pelts down, heavily.

"Mrs. Storr," Nate says, returning to her. "Is there anything I can do to help you?"

"I had no idea, I was astonished to find you," exclaims my mother forcefully, as she follows Nate through the labyrinth of housing. She burns with humiliation. "I am so looking forward to seeing your father and mother and Miss Lark, it has been such a long time. They'll be surprised to see me, won't they?" She pays little attention to what she is saying. Her mind is busy looking for ways to cover her tracks. "I'm in Cologne to see Gerhard, did I tell you? He is here, as you know, studying music. How wonderful, though, to find all of you here, too. It will be just like home!"

The last of the lightning ripples through the sky. She remains unstrung by Nate's likeness to Bill in his prime, although Bill was never so slender. How could she have been so foolish? She aches to say to him, "I gave you my secret—it is up to you to keep it," but she can't. She says, instead, "When will those animals stop!" If they don't quit screaming soon, she will scream herself.

"Here we are." He halts. The curtains covering the little windows of the wagon are drawn, but through them glows rosy, warm lamplight. To make matters worse, she can hear, through the thin walls, the sound of laughter and some other noises, not quite identifiable, but equally, hurtfully, pleasant. Nate knocks.

"Enter, sons-of-bitches," shouts Bill Bone, throwing open the door at almost the same moment. It swings wide to reveal a *gemütlich* tableau. A settee against one wall, heaped with clothing. An oilcloth-covered table in the middle of the room with several chairs drawn up to it. On the table, as well as lamps, are the remains of a meal and two half-empty wineglasses. Seated, and appearing years younger than she is, is Mildred Lark. On her lap she holds the child, Elizabeth. Although my mother, of course, has no idea who the toddler is.

My mother gasps. Nate says that it is as if she has been stuck straight through with a knife. He half turns to look for the assassin.

Bill breaks the shocked silence. "Friedl Storr! A sight for sore eyes, come in! Give me a squeeze. Don't leave the door open for gawkers." He grabs her, hauls out a chair, and helps her to it. "A glass of brandy to celebrate?" He has caught Nate's eye. Without waiting for an answer, he brings a bottle out from under the table and pours her a stiff one. He sets it in front of her and waits for her to drink. Mildred Lark, who is not without compassion, and to whom the whole sorry tale is all too evident, murmurs, "Drink up, lovey, it will do you good."

My mother doesn't move. Her pasty face is death warmed over. Bill keeps talking. He asks questions about acquaintances in Winnipeg, and when there is no response, he carries on. Does he suffer on my mother's account? I doubt it, but he is not—at least, not often—gratuitously cruel. Even his treatment of Nate, years before, had had its reasons, oblique as they were. He does his best to smooth over the awkward moment without quite grasping what it is. How could he? She is not part of his life; she has not been in his thoughts for years.

Which just goes to show you.

After several more minutes, when the strain is beginning to tell, even on him, Bill says, "Well, Friedl. Why don't you stay for the show? We can go out for supper afterward." He is trying to be kind. It is the kindness one shows to strangers, or poor relatives.

My mother turns her burning face, looking round, but not seeing the room. She is adrift, loosed from a net that she hadn't known held her, an accidental form of life suddenly without meaning. She is not real. Her children, husband, dreams: they are not real. They never were. Her gaze returns, magnetically, to the girl, Elizabeth, who is squirming on Mildred's lap and banging a spoon on the table. "Whose child is this?" asks my mother.

Mildred eyes Bill. Bill, Mildred. They cast querying glances at Nate, who has remained standing in the doorway. He shakes his head.

"She's mine," says Mildred. "Look how beautiful, she's gonna dance with tigers like her mama." She smiles, smooths Elizabeth's pale hair with a hand crisscrossed with scars. "Isn't she a darling?" she asks my mother. "Who'd have thought it, at our time of life." She winks. "Bill's a dab hand with wild animals and women, honey." She gives the toddler a kiss, *smack*, on top of her head.

"Who is the father?" asks my mother. Her voice has dropped in pitch; it comes from so deep within her that it makes Nate think of Mr. Fergusson speaking through Pince-Jones. A voice without residence, both fraudulent and chilling. Mildred Lark narrows her eyes, picks up Bill's smoldering cigarette, puffs at it, and blows a fist of smoke at the ceiling.

"Jesus Murphy," says Bill in disgust. He has had enough. He unbuttons his shirt, beginning to change into his costume. The shirt drops from his shoulders. My mother's eyes fix on Bill's stump where the skin is pulled together, ridged and purple, like a drawstring purse. "Friedl, you're a bitch," he says. My mother's face slips its moorings.

"But a child!" she wails. "You should have told me! I feel like such a fool!"

Bill takes the burning cigarette from Mildred's fingers and stubs it out. "Go home to your family, Friedl," he says. "Go home where you belong."

Home? Where? With whom? She thinks, when she becomes aware of herself again, beyond the circus perimeter, in the stretch of wet wasteground where fires still smolder, and men and women shiver together, sharing damp blankets and coats, that she would like to join these outcasts. Where, of all the sins represented, hers would be among the smallest, wouldn't it? To want what isn't yours? What's so bad about that? The architect planned and the builder wrought, and what choice did she have when it came to her heart? She didn't invent herself, did she? It isn't her fault. She has done her best, but she is still in that *deserted banquet hall alone.* She hates her life. She does not want to be a good wife or mother any longer. Shame runs like molten lead right through her, burning out her insides, exposing the empty core, the nothingness from which nothing can grow. She knows that they are talking about her, laughing at her, even now, as they get ready for their performances. Poor old Friedl Storr. Once a pretty girl, now nothing at all. Look at her.

"Friedl! We've been waiting for you! We thought you were lost. I was going to send out a search party, wasn't I?" Fritz laughs, but the look he gives her is venomous.

"I'm sorry, Fritz," she says, dropping into a chair, not even removing her coat, "but I really couldn't help it." She rubs her hands together, like an arthritic old woman, and keeps her eyes fixed on her feet. Steam rises from her wet garments.

"So, I can see you have had an adventure. You must tell us all about it." He smiles, showing his good teeth to the guests, a man in a black and silver uniform, standing in front of the fire, and a young woman who sits in a chair well back in the shadows. Fritz half helps, half pulls my mother to her feet, and removes her coat.

"I've been telling our guests that I sent you out into the city to see what it is to be a German these days. Now we are waiting for your impressions. You have our ears." He puts a glass in her hand and leads her to the center of the room. The man in uniform—she recognizes that he is SS—nods encouragingly.

"But you haven't introduced us, Fritz," says my mother, regaining her manners. There is time to think that the room is far too hot, that the young woman has lovely legs, like her own, and to say to them, "I have been to the circus," and then she faints.

When she comes to, she is prone on the couch. The young woman bathes her forehead and wrists with eau de cologne. Fritz, with a face demonic with fear, stands over her. My mother begins to sob. Fritz presses a drink on her, and makes her swallow half of it. When he tries to force her to drink more, the officer stops him. "Fritz!" he admonishes. "There is no need. Please, let me." He sits beside my mother.

"Frau Storr," he says, "I am pleased you have returned safely. I don't know what your brother was thinking of, letting you wander in the city alone. Even in the new Germany, there are dangers, uncontrollable foreign elements. As for the circus, it was not wise to go there, as I'm sure you know, although I can't really blame you. Some of those people are quite talented, they are excellent entertainers, to be sure, but they are not like us. They are not the sort of people with whom you should associate." My mother doesn't know what he is talking about.

"But it is not a European circus," she says. The officer smiles at her ingenuousness.

"Circuses are magnets for undesirables, for Jews, Gypsies, mixed races, my dear," he explains. "If ever you think of going to such a place again, I beg you to go in company. I will go with you myself if I am free." My mother nods slow agreement.

"You are kind. It is all so different."

He moves closer to her and takes her hand, motioning the young woman away. "I attend the circus myself, occasionally, I confess," he says. "I have even picked up some tips."

"Tips?" interjects Fritz, astonished, his face relaxing a little. "What could such people teach you?"

"Ah, you must take life as you find it, Fritz," says the officer. The heavy silver braiding of his uniform flashes as he turns. He waggles his finger at my uncle. "You must be careful of making assumptions. There are good things to be learned, even in bad company. Isn't that correct, Frau Storr?" He pats my mother's arm and helps her to sit. "I am told that these circus people can erect, tear down, and entrain their equipment in no time at all. The Wehrmacht would like to be able to do as well."

"Then you know them," says my mother faintly, "you do know these people."

"As I said," he answers. He has crossed one leg over the other. His boot swings back and forth rhythmically. "Now, dear lady, please won't you tell me what has happened." Both the young woman and Fritz have withdrawn, leaving my mother and the officer alone.

When she has wiped her eyes and sipped again at her drink, my mother tells her story. How she had come upon the circus by chance, that she knew one of the performers, a former neighbor of hers in Winnipeg, that when she had seen him, she had been shocked to find a child with him. "Such a pretty child," she says. "She is blond. But the parents!" Friedl shakes her head.

"Tell me about them."

"The mother is unmarried, a woman of no morals, who has known nothing other than circus life. From her name, one supposes she is Jewish. The father is of mixed race, partly Red Indian." My mother says that it makes her ill to think of such a beautiful child growing up with such people in such sordid circumstances. She is a mother, she has a mother's feelings. She wishes there were something she could do.

"But there *is* something you can do," says the officer. "You can tell me their names."

So my mother does, and may or may not notice the intensification of the officer's interest when he hears them. The young woman returns with glasses of water. "Your old friend is up to his tricks," he says to her. "You remember? Your playmate of the woods." She grows white around the nose and lips. Fritz notices and puts out an arm to steady her. But my mother doesn't notice. The officer is good-looking, he is sympathetic. He looks straight into her eyes, and asks questions. He nods warmly, encouragingly, at her answers.

"Give the matter no more thought, my dear," he says at length, delivering a final pat to her hand. "Go out into the city again, but go with a friend this time. In a few days, you will see your son— a fine boy—and you will think only of him. Yes?"

"I am so sorry about last night, Fritz," my mother says in the morning as she enters the kitchen. "I'm afraid I spoiled your evening, although your guests didn't seem to mind. They were so charming." She rubs at the headache in her temples. Two long braids, tied with blue ribbons, dangle down the front of her dressing gown.

"Never mind, Friedl," he says sourly, pouring coffee. "I suppose it couldn't be helped, although I can't imagine what you thought you were doing."

"Doing? Whatever do you mean?" She halts mid-sip, raising her eyebrows. "As I said, I thought your guests were charming."

"You made us look bad last night," he says. "A woman of your age should have some self-control. You are lucky things turned out as well as they did."

"I? I made us look bad?" She can't believe her ears. She thinks back over the evening. Nothing in her memory fits with what Fritz is saying.

"It could have an effect on Gerhard," Fritz elaborates, searching her face for signs of understanding. Seeing none, he turns away from her, wearily.

"But it was nothing to do with my son! You will have to explain, Fritz. I cannot make head or tail of this innuendo."

"Who was the woman who was here last night, Friedl? Tell me." His back is to her. He looks out the window, over the rooftops of the city. He can see a housewife across the way beating pillows.

"Last night? The woman? I don't know. You did not introduce her. She was young, out of her depth in the company, I thought."

"You didn't pay any attention to her. You gave me no chance to introduce her to you. She is the mistress of that very important SS officer whom you entertained with stories of your 'friends'— Jews, half-breeds, circus freaks!"

Now the ready tears come. "You were always so cruel, Fritz. I hoped you had changed." She lifts her chin, defying him to deny the pain he inflicts on her. Fritz examines the wounded countenance of his sister.

"The woman is your daughter, Charlotte," he says to her. "She is the mistress of that SS officer. Gerhard's future is in his hands. So far, Major Hoss has taken a benevolent interest, because of Charlotte, but now, after your performance, I don't know . . ."

"You didn't tell me! It is your fault! If I had known!" Desperately, my mother tries to recall details. But it is true. She had scarcely glanced at the girl once the officer had shown an interest in her story of the circus. "It is your fault, Fritz," my mother insists. "You should have told me!"

"I told you enough, if you had listened. You think too much about yourself. I was counting on your good behavior, your upbringing, to carry us through. Now it is for nothing. I don't know what will happen." He buries his face in his hands in despair.

"You exaggerate," she says. "You are making this up to hurt me. I did nothing wrong." But a seed of doubt begins to grow in her mind. Was there more going on than was apparent on the surface? Was Fritz telling the truth?

"Will I see her again?" she asks him. Fritz looks up blankly.

"My daughter, Charlotte."

"I don't know. It's not up to me. I imagine he wanted to know if a reunion was in Charlotte's best interest. I'm not sure."

"Why doesn't he marry her?" asks my mother, taking up her daughter's cause. She begins unplaiting her hair. "She is a beautiful girl. She could do better than him."

"My dear sister," says Fritz, getting up, buttoning his coat, searching in its pockets for his pipe in preparation for leaving for work, "her lover already has a wife. He will not be leaving her for Charlotte, I assure you."

"Then she should leave him," says my mother, as firmly as once, long ago, she had advised Bella Bone to end her marriage to Bill. "She should start a new life."

"There are no new lives for a woman like her," Fritz tells her. "He talks to her. Maybe he tells her things that he shouldn't. When he tires of her, that will be the end of it, if she is lucky. If she isn't . . ."

"What, Fritz? What could happen to her?"

"It is better not to think about it," he says. "I had hoped you might be able to help, to convince him to let her leave the country, in your care. That hope is gone. Let us hope, now, that at least she has saved some money."

Magnetism, says my father, is a conversation between the universe and ourselves, the pulses of creation answered by the snap and tingle of cells. When all is well, the conversation is musical, and we lose our loneliness, buzz with electrical exchange. Circuits intersect, support each other, information passes back and forth; lines of origin are guy wires to the soul on its journey through possibilities. Infinite energy. Nuclear fission.

The head is an important network of receptors, and we must work to locate precisely those that are disturbed. Else we have disconnections, short circuits—at the very least receptors with static electrical potential, lacking the organized arrangement necessary for any wave motion. This is what my father says. This is what is wrong with the world.

Explanata wakes Nate three times in the night. She makes him check on Elizabeth, sleeping on the couch in the circus wagon, wedged in by pillows. Nate unwinds a blue ribbon, sewn with red stars, where it has tangled round her wrist, listens to the breath, light as confectioners' sugar, that sifts through her lips. The second time, Nate moves quietly through the web of snores cast by Mildred and Bill in their curtained-off alcove, and stands at the open door looking out into the circus ground. He is aware of the child in the room behind, of her almond smell, the footprints of her dreams, the meteor fragment suspended round her neck, of the African elephant, Romeo, restless in his stall, the tigers, the bears, awake, waiting, as he waits for Explanata to tell him what she wants, to find out what is different in the air around them. Cut wires, for one thing. The circus is in blackout.

He wakes up, the third time, hearing Explanata's scream a second before the light shines in his face. A half-dozen armed men, hiding behind flashlights, and three other figures in white coats, crowd inside. The woman among them snatches up Elizabeth even as Bill Bone, shaking the fuzz from his brain, lurches through the curtain. "What the hell! Mildred!" he calls. "Wake up. Find out what they want." Nate knows. Explanata knows. There is a pistol at Nate's head to keep him quiet.

"They say they're from the health department. Elizabeth has been in contact with an infectious disease. They have orders to put her in quarantine." Mildred has the woman repeat it three times to make sure she understands. She puts out her arms to Elizabeth who has started crying, but the woman holds her away and passes her to one of the armed men.

"Bella!" bellows Bill. And to Nate, "Where the fuck is she?" Nate doesn't answer. He doesn't need to. Bella is with the horses. Elizabeth, is his responsibility—his. He tries to get up, is shoved back. The mouth of the pistol, cold on his cheekbone.

"Their identification—did they show it?" The child's crying is so loud now that Mildred has to cover her own ears just to think. She must think. She steps forward, ignoring the light that one of the men shines on her nightdress, up and down, focusing on her breasts, her crotch, showing darkly through the silk.

"What is your authority?" she asks them. Her German isn't good, although it is better than Bill's or Nate's.

"Her papers!" insists the woman. "Give us her papers. Passport. Birth certificate."

"She doesn't have a passport. She doesn't have a birth certificate. She's a baby. She travels with her mother."

"You have nothing to prove that she is yours?"

"Of course she's mine," says Mildred.

"You're a Jew," says the woman, flatly. "This child has been
stolen. This is a German child."

My half-sister, Charlotte, has a boyfriend. He is SS Major Jurgen
Hoss. The time is Gerhard's first winter in Germany—two years
before the night Elizabeth is taken—when Hoss invites him to
join the couple one weekend at a hunting lodge. Uncle Fritz
drives Gerhard to the *Gasthaus* in the Eifel mountains where Hoss
will meet him. It is snowing lightly. The leaded glass panes of the
inn leak warm light onto the wet street. There is a stone
horsetrough near the entrance half-filled with water and ice.
Gerhard stands in front of it, reluctant to go inside to the smells
of sausage and beer. He looks over the rolling white and green
hills, the stone farmhouses, the ruddy-faced foresters in blue over-
alls down the hill who stack logs into a cart at the edge of a wood.
Their breath puffs signals into the air. His fingers itch with the
need to make music, to play something that will express what he
is feeling: how this is home, and not home. That he has left his
childhood behind. Mendelssohn? No—the Jew is out. Strauss?
Yes. Gerhard can hear the clattering pots and pans, the bleating of
sheep and cackle of geese in a Strauss tone poem. He hears violins
begin the song of the outsider, an elaborate melancholy loneliness. They are tender and reflective. But perhaps even Strauss is
not a good choice. Gerhard already knows that there is music he
will never play, that a future as a musician, once so certain, is

beyond him, but the memory in his fingers takes him into a
Bartok folksong and through his part in a string quartet. It fills
him with love, and with memories. Cold silver sunlight falls onto
a small slice of field below. A hawk spirals all the way to the
ground. Behind my brother, the door of the inn swings open.
"So!" says Hoss coming out, releasing a whiff of beer and meat,
rubbing his hands together. "There you are!"

Charlotte is not with him. Hoss and Gerhard climb into Hoss's
jeep and the driver speeds them out of the village. They drive
southwest along back country roads, dipping into shallow valleys
where the light snow turns to icy fog. Gerhard catches glimpses of
fallow fields, mute cattle standing in ragged circles, a cat huddled
at the side of the road, stone mile markers. They drive through a
village, deserted except for a knot of old men, their faces masked
with scarves, and a truckload of squealing pigs. Even the church
is shut, the door barred and padlocked. Further on, rising out of
the fog, they come to a gate. The driver stops and opens it. They
follow a wood-cobbled path through a forest all the way to the
lodge. It stands a short distance away from a working farm, set up
with stone and timber out of the mud.

As they mount the steps, Gerhard hears snatches of music, the
same Bartok folksong that has been in his mind! "I hope you will
feel at home," says Hoss. "Your sister is looking forward to this
special time with you." My brother says nothing, but his heart is
beating rapidly. The music grows louder as he follows Hoss down
a central hallway. They come to an open door and look in. The
room is full of men in uniform. The violin is played by a young
girl who sits, smiling, on a marble pedestal. One of the men,
dressed in white, lounges at her feet. He holds the leash of a lion
cub. Another figure appears to be a man dressed as a woman. This

person, clearly drunk, comes to the door and cups his hand under Gerhard's chin. "Who is the pretty boy, Jurgen?" he asks. "I didn't know you had such good taste." The hand slides up over Gerhard's mouth, nose and eyes and into his hair. Hair the color of sun-bleached grass. Hoss smiles, tucks his hand beneath Gerhard's elbow, and moves my shocked brother on.

"You don't have to concern yourself with that," he says. "We will be on our own." They pass all the way through the lodge and out the back door into a courtyard. At the far end of the enclosure are the stables. "There," says Hoss, pointing to a series of prettily shuttered windows at one end, "we have our own cosy quarters. Charlotte prefers her privacy."

As Gerhard follows Hoss, he tries not to stare. Filling the body of the courtyard are several score of people and animals. An extraordinarily tall woman, wearing a toga and carrying a bow, stands beside a man who is so thin that Gerhard can see the outlines of his bone structure through the old-fashioned black bathing costume he wears. His head is a death's head. His eyes sit deep in their sockets. His lips collapse round the bow of his gums. He and the woman are shivering, rubbing their bare arms in a hopeless attempt to warm themselves. A short, stocky man, dressed in a leopard skin, adjusts a water barrel. He ties a strap to one end, puts the strap in his teeth, and lifts the barrel. Sweat melts down his face, but he keeps the barrel aloft and staggers a few steps forward, backward. There are several goats in red harness, a mule, dogs wearing skirts and pompons, clowns examining their make-up in mirrors hung under the eaves, a complete brass band, its members in red uniform embellished with gold braid, white horses decked out with pink ostrich plumes, acrobats in sequins and spangles, two midgets practicing tumbling: in short, most of the performers of a circus.

Hoss leads Gerhard through the crowd, which parts to let them through. As they near the stables, Gerhard can hear rustling and stamping. Over in a corner, beneath a shed roof, is a tethered elephant, and farther back, beyond the stables, at the edge of the woods, Gerhard can see two cages. One contains two pacing tigers, and the other a standing bear. Near them, unmistakable even at this distance, are Mildred Lark and Bill Bone. Bill Bone! Gerhard's heart begins to thump even more loudly. He does not know whether to say that he knows these people or not, but exercising the caution that will ultimately see him through the war, he chooses silence.

"I have a surprise for you," says Hoss as they climb steep wooden steps to his rooms. He opens the door, and there stands Charlotte, thin, blond, in tailored trousers and silk shirt, and with a merlin on her gloved fist. The bells on the falcon's legs jingle as the hooded bird senses Gerhard's approach. "Oh!" breathes my brother, entranced, as Charlotte shifts the bird from her hand to a perch. She attaches a leash to the jesses. "She's lovely!"

Charlotte puts a hand on his arm. "Do you like her?"

"Oh, yes!" He remembers a white gyrfalcon, one of the glorious birds he had observed over the prairie, as a boy: the cool fall light on the gold prairie, the air full of spores and must and dust; the threat of ice in the bird's eyes.

"She's not for you, boy," laughs Hoss, delighted at Gerhard's wonder. "The merlin is Charlotte's, although, if you speak nicely, she may let you fly her. But don't worry, I have something special for you in the mews." He hands Gerhard a falconer's glove and a hawking bag.

"It's my dream! How could you know?" says Gerhard.

"Every boy wants to control a wild creature. It is not so unusual."

"There's just time to see the weathering ground before dusk," says Charlotte, drawing on a heavy jacket and boots. "Come, Jurgen, let's not waste precious time."

The real surprise *is* a gyrfalcon. It is as if Gerhard has conjured her with his desire. She is white, with a deep sternum and broad wings; her beak, eye, and claws are almost the same gold in color. Gerhard learns to use the lure, swinging the set of wings tied back to back on a length of line, half frightened, half exhilarated at the great bird's swift stoops at it. He watches Hoss send the bird ringing up, sees it spot and start for its prey almost as far away as it can see, climbing steeply until it is above the quarry, then twisting abruptly downward, almost smashing the prey into the ground when it strikes.

On the final day of Gerhard's visit, Hoss gives him permission, in Charlotte's absence—she has gone to the village to shop—to go out on his own with the merlin, and a dog to mark the game. Gerhard knows that the bird, normally used for larking, is unlikely to find much beyond field mice to hunt at this point in the season, but he does not mind. Never has he felt so sure of himself, so certain that he is in the right place and at the right time.

At Gerhard's signal, the merlin releases its grip on the short merlin glove and rings up, gaining height in short bursts, angling toward a wood, and then, inexplicably, stoops and disappears from sight. Gerhard turns to send the dog after it, but it, too, has slipped away. He doesn't know what to do. He doesn't know how to call them back; he cannot return without them, and there is no one nearby to give him guidance.

Gerhard sets out over the muddy field toward the forest. The small, straight pines are set close together on the perimeter of the wood, but farther in they are more widely spaced, and there are clearings. In some of these are the remains of fires left by Gypsies, or foresters, or charcoal burners. After an hour of fruitless searching, Gerhard squats to rest near just such a pile of ash and stone. He fishes in his bag for meat with which to lure the merlin, still hoping against hope to catch sight of her rich brown plumage, reluctant and too ashamed of his failure to give up. He has been still, listening for half a minute when he thinks he hears the merlin's bells. He listens more closely. As quietly as he can, he approaches the sound, and as he does so, he becomes aware that there is someone else not far from him, also approaching cautiously. He freezes. Only a few yards away, his head turned towards an opening in the forest, is Hoss. Gerhard hears the jingle of the bells again, and then he sees what Hoss is watching from behind a pine. In the clearing, there is a small forester's hut, and standing at its entrance reaching out her hand to where the merlin perches on a branch is Charlotte. Charlotte! Who is supposed to be in the village! Her cheeks are flushed, her blond hair falls smoothly to her collar. Worst of all, behind her, still in the doorway, blinking at the light like the great blind bear that he is, is Bill Bone.

Gerhard dares not move. He scarcely breathes. He does not know how to understand what he sees. He knows his sister is unhappy, that she has been on the verge, several times, of confiding in him, but he does not know what she wants. He can only watch, horrified, as Charlotte takes the merlin on a fist wrapped with a sweater, and Bill's hand comes up to massage her shoulders. She leans a cheek against the bird's wing, and Bill bends forward to press his mouth into the nape of her neck.

What does this mean? Why is Charlotte willing to risk so much? What could be so important? For it is not love; Gerhard, who can see his sister's face, is certain of it. But what will Hoss see? And what will Hoss do?

Hoss is one with the shadows and broken planes of light in the forest. For now, he does nothing.

This is the moment that returns to Gerhard when Nate, distraught, finds him outside the Langwasser, the great tent city of Nuremberg, among the nearly fifty thousand Hitlerjugend (each with his own bunk number and marching order—which is how Nate has been able to find him), and pours out the tale of the mystifying circumstances of Elizabeth's disappearance. Gerhard sees at once the strong lines, specific as a creance, that link them all: Bill Bone, the SS major, Charlotte, Friedl, and Elizabeth; and how our mother has played the swivel, bringing into play, as the instrument of Hoss's revenge, the child. To Gerhard, if to no one else, it makes perfect, frightening sense.

"If she has no papers," he says to Nate carefully, "there is little you can do. There are laws that permit the state to protect German blood and the hereditary health of the nation. If she looks German as well . . ." He does not finish the sentence. He is teetering on the edge of a decision that will determine everything.

"Can you help? Is there anything you can do?" Nate is sick with anxiety.

Only his desperation has given him the strength to come here. He has failed, terribly, to do the one thing he had promised himself: to protect the child with his life. Explanata's fury is excoriating: he cannot bear it.

"I?" My brother's snowy skin is screened with sweat.

"Gerhard, please?"

Gerhard sighs, a sigh as when one breathes out a soul. "I have a woman friend who works for the NSV, the Nationalsozialistische Volkswohlfahrt, which is linked to the Central Social Welfare Office. It is an organization entrusted with foreign children suitable for Germanization. You will understand that if the child has been placed with a German family, it will be like looking for a needle in a haystack."

"Ask your friend. Ask her to look at the files."

"It will be dangerous."

"What about Charlotte? Can't she help?"

Magnetic lines arc out from his place of birth and reel Gerhard in. He feels a darkness, deeper than music, as he steps through the door he hadn't known was in front of him. "If I am to help," he says to Nate, "you will have to tell me everything."

7

THE VITAL
EYE

MAY 10, 1960

Eighty-seven degrees north. Nearly halfway to the nearest landfall from the Pole. Fika carefully folded away the charts and wrapped up her instruments.

Earlier in the morning, there had been a brief freezing rain that had covered her and her equipment with a light crust of ice. Then the sun had come out and quickly melted it. It had grown so warm that she'd been able to leave her container of sugared tea on top of her pack where she could reach it as she worked, without danger of it freezing. She drank as much as she could. She was always thirsty, always plagued with the urge to void.

Ekaterina, the biologist, had told them about the physical changes they could expect during the expedition. She'd said the changes were a normal part of mammalian adaptation to cold weather. Decreasing temperatures made the system try to rid itself of fluid so as to increase the insulation value of the skin and hair. Fika hadn't minded so much when there were the other women to complain to when she'd had to stumble out of the tent, half asleep, at the urging of her bladder. She'd know, when she'd gone outside, that the others would be waiting for her, willing her back to safety. Now, minor discomfort that it was, it made her dread the attempt to sleep. She would begin to sleep, to dream, and then her body would wrench her awake, her heart clenching with fear, her bladder tight and painful. This happened not once, but six or seven times during the night. She would lie there, fully awake, desolate with grief, as if buried alive in ice, until the infinitesimal spark that was her life, her hope, grew stronger. Then it was struggle out of the bag, out of the tent, making sure that the tent opening was fastened tightly behind her to keep in the warmth. Then that step into the white world, a world without faces. A world she had to create afresh from memory each time.

Marina had asked that they be given an apparatus similar to one the female cosmonauts used, but adapted to polar conditions, so that they could urinate without having to leave the warmth of the sleeping bag. Her request had been turned down. There was no money for extras. She'd been told to ask again, next time. That is, after the women were successful. Only then would anyone care whether they could pee indoors or not, or that there were times when this might make a life and death difference. Fika sighed, driven by thirst to drink again, and knowing that the urge to void would follow within minutes. Homo sapiens was a poor species, less adaptable than reindeer, foxes, or polar bears; less vigorous than bacteria or the blooms of fungi that splashed the snow red. Humans were hairless, pitiable aliens here in the far north, relying on the unreliable—their prone-to-malfunction brains.

It made her feel like a child again, she thought, as she placed the remaining items in the pack and tried to ignore the increasing pressure in her bladder. In the orphanage, at the Château de Froid Coeur, where she had spent much of the war, she had been punished for getting up in the night. Since she was also punished for wetting the bed, it had made for a dilemma. She had welcomed the air raids, when they came, for they meant she could slip away unnoticed to urinate, and then crouch afterward near a colored, leaded-glass window to watch the light of the explosions. They had fascinated her; they had not made her afraid.

There were few memories from before the orphanage, although Gerhard had told her she had first been placed with a shoemaker in the small village of Bleialf near the west wall of the Siegfried Line. Only the priest had known her identity, and it had been in the church that she had met, several times, the young soldier, Gerhard, and, more frequently, the pretty blond woman she had thought must be her mother. She remembered a walk with the woman down a hill, and along a winding road in the fog. There were glimpses of fallow fields, and the looming shapes of horses. The woman had given her a warm coat, and an orange, which Fika had peeled right there so it could be shared. She had seen the woman several more times after the move to the orphanage, and on one of these visits the woman had told her her name—Charlotte—and that she wasn't Fika's mother at all, but a friend of a friend who had promised to look after her.

"Promised who?" Fika, by then aged ten, had asked. But Charlotte, thin and frightened, hadn't answered. She'd said Gerhard would come for Fika at the end of the war, that a new home would be waiting, in Canada, that there was money sent ahead for her care. Charlotte had wept out of tiredness and hunger, adding that she would have liked to be Fika's mother, but that Fika—of course she hadn't used that name, because that name had been given in the labor camp—already had a mother, and that one day Fika would find her.

"Do you have a mother?" Fika had asked her. At this, Charlotte had wept harder, then wiped her eyes with her dress.

"Go into the woods when the soldiers come, and stay there. Wait for Gerhard."

And so, when the bombs were falling, and the others were huddled in the Château cellar, Fika had slipped outdoors to the forest and built tunnels in the snow, hidden food and scraps of clothing, prepared herself for the siege. Never frightened, always exhilarated, and full of hope.

Hope. Although for so long afterward, hope had seemed far away. In the labor camp, at night, she would lie in the fetid darkness, listening to the breathing and snoring, the fragments of nightmares and whispers, that seemed, sometimes, like an element of nature: a coarse, busy wind from which there was no shelter. She would try to hold on, afraid to cross that sea of restless noise and breath, of cries and weeping, of suddenly outflung limbs, by herself. Finally, when she could put it off no longer, she would get up and make her way to the bucket, taking care not to disturb Gerhard: once awake, he would cough and get no more sleep that night.

How she had longed for privacy. What bliss it would be, she had thought, to be alone.

———————

She sniffed at the wind. It was fresh, without animal or vegetable odor, and blowing just enough to keep the ice steady and the pans joined together. Today, she had encountered little open water. Yesterday had been a different story: only luck had saved her. A cornice overhanging a lead had broken off, taking her with it. She had fallen into the water on top of the snow, but had flung out her arms to bridge the gap, and so had kept her upper body and her pack dry. After hauling herself out, she had put up the tent, lit the stove, and changed her clothes. She couldn't have managed by herself in colder temperatures. She had eaten some extra sugar and fat to try to stop her shivering.

Fits of trembling still shook her occasionally, as if her body could not forget the shock of icy water and the narrowness of the escape. Fortunately, she had spare skis: without them, the accident, resulting in a broken ski-tip, could have proved disastrous. The bindings on the replacement ski looked worn, but she could always fashion a new one from rope. She had done it many times when she had skied with friends near Yakutsk, or on trips into the mountains where, on the lower slopes, there were great swaths of stony scree, often only thinly covered with snow. Everyone broke bindings and skis now and then. It meant nothing.

Sometimes, Fika had ventured on such trips alone. Once, in Yakutia, when the tundra was still covered with snow, but the first thawed patches showed on the hilltops, she had watched the Siberian cranes arriving from their winter quarters in Iran, India, and China. From a distance, through binoculars, she viewed their courtship dance, the male dropping his wings, rustling his feathers, and raising and lowering his head with his neck and bill stretched out, circling the female, crying loudly. Years before, there had been many more cranes, but the war and industrialization of parts of Siberia had destroyed much of their habitat. Many of the huge hydroelectric dams that had contributed to this damage by draining the marshes had been constructed with forced labor. The dams were formidable achievements, but at such a cost. The birds, with wingspan wider than a man was tall, needed large areas of wetlands—damp, lowland grassy tundra, or moss-covered moors and swamps—in which to breed and nest. They did not reproduce at a rapid rate, in any case. Rarely more than one of the two eggs they laid would hatch.

Fika had stayed quiet, counting the crane pairs. The patches of bright red skin on the front of their faces flashed as the males circled the females, uttering shrill cries. They were wary birds and would flee if she made a closer approach. She remained still, as still as Gerhard had said he'd stayed to watch the gyrfalcon that wintered over on the prairie near his home. He had told no one, not even his brother, about the bird. Watching its rise and fall in phrases of movement, its sudden stoops and kills carrying the full emotion of life, was, he'd said, like hearing a symphony. To comprehend it, you had to enter the secret world from which it sprang.

They had decided that Fika was going to be a doctor. Doctors were always needed. They didn't have to do heavy labor. They lived in clean, warm quarters and had plenty of food. There were sheets on their beds. Gerhard had helped her with schoolwork at night after each long day of toil. Fika had studied hard, spending hours reading by candlelight after the lights were turned out. For a short period, she had helped in the medical quarters of the camp, washing and scrubbing floors, sterilizing equipment, cleaning windows and tables, and emptying and changing surgical trays. She was allowed to bathe, in hot water, every day. But she had lost her place in the clinic when she'd been caught stealing vitamins from the pharmacy. The poor diet and heavy work meant that everyone was always hungry and malnourished. She had been trying to help Gerhard.

Every morning at five, the siren sounded, waking them. She'd leap up and run to get to the wash water among the first, soaking a cloth in the relatively clean water to take back to Gerhard. The two of them gulping down bread and *kipiatok,* or boiling water, then stumbling through the three-mile march to the factory. There, she sorted nails, broken bricks, sticks of wood— anything that needed to be ordered by size. In the coldest weather, because of her youth, she was permitted to shelter in a construction shack with the foremen. Poor Gerhard. Nothing could be done for him. He had loaded wheelbarrows with earth and rock, dumping the loads into trucks or over embankments, learning the routes by heart. It was grueling work in the winter, even for men in good physical condition. For him, ill with his cough and suffering the inevitable daily accidents caused by his blindness, it had been a death sentence. They had been hard on him because he was German, because of the war. They had said he was guilty of war crimes.

Later on, as the structure of the factory took shape, he had been given a job working high up, on the roofing. There were frequent falls as men failed, in their weakness and the cold, to keep a safe hold to the scaffolding. Every day, Fika lived in terror of Gerhard's falling. She had seen a man fall. She had looked up from her work at his scream. Once he had landed, he was nothing but a doll that had had a moment of freedom.

Fika took a final drink of tea, walked a few steps away to relieve herself, and then finished fastening her pack. She had been standing there, in one spot, long enough. Standing, in fact, on the edge of a great slab of rough ice while she planned the best route. It was like a game of chess, with each move having definite consequences. If her choices were poor, the journey could end almost at once.

On an open lake to the northeast, the wind was making ripples. But where she waited, sheltered from the wind by a pressure ridge, she was so warm that she felt she would fall asleep if she closed her eyes for a moment.

Carrying her gear, Fika stepped out into the prisms of color that the sun spilled on the ice, beginning the work of climbing ridges, slipping and sliding down, sometimes sinking in pockets of deep, soft snow nearly up to her waist, that would characterize her day. Repetitive effort for which the labor camp had been good training.

She floated free from her body, gifted, at moments, with almost magical lightness as she crossed fragile surfaces. Higher and higher, like a balloonist, or a cosmonaut attached by the slightest of threads to an insectlike capsule, she felt herself drift. She watched the shadows that the strange creature cast, fascinated. It was a butterfly, one of the Apollo species, fluttering lazily over a high mountain meadow of brightly colored wildflowers. It rose farther, through the magnetic band that circled the earth, into the zone of electricity, igniting with its wings the cap of gases that shielded the pole into glorious color. The aurora borealis. Pure energy and flame.

8

INSTANTANEOUS PERSONAL MAGNETISM

THE WAR

Fulminating illusions, visionary encounters, dreams—the psychic life of the nation is flourishing as the war clouds in Europe roll in. We see it, daily, in the long lineups outside Pince-Jones's house. Every family has its table-rapper and card-reader, but there are many, mostly women, who require more professional support. Pince-Jones's business is booming as sons are sent overseas, and lovers vanish into the anonymity of the armed services. Everyone wants to know what the future holds and how she (or he) can tip the balance in her (or his) favor. Pince-Jones can help them: she knows how to keep a secret: she'll take it with her to the grave. I throw a look of despair at my father as he goes next door, waits his turn, and moves slowly to the head of the line to go straight in Madame's front door. He looks more puzzled than upset when he gets out, and sits down in the kitchen to chew a matchstick, mull over events, and wait for my mother's return.

But my mother does not come back, and my father is a fool. Every day, he leaves for the Quonset hut laboratories, near St. Boniface hospital, where he now works to adapt his magnetic survival kit for the military, and every evening he returns, cooks us bacon and eggs, and troops next door to hammer loose doorframes, put soap on sticking window tracks, and make the thousand and one repairs that a house without a man requires. He also suspends chains from nails over the doorways so that he can measure the angle of deflection from the perpendicular of the pendulum swing, depending on who is approaching Pince-Jones's house. He calls this an alarm system, and has convinced Pince-Jones that it will show her who it is safe, and who it is not, for her to see. I do not ask, but he volunteers that old Ukrainian women—of whom there are many—carrying carpetbags of old photographs produce the greatest effect. I do not ask him what this means, because I don't want him to think that he can ask *me* questions: such as why Mary stays with us and not at her mother's house when she's on leave, and when we will be getting married. Mary has completed her medical training and works in research at Connaught Laboratories in Toronto. She comes back every six weeks or so to see me. Prudence has moved home to stay with her mother while Charlie is away. Charlie flies C47s in the Far East, on the Flying Tiger supply route between India and China, to General Stillwell's Chinese forces, and even though we have recently heard that he's missing in action, I am envious, sometimes bitterly so: I would cut off my right arm if it would *help* get me flying.

But there are things in the way. Such as a mother and a brother in Germany.

I go upstairs, leaving my father to his musing. Mary is lying on the bed. "Never mind them," I say, when she sits up and looks out the window to watch my father slide next door to speak, on the porch, to her mother. I sit beside her and kiss her, feel her small bony shoulders, the pattern of her ribs, and slide caliper fingers over her fairly nimbly. I always used to be able to make her laugh, but now she laughs rarely. Mary has dark shadows beneath her eyes; she no longer talks about what she does in the laboratories, but she gives me her cat's mouth to lick. In a while, we are lying quietly, watching the drift of shadows from my old model airplanes circle the ceiling. She says, "We'd better find out what she's up to."

I rub a lock of her short dark hair between my fingers. It is so smooth, it catches on the rough skin of my hands. "Why? Why should we bother?"

But she's already up. She puts a finger to my lips. It feels like a soft cat's-paw. "Be quiet. Follow me."

We tiptoe downstairs. My father is back, reading, yawning as if he'd never left the kitchen. His badly washed shirt and pants drip dry over the stove. His sharp shanks show through the thin, baggy pants he wears, as he swings a leg hooked over one knee. He looks up, but scarcely registers us. The remains of a meal molder on the table. In an instant, I take notice of all I've shut my eyes to: the dirty carpet, the layers of dust, the stench of sour milk and garbage. The stultifying fumes of neglect. Without a second's second thought, I lay all the blame at my absent mother's door.

We creak open the back door of Pince-Jones's house, creep past the rows of empty chairs set in the hallway—it is after office hours—and peer through a crack into the consulting room. "Good," whispers Mary, "it's empty." She leads me to that private closet—the door I still see in my dreams the moment before I wake up hard and lost and reaching for Mary—the camera obscura, Latin for a dark room.

"She's using the parlor now," says Mary. "I want to see what she's doing."

"Why, sweetheart? Who cares?"

"I do, I care!" she says fiercely.

"But why? It doesn't hurt. These people want to be fooled."

"Don't you know, Albrecht? It's not people she's fooling this time, it's Pru! Charlie's been taken prisoner. His plane crashed, but he's alive. He's in a POW camp in China. Pru thinks the spirit world can tell her what's going to happen."

"But that's good news. Then he's safe!"

She just stares at me as if I've landed from another planet. "It's a special camp, Albrecht. They conduct experiments on human subjects."

"What? Who does? How do you know?"

She slumps onto a chair. "It's been going on for years. The Japanese have used biological toxins in the food and water supplies in cities in China since the thirties."

"But what's that got to do with Charlie? He's in a POW camp. There's the Geneva convention."

"There's a war on, Albrecht, or did you forget? He's in a camp near Mukden, with other POWs. They've been given injections, and some of them have been operated on."

"But they can't do that!"

"Why not? Why can't they do that? What's to stop them?" Once more, she regards me as if I've just hatched. "It's nothing to what they're doing to the Chinese and White Russians there. Believe me. You don't want to know, Albrecht. They call them logs; they don't believe they have human feelings. They use them up and throw them away. Women and children, too."

"But how can we stop them? What can we do?"

"We're fighting fire with fire," she answers, and my entire body goes cold.

The room we see through the lenses is nearly dark. Only one small lamp is lit. The walls and windows have been shrouded in black-out curtains and lined with mirrors. Pru sits stiffly at a little table littered with photographs of Charlie. We see Pince-Jones slip from the room.

"We're too late. We'd better get out of here," says Mary. Quickly, we put the cupboard to rights and slide out of the room. We are scarcely back in the hallway before we hear the slushing of Turkish slippers on the floorboards and smell the heavy scent Pince-Jones wears. I start guiltily at her voice, deep and raspy as if it had just crept out from under the covers. "What are you two doing here?"

Shame takes various forms. For me, it is simply the sense that I am wrong, wrong in every way, mostly for being Albrecht Storr with nothing special about him but a predisposition for getting in trouble. I give a weak smile. For Mary, though, shame—if that is what it is—takes the form of anger.

"You wicked old woman!" She stares straight into her mother's eyes. "You thrive on other people's suffering! Why can't you leave her alone?" Her clean little face has sharp edges to it, and looks as if it could chop right through Pince-Jones's soft roundness.

"What are you saying? You know I'm trying to help. I'm doing my best for Pru. Why don't you want me to help her?"

"Help her? By filling her head with nonsense?"

"She may see Charlie there, in the mirrors, and find comfort. She can talk to him as if he is with her. She is lonely and frightened; she doesn't sleep at night, she's so worried."

"He's not with her, Mother. It's a lie. We don't *know* how he is. In fact, from the little we do know, for all the good he'll be— *if* he survives—he might as well be dead. She'd be better off facing it now."

"How can you be so cruel?"

"How can you be so unbelievably naïve? You think you're bloody God. It's not a game. You can't fix this one up with table-turning and cards. You're a fraud."

"I don't see anything wrong with offering comfort. There's little enough of it in this world. I don't do any harm. I never thought I was God. You're a person of no feeling. And what's more," the clairvoyant adds, to my surprise, "you're a little bitch. I hope you know what you've got here, Albrecht." She sweeps away down the corridor, her velvet cape raising dust. Once she's gone, I can hear, from the room where Prudence sits, a sound like mice searching out scraps of cheese. The scrabbling, nail-peeling sound of grief.

———————

I want to ask my mother, when she finally comes home, what took her so long, but I don't get a chance to ask, because I'm told. Major Hoss, Charlotte's friend, had forbidden my mother to see Gerhard; my mother would not leave without seeing her son; there was an impasse. Major Hoss could do whatever he wanted, and what he wanted most, in the end, was for my mother to sail on the last ship to leave Hamburg for Montreal.

"Without seeing Gerhard?"

"I was able to say good-bye" is all she tells us. My father and I look at each other, stunned.

She didn't have time to let us know she was coming. She is sorry if it isn't a nice surprise.

My father can scarcely raise his eyes once more to meet mine. My mother's face is a closed fist. I think we are a little afraid of her as we watch her unpack silk lingerie, soft angora sweaters, and bars of chocolate. I half expect to see gold bars when she reaches the bottom of the case. Perfume wafts from every fold, every movement.

My father clears his throat. "People paid thousands of dollars to be on that ship, Friedl. Their desperate stories were in all the newspapers." I want him to go on, to ask her how *she* had managed it, and if she could wangle it for herself (or Hoss for her), why not for her daughter, Charlotte, and why not for Gerhard? Surely she hadn't intended to leave them both behind? But my father loses courage under my mother's basilisk glare.

"There's a war on, Wilhelm, or didn't you know that?" She slams closed the lid of her new leather trunk and begins to hang up dresses.

My father tries again. "We've heard nothing from Gerhard. Not even a postcard."

My mother whirls on him. She's lost weight. Her body is rapier thin and her expression is vicious. "Nothing! Of course you've heard nothing! There is nothing to hear. There is no more Gerhard, there is no more anything." Suddenly, to my astonishment, the white mask of skin crumples like a folded dollar bill and she slumps on the bed, an old woman. "All my sacrifice, my youth, the love of my children, all gone, for nothing. I am all alone!" Months, maybe years, of stored-up pain spills out of her. It fills up the room, ruining my plans. I had thought, with my mother back, the RCAF might take me. I can see she is on the edge of a breakdown, and I foresee a dim future nursing both parents—my father looks ancient, frail, and half-dead—while the war goes on without me. He helplessly runs his hands through his hair. Steeling myself, I touch my mother's shoulder.

"Mother, what is it?"

"You!" she says bitterly. "Why are you the one left?" Once more, the sorry face is buried in her hands, and I retreat in shock.

There is more going on than I understand, but I do see that my parents are like children on a seesaw. When one rises, the other sinks. When my mother pushes us both away and cries out, "I am an old woman, let me die!" my father perks up. Within hours, he has scrubbed the kitchen table and floor, polished the stove, cleaned and aired the larder, removed the garbage to the back lane, fed the hens, and swept the porch. He displays the results with pride. My mother, who is fifty, and until only a few hours before seemed healthy as a horse, lies helplessly in bed. He has cleaned her room, too, so that it shines.

"She has taken to her bed. She is a strong-willed woman. I do not think she will leave it," he confides to me over a bang-up supper. I nearly choke on my mashed potatoes, but he may be right. He stays up all night to be sure of her, and only goes to bed when my mother staggers forth from her room to use the toilet at first light. Soon they are into a routine that depends on my seeing to her every need. He is away at work all day, and in his leisure time, he potters next door.

One morning, though, when I rise, I find my father snoring, still in yesterday's clothes, among the piles of metal, screws, the tangle of rubber bands, and balls of tinfoil that overrun his room. I shut the door so as not to awaken him, and take my mother a cup of tea.

"Don't think I don't know what you're up to," she says to me, her eyes inches deep in the bone of her face, glittering up at me. "You only want to get away. You want to leave me, too."

"Mother!"

"I don't entirely blame you, Albrecht. I have not always been kind to you in my time. But the moving finger writes and it has written me off. My time has gone. By now, if things were as they should be, I would have grandchildren. Instead, I have no one. " She turns her face to the wall and rubs her eyes. There are tearstains on her face, but I note that she has washed, put on a clean night-gown, and made an attempt to tidy her thatch of braids.

"I suppose you hate me," she says sadly.

"Mother!" I repeat, but in truth, I do not know what to say. I don't hate her, but I do not think I love her. Still, I am a good son, trained to respect his elders, grateful to be alive, and my mother, whatever her failings, is no more than a dim, fading star on my bright horizons. She doesn't matter anymore. She has lost the power to hurt me. I have had a letter from Mary, who will be home in a few days but who is being transferred to Alberta. Which is where I'll be going too, for training, as I have had my RCAF acceptance at last. They had called me into the recruiting office to say they were sorry for the delay. It was because my mother was a German alien who had never become a Canadian citizen. But now that she was back on Canadian soil, all was forgiven. There were ameliorating factors, it was implied. Winks were exchanged, references made to my father's important war work. I had breathed out my relief and floated home, for once grateful to my father for his peculiar obsessions, and whatever use they might be in the waging of war.

Just now, though, my mother's hard blue eyes are staring right through me. "I will be sorry if you hate me— it is not natural for a son not to love his mother—but it won't change anything. I have eyes and ears, Albrecht. I know you bring a woman here. This is a decent home, not like some I could name." My ears burn. I can feel them pulsing.

"Well, it is not so bad," she says, reaching out and patting my hand. "You are young and you will do the decent thing and get married. I will not hold her background against the girl. It is not her fault." She is talking as if the woman is a stranger, but she has known Mary all Mary's life. Before I can think what to say, she goes on. "The days of marriage are over for me." She sighs, and I hear with that outgoing breath the exhalation of dreams. She shuts her eyes briefly, as if she has finished and closed a too-lengthy book.

"Your father and I have had a talk. Please don't be afraid for me. I am at peace."

"What do you mean?" I'm confused. I had thought we were talking about my future.

"I will be starting over, Albrecht. He can make a fool of himself if he chooses, but it no longer has anything to do with me."

"Start again?" I feel stupid, a boy who cannot grasp his lesson.

"Bella Bone will be living here with me. You won't need your room any longer as you will be going, too." I am astonished, again—how did she know about the air force?

"Bella?" I'm like a trick dog that can only respond to its master.

"Bella is my best friend. We work well together. We think the Rebekahs can be a great help."

"Help with what?"

"With the war, Albrecht, what else? We can't all stand by like drugstore Indians!"

Where have I been? What have I been thinking of? My father, it turns out, has been carrying on.

"I don't believe it! With who?"

"Don't shout, Albrecht. I am not bitter, although some would be," says my mother, looking stronger every second. She swings her feet out from under the blankets. She is wearing shoes, small black lace-up shoes. The nightgown comes off in a wink. Underneath it, she is fully dressed. Whatever role this is, she is ready for it. She walks over to her dresser and takes her Rebekah decorations from a jewelry box. She slips a big one round her neck and breathes in and out several times, deep chest-expanding breaths, becoming, in the process, larger. She is inflating herself back to size.

"He is the lover of that woman next door, the whore of Babylon, a person who I thought was my friend, who insinuated herself like a snake into my bosom."

"Madame Pince-Jones?" My voice is a squeak. I will have to ask Mary if she saw this coming, but even as the question forms in my mind, I know she has always known, and so have I. It is true what they say about opposites.

"You cannot trust them."

"Mother, what are you talking about?"

"They do not think as we do. They do not think for themselves. They obey the pope like automatons. You should think twice about marrying a Catholic, Albrecht. I tell you only for the sake of your future happiness."

"Mother!"

"A snake in the grass," she repeats almost joyfully, having had her worst suspicions confirmed. "Wilhelm himself, before he took leave of his senses, before she ensnared him, warned me many times against them. They are not like us. What a fool I've been. I should have known. If I have been so foolish," she muses, wonderingly, "is it right that I now blame him? Can the blind call the blind to account?"

I sit down on the bed, overcome by her philosophy. The odor of talcum powder and sweat rises like steam. I have to think. I stand up and throw open the window. "Tell me what you are trying to tell me, simply, please."

"Your father has revealed his true colors." She shakes her head, some of the hairpins falling loose, as if to say, Imagine me, clever Friedl, being taken in like that! It is scarcely believable. I grip her shoulders, restraining myself from shaking her.

"Speak plainly, Mother."

"Don't tell me you didn't know, Albrecht."

"Are you saying that my father and Pince-Jones . . . ?"

"He is packing his things right now. He is moving in with her."

"He's asleep. I just saw him."

"Look for yourself."

I throw open the door. The house is silent. The door to my father's room is open. The room is empty. There are still piles of junk, but he is gone, and so are his clothes and so are all the implements of magnetism. I feel anger, hot as shrapnel, the burning skin of an airplane, a plane that I could be flying, sting through me.

"I'm not staying. You can't make me."

"I told you," says my mother, smiling. "Don't you understand? Bella and I are starting over. We will build an orphanage for all the little children of the world who have lost their homes. It is the least we can do, as mothers. It is wartime, Albrecht. We must all do what we can."

As if at a signal, there is a knock at the door. I open it to find Bella Bone on the doorstep, dressed in black, as always, wringing her long, pale, shapely hands. "I hope I'm on time?"

"No time like the present," I answer, and invite her in. The taxi driver heaves Bella's trunks up the stairs and into my room. Within seconds, it seems, her sensible shoes are piled on my bed.

"How's Bill, Bella?"

"They are all gone, Albrecht, because of the war. Everyone. Nate, too."

She throws up her hands as if they had all—and I understand this to include Mildred Lark—vanished like dust one bright California morning.

"But where are they, Bella?"

She puts her finger to her lips. "Shush, Albrecht. The walls have ears. I must not say."

I give up and go downstairs to corner my mother. "How will you do it? How will you build an orphanage out of nothing? You need a building, and staff. You need money, lots of money!"

"The Lord will provide," says Bella, coming down the stairs and overhearing us.

"I have money," says my mother. She licks her dry lips and stares at me with the face she has brought home from Germany. My mouth goes dry.

"Where did you get it?"

"It was a gift from your sister, Charlotte. She was so good to me, your sister, she wanted me to have it."

"Why didn't she come with you, Mother? Why did you leave her behind? If there is so much money, surely she could have come with you? What about Gerhard? If there is money enough for an orphanage, what about him?"

She will not meet my eyes. "She could not leave her obligations."

"That takes care of Charlotte. What about Gerhard? I asked you about him, too."

"I do not have to answer your questions. Gerhard is a soldier in the German army, as you know. Unlike you, he is fighting for what he believes in."

It is a struggle, but I ignore the insult. "What kind of money are we talking about? Is it gold? Where, and how, would my sister get hold of gold?" I am shouting suddenly. Bella backs nervously up the stairs, but I do not care. I believe, at this minute, that my mother is capable of anything. Bits and pieces, things my father had read to me, hints from Nate about what had happened when my mother was in Germany—hints he had given when he'd passed through town on his way to his posting—these draw a cartoon outline with the caption *Blood Money*. Gerhard and

Charlotte were left behind because of something my mother had done, something she was paid off for. I am sure of it. You don't get something for nothing.

"What is it to you, Albrecht Storr? You do not know the cost of anything! You have never had to pay your way. Well, let me tell you," she hisses, "you are now on your own."

I have been through ground school, elementary flying, first solo, instrument flying, aerobatics, night flying, and cross-country, training out of the aerodrome at High River, Alberta. I am in my lucky plane, a Cessna Crane, number 7393. In her, I have passed my wings test. I start her up and take off, climb to five hundred feet, and then begin a climbing turn. Within a few minutes, I am far away, the engine thrumming toward the night, the small flames of farmhouse lamps starting up below. For the hundredth time, I'm aware of the shadow I carry with me, the shadow of my brother, Gerhard. Beautiful Gerhard, fair where I am dark, straight where I am stooped; narrow-boned, acute, handsome, sensitive, gifted. Gerhard, who has ruined my life. I am always two steps behind. Even in the plane, he sits ahead of me, on the nose, weighing it down. I feel the machine slipping into a dive, and I want to let it go, to follow my brother's perfect white smile in a straight line, nose-first into the ground. Then it would be over.

"We didn't know your brother was in the Luftwaffe," the officer, whom I had never seen before, told me. We were in the CO's office. He sat on the edge of the desk, legs crossed, swinging his foot. "You should never have gotten this far." He wagged his finger at me, as if I were a naughty boy.

"I was cleared, sir. Right at the beginning. I was told it was all right."

"What you *said* Storr, was that you had a brother in the German *army*, a footsoldier. No big deal, you said. It may be news to you, Storr, but there's a difference between the army and the air force: we don't want *you*, flying one of *our* very expensive aircraft, to be wondering if the pilot of every German aircraft you meet might be your nearest and dearest. No, no, no"—the finger-wagging went on—"it simply won't do."

I didn't bother to say that I had told them what I had believed to be true—what my mother had told me. To the officer, I had been caught out in a lie. From now on, whatever I said would be said by a *bad boy*. "There are other men with German relatives. You're not washing them out."

"You're not *washed out*, Storr, you're gone. We don't want you." He picked at his teeth with a pencil. Clearly, he had more important things to do than talk to me, the scum of the earth. He was a plucking runt, and I had snapped him a salute that whistled when I came in, thinking I was about to get a commission.

"We need pilots, sir. I'm a good one."

"It's out of the question." He shut a file that he hadn't let me see.

"If I can't fly a fighter, I can fly bombers. Surely you'll let me fly something!"

"We could probably find *something* for you to do," he said, leaving me to sort out the implications of *something;* then added, "but you wouldn't be allowed near an airplane." His teeth were nicked with black from the lead he tapped against them. Lead poison. No wonder he was brain-dead.

"Give me a chance and I'll kill the son-of-a-bitch myself. I'll stuff the frigging Luftwaffe down his throat."

"That's enough, Storr. You're not welcome here as a pilot, and you'd better face up to it."

I stood as he left the room, and then I walked outside into the last of the sun on the airfield.

I know people down there. People I've met in pubs, families who've had me to dinner. Girls I've slept with. The shadow on the nose keeps smiling like a poster boy. Nazi poster boy.

"Get off my back!" I shout, but the words go nowhere, and the shadow stays right where it is, rosy now where the last light glints on its whiteness, and murky as blood everywhere else. I could head north and not stop; I could descend and fly along the railway line at low altitude until I slam into a grain silo. I could land the plane in a field and walk away, just to see how far I get: west, maybe, to the ocean, or north to the icecap. Somewhere where it isn't my fault.

Then there's this funny thing I remember, for some reason— the look on Gerhard's face when my mother spoke German to him, a look as if he'd tasted medicine, but was being good and swallowing it. And I wonder what, if anything, has happened to him because of me, and if he is still being good wherever he goes, and how he decides what good is; and if he remembers the things that I did, the way I remember what he did. Like the day before Lily Bone died, when he'd taken her for a walk, and she'd told him she saw Jesus sitting on top of a flagpole, waving to her; and then, after she died, how I'd run away from Bill Bone with Nate to West Hawk Lake, and we found a meteor. How Gerhard only nodded, and didn't ask stupid questions, when I told him. How it was that the strangest things could happen out in the world, but once you were safe at home, you were safe, it was fine. Fine, just fine, as Bella Bone always says.

I land on two wheels, setting down soft as a shiver. The tail wheel shimmies gently as I taxi past the tower and turn the Crane over to the ground crew. Everyone knows what has happened, but nothing is said. They know what it takes to get this far. I can thank the air force for that.

And so, after some thought, I join the Royal Engineers, who seem glad enough to have me so long as I serve in Pacific Command and not overseas. We go to Vancouver, then to Nanaimo on Vancouver Island. Most of our labor involves road-building for troop movements and possible civilian evacuations in case of a Japanese Pacific coast attack. In late August, a submarine shells a lighthouse at Estevan Point, making us feel, briefly, useful.

I take a bomb disposal course given by the navy on HMCS *Borradaile*, at Esquimalt, near Victoria. I'm good at it, so I'm sent to the new army/navy bomb disposal school in Chilliwack. Nate Bone is there, too. He's involved with jungle warfare training at a Vancouver Island special operations camp—a lot of the circus people are there, their skills put to use in camouflage and deception and other intelligence techniques. He says that he's still working with elephants. "We could use Madame Pince-Jones," he says. "Nobody I know in the army knows what's going on."

"Yeah, well, she's too busy."

"Busy?"

"Keeping my father happy."

He blushes and looks down. "I've heard about your father's research. They think it could be important."

"No kidding." We don't talk anymore about our families, and I don't tell him what I think about my father and his various forms of "research," the main one being how loud he and his mistress can be in their room next door at night. It's what Mary calls "sound instincts." My last night at home, I had to get up and shut the window. Then I lay awake for hours, trying not to feel like a lost and lonely child.

Nate can pull strings. He's near the top of some ladder I barely know exists. He's a wallah, it seems, in Intelligence—despite his relative youth—and he must have spoken to someone about me, because when my company is put under warning order for overseas and moves on to Winnipeg, leaving me behind, I'm transferred to the 22nd Field Company, posted back to Vancouver Island, and sent immediately to Nate's special operations camp to teach bomb disposal.

From the air, it looks like a whole city, but on the ground you can see it is only painted sheets of canvas. The landing strip, littered with airplanes, is paint and wood. In the field, it can lure enemy bombers to drop their bombs harmlessly, miles off-target. They say that the founder of the camp, a British magician named Jaspar Maskelyne, conjured German cruisers at work in the little bay, creating panic in visiting politicians. He calmed them, they claim, with an image of Prime Minister Mackenzie King projected onto the clouds. It worked for the politicos, but it emptied out the pubs for miles around.

I find Nate, with the elephant, Romeo, near the firing range. He is teaching the animal to stay calm and obey orders, despite the spatter of small arms fire. By the end of the training, Romeo should be able to pass through a field under artillery fire, without fear. We work together, for a while, demonstrating bomb arming and disarming techniques to a group of Yugoslavs, then he shows me more of what he and Romeo have accomplished. Romeo can carry bombs, strapped to his legs, and drop them at given distances; he can charge a machine-gun nest, and he can carry, slung beneath his belly, half a company of commandos. Nate talks a little about why he's doing this: about children put into heated chambers until the flesh desiccates on their bones, and pregnant women who are forced to give birth and then watch as their infants are subjected to immediate cold-water experiments. We talk about Charlie a bit, too, but there is no fresh news. I hope Nate and his group have some plan to stop these horrors, because nobody else seems to have one, or to know or care much about what's going on.

I wake and fall into the dream again half a dozen times during the night, carrying with me the snuffles, half-cries, and weeping of the score of dislocated men—Hungarians, Italians, Rumanians—with whom I am bunking in the camp. In the dream, I have gone to Lac Sioux with my father and brother and Nate and his father to cut cordwood. It is minus sixty degrees Fahrenheit—too cold to use the horses. Their nostrils freeze, and when they breathe through their mouths, the cold sears their lungs. We huddle for warmth in the caboose of the sleigh train. My father and Bill Bone are checking the runners on the other sleds, I am cooking breakfast on the oil stove, and Gerhard is polishing harness. He shows me some cuts on his hands. "Will I be able to play the violin again?" he asks. He smiles, but I know he is worried. Some of the cuts are deep and should probably be stitched.

In the dream, I remember that, the day before, we had been following the poles that marked the trail across the ice to the cutting lot, when the horses suddenly plunged through the ice into the water. One horse died instantly; it didn't even scream. It floated for a minute, then started to drag the other one down.

"Cut the harness!" cried Bill Bone. He was making a noose at desperate speed. I live through it again and again, watching helplessly as Bill casts the noose around the horse's neck and pulls it tight. As soon as the horse loses consciousness and stops plunging, Gerhard is there with a knife. He saws at the leather, up to his knees in freezing water. His hands bleed from the ice that is stuck in sharp, broken plates all over the horse's head and neck. It cuts him as he works. We strain to pull the horse out, then I jump on its back and ride it at a gallop across the lake and back to warm it.

In the dream, time twists once more, and now it is Gerhard dreaming, standing up on the bed, shouting, waking me with his usual nightmare. Dogs are chasing him. His bandaged hands flail at his invisible pursuers.

Bill Bone and my father appear, pulling back the canvas cover of the caboose. Their breath steams, joining in a cone that floats upward. Bill Bone climbs into the caboose with us. He takes Gerhard in his arms. "It's all right, boy," he says, soothing the hurt hands, speaking softly as he would to his animals, and wrapping Gerhard in a blanket. "Never mind." And I see how Nate looks as

Gerhard drinks in the warmth of Bill's concern. My father's face is just as desolate. As for mine, I can't feel it. It is frozen.

I return to road-building. We construct a road from Shawnigan Lake to Port Renfrew, where there is a small naval establishment. We also cut roads between Ucluelet, Tofino, and Alberni, slicing through the forest of giant Douglas fir and cedar, and the thick underbrush of tough salal and Oregon grape. We build bridges, engineer water supply and sanitation systems, string communications wires of all kinds, and blast rock to the heavens when the mountains stand in our way. But I've done this before. I'm sick to death of the bush, and I'm lonely. And I am still light-years away from the role I had envisaged for myself, downing the enemy in fighter-plane dogfights. I'm not going to get anywhere, not here, which is why I break a cardinal military imperative—never volunteer—and step forward when we are asked if we want to assist our country in a scientific experiment. We are needed at Suffield, Alberta.

Suffield is where Mary is posted. She's employed in the biological materials lab there. I'm not sure exactly what I have in mind: maybe just to get away before I do something to get me in serious trouble. Or maybe to be close to Mary, to be near somebody who thinks that who I am and what I do still matter.

There are a hundred of us volunteers from the army, Pacific Command, and we are glad to be here, away from the rainforest where the air is thick as gravy, and the mountaintops offer unending, deadening vistas of forest and a wrinkled expanse of elephant-gray sea. Here, at Suffield, in a thousand square miles of the Palliser Triangle, there is open space, clear skies, and sweeps of weather that you can watch gathering force five hundred miles away; and there is semi-arid grassland, flat prairie, and rolling hills, ponds and sloughs—much of it alive with rabbits, wild horses, and flocks of duck.

Even the food is better here. We eat Alberta beef and wheels of farm cheese and homemade pie. We do not know exactly why we are here, at the Experimental Station, but we stand at attention as ordered on the test site, dressed in winter-issue battle dress against the cold. We face downwind, and when an airplane approaches overhead, we don our gas masks, as ordered. I delay a moment to look up at the plane and remember what it is like to fly. Then I cover my face with the rubber contraption and wait. Mary will come and see me when whatever this is, is over. I have a note from her in my pocket. We stand as quietly as the cows on the horizon while the plane passes over us several times, and we keep on standing until we are told to move. Then we march the three miles back to camp, where we are instructed to change our clothing.

I feel tired, that's all. Then my eyes begin to hurt. I rub them, and soon my eyelids have swollen until they are shut and I cannot see. I break out in blisters, great bloody burst saucers all over my back and on my right side and thigh. I have burns and blisters between my buttocks, and down my legs and forearms. Something similar is happening to us all.

I cannot see my Mary when she comes. There are bandages over my eyes, and I'm afraid that I will be permanently blind. She tells me that she has seen this before, and that the men always recover. She tells me she is proud of me, that the spraying of mustard gas on us will help bring the terrible sufferings of this war to an end. I don't understand, and I ask her to explain to me how the burns on my buttocks will save a single human being. If they will, I'll stand out there on the prairie again and again like a piece of shit, and they can drop whatever they like on me.

I hear the creak of her starched lab coat as she shifts on the chair. She puts her lips close to my ear and whispers. The words hiss like steam escaping under pressure. She tells me secrets I don't want to hear; they enter the small chambers of my ears and stay there. I do not want these words—anthrax, tetanus, typhoid, dysentery: the names of the diseases of her war work—nor the vermin and a dozen different kinds of insects that she also invokes, and that crawl from her mouth to nest in my body. Some changeling has taken her place. This is not my Mary. There is nothing to say to such terrible words as these. I can only feel desolate, and remember the touch of her hands, the scratch of her nipples under my palm, her tongue licking salt from the corners of my eyes.

She tells me then about Nathanial Bone. How he was sent to work with a commando force of Chindits—the army irregulars who carry their own supplies and undertake operations behind Japanese lines in Burma.

"He wanted so badly to help, because of Charlie," she tells me, and I think about Charlie who was captured in Burma and is rotting in a POW camp in China. "The commandos were going to liberate the prisoners in Rangoon first, and go on from there over the border to the other camps, but the Japs got Nate, too."

"What happened?"

But before she will tell me, she must whisper again. I do not try to stop her, for I know she cannot help herself. This time, the words are of lethal injections, surgical experiments, vivisections, pressure chambers in which the eyes pop out of their sockets, then rupture, and where blood flows through the pores of the skin; children whose blood is siphoned off and replaced with horse's blood, children electrocuted, boiled alive, killed in giant centrifuges. "This is what they're doing, Albrecht. This is what's going on."

"How can they do this? It isn't possible."

"They follow orders," she replies. And I weep through the slits of my swollen eyes, into the bandages, for all those following orders, for the dead and the dying, and for those about to step into the flames.

"Some, they inject in the genitals with toxins. They've taken some of the men and cut off their testicles. To see what will happen. If Charlie Rivers comes home, if he stays alive and comes home, he will never have children, Albrecht."

I lie in my hospital bed, immersed in black night. Although I've not given much thought to it before—except to assume that Mary and I will have children—I know that a world where I'd be denied the possibility of children would not be worth living in. That's how I feel. I don't know why.

Slowly, as Mary's small, dead voice goes on to recount its worries about the ventilation system at the Suffield lab, and the possible escape of bacteria, and how she has become so afraid to breathe that she has to force herself, especially at night when she is by herself . . . slowly, I escape into my dreams.

The spatter of words is nothing but a handful of stones scattered over a wide sea of sound. I am listening to music. Gerhard plays the violin. My mother sits on one side of me, with her arm around me. My father is on the other side, dozing. Then my mother recites German poetry to help *me* fall asleep. A deep, deep sleep, in which I hear the cawing of crows, the screech of ravens at the moment of creation, the innocent sounds of grasshoppers and chickens, the washing of dishes. I take back the world with my memories. I shut Mary out.

Some weeks later I take a drive with Mary to Lake Patricia, near Jasper, in the mountains. The trip has been recommended by the doctor as something to take me out of myself and lift my spirits, which have remained apathetic and depressed since I was an experimental subject for my country. This is not how Mary likes me to put it, but it is how it was.

She is taking me to see a new project on which she thinks I might like to work. A man named Pyke has caught the interest of Churchill with a scheme to build a fleet of ships made from ice mixed with sawdust. Pyke has called the material pykrete, after himself. In his scheme, these ships will sail from the Arctic and launch attacks on German and Japanese ships and ports. They will do this first by spraying enemy fleets with super-cooled water, immobilizing them in ice. Then, when the iceberg troop ships reach the ports, the troops will build barricades of pykrete twenty feet high and thirty feet thick around captured areas, providing themselves with a safe zone in which to mount other necessary defense installations.

The project is called Habakkuk, after the Old Testament prophet and his vision of the Lord God's vengeance visited on his enemies. Churchill thinks that the ships should be built here, in Canada, where it is cold; and besides, we are just the people with the get-up-and-go to do it.

"You've got to be kidding," I said, when Mary told me. But I agreed, in the end, to go along anyway, just to get away from the sight and sound of the other men, and their suppurating wounds, and their faces like loyal dogs whipped by their masters.

The atmosphere between Mary and me is . . . cool. She is smoking a herbal cigarette. Because of the cold, the car windows are shut. I roll one down, risking frostbite for the sake of a few breaths of fresh air.

"Would you roll the window up, please?"

"Hey, things are looking up! You're talking to me again."

"Don't exaggerate, Albrecht. I was never not speaking to you. Now, please, shut the window." Her hands are shaking. An inch-long worm of ash trembles at the end of Rose Peony or Cow Dung Leaves or whatever her coffin nails are called. I sneeze, take three deep breaths of good air, and do as I'm told.

"Any news of Nate?" I can ask her that. I can ask her anything about the war and she won't mind.

"Not really. We know that he was taken to Mukden, where most of the other POWs are."

"Where there are experiments on human subjects, you said. You told me about Charlie." I say this because I'm not sure what she does and doesn't remember. Talking to Mary is like talking on the radio to a pilot flying in and out of heavy cloud. Reception comes and goes. I'm told, by people who should know, that she does an excellent job at work.

"He's not with the same unit as Charlie. Sometimes they go easier on the Europeans. It all depends."

"He could be okay?"

She looks at me just long enough to remind me that we're on a jaunt and our friends are in prison camp. So I oblige. "You know what I mean. It could be worse. Nothing is okay— I know that. But there's a possibility that, if he survives, he might be all right?"

"It could be worse, yes, you're right."

That's as much progress as we make. Of course I'm bitter and I'm angry, and when I think about it, which I try not to do, I don't see how I'll ever forgive her for letting me go with all the others like a lamb to the slaughter, for the sake of some abstract bull-shit science that I think is crap. But why should it be any different for me? Why should I be singled out for rescue?

When we arrive, I am introduced to the engineers who have built, in Lake Patricia, a model pykrete platform and some experimental pykrete beams. The beams are about fifty feet long and six feet thick. It is a bizarre project. As I can see, and as one of the engineers confirms, it takes enormous reserves of power to produce and maintain the pykrete. There are other problems: an iceberg ship would have to sit fifty feet above the waterline and be around five hundred feet thick. It would weigh over two million tons and need water at least a hundred and fifty feet deep in which to float. You don't have to be in the navy to know there are only a few ports in the world that such a ship could approach. To make the iceberg carriers would require a major part of Canada's production of pulp.

"Come here, sweetheart," says one of the younger engineers to Mary. She glances at me. She must be freezing, clad as she is in skirt, sweater, and labcoat. I nod, and she goes over to him, and he brings a service revolver out of his pocket. "Can you aim?"

"I've shot a gopher or two in my day," she says, with a wry smile that cheers me.

"See if you can hit that." He points at one of the beams.

"I'm not sure I want to."

"Don't be afraid."

"I'm not afraid. It could be dangerous."

"Ah, come on, honey, go ahead. It's a demonstration for your boyfriend."

She gives him a look that stops him chewing gum, but she lifts the revolver and aims and fires. The bullet strikes the beam, bounces right off, and zings back at us to nick his ear. Without comment, Mary hands him a handkerchief to stanch the copious flow of blood, and then she walks back to the car.

"So, do you want to work here?" asks the senior engineer who has been watching us from a safe distance. I pick myself up from the ground where I had flung myself when the bullet ricocheted. "I hear you've been building roads. I'd say you've done your time."

"It's a fascinating project, all right," I say. The junior engineer has slunk away toward a hut with a red cross marked on it.

"I can fix it, if you want."

Suddenly, I'm tired. Maybe it's a holdover from the mustard gas. I don't care anymore. One form of madness is as good as another. "Why not? Why don't I just stay?"

So I do, kissing Mary good-bye and letting her drive off on her own. I look at the models and drawings, wondering about the limits of the possible, until it's late afternoon and then I can catch a lift "home."

After a period of time, we find out what we already know—that the ships can be made more efficiently and less expensively out of reinforced concrete. The project, after a tremendous investment of time and money, is called off.

There's only one more brief flurry of activity for me. A series of balloon bombs floats in over the Pacific from Japan, each ballon armed with a small explosive payload, and sets off fears of a biological warfare attack on the west coast. I'm called in to disarm them, and then the war is over. We have dropped the biggest bomb of all, on Japan.

9

PREPARING
THE WAY

She was being bothered by a dream of a small, cold boy. For a minute, when she awoke, she could feel him in her arms, with his dark, cold head against her breast. He seemed impossible to warm.

She felt for the zipper on the sleeping bag, already thinking ahead to the painful task of unthawing the frozen zipper head with her bare hands, easing it down through teeth jammed with frost; then lighting the primus and making tea while the frost on the tent ceiling melted and fell like rain—a small penalty to pay for the warmer days of spring. But her hands encountered nothing. Slowly, through her puzzlement, she realized that the dimness around her was not caused by the snow-covered walls of the tent, but by the goggles which, inexplicably, she was still wearing. She kept them on outside all the time, even on cloudy days, in order to avoid snow blindness, but why was she wearing them now?

She had first seen what snow blindness could do on the march to the camp from the terminus of the Russian railway line, at the end of the war. So much blinding light after the days in the windowless transport train, and men who hadn't known enough to protect their eyes, had been sitting on the ground, hours later, rocking back and forth in helpless pain, pressing the heels of their hands hard against their eyes.

It had been Gerhard, who could see nothing, who had told her what to do.

She was not in the tent, not inside the sleeping bag. Her pack was still on her back and she was half lying, half sitting fully dressed on a wide prairie pan of ice and snow. Her disorientation was complete. She was grateful that it was light for twenty-four hours a day—to have awakened unsheltered and confused in the dark would have been terrifying—and that the wind had dropped. She could easily, far too easily, have frozen to death.

Fika cleared the snow from her goggles. She had no idea how long she had been asleep. The sky was white, and it was snowing lightly. A thin layer of powdery snow, light and fluffy, lay over her. She could see the lower half of her body, the long mounds of her legs, and the lines of her skis, but they seemed to have nothing to do with her at all. Slowly, and with great difficulty, she managed to move the skis from where they lay frozen into the ice. Even more slowly, and with tremendous cost to her stores of energy, she struggled upright. Her poles, under their dusting of snow, lay neatly arranged nearby, as if she had deliberately placed them before laying herself down for a nap.

Resisting the temptation to start walking and make up lost time, and fighting back the tears that were further evidence of her physical deterioration, Fika began to erect the tent.

When she had finished, she lit the stove, made tea, and drank it liberally mixed with condensed milk. She ate some oatmeal, then turned the stove up higher and stripped off her clothing. She took out the small mirror she carried with her and examined herself inch by inch, finding new frostbite on the tip of her nose and chin, on her ears and on her toes. The rest of the exposed skin of her face was white and puffy, and she had rashes and bacterial infections in the folds of her flesh. She thought she had put on weight: there were small rolls of fat around her middle. She was adapting to the cold, just as Ekaterina had said she would, by putting on an extra layer of insulation. The only substantial worry was the bleeding, both from her nose in the mornings, and from her monthly bleeding which, once it had begun, hadn't stopped. From this, as well as from the poor condition of the mucous membranes of her eyes and mouth, she suspected she was anemic. She took out the small emergency medical kit and gave herself a shot of vitamin B_{12} and iron.

What she really needed was fresh meat, and fresh fruits and vegetables. But there was no chance of such food before landfall and civilization.

As she rested, waiting for her strength to return, she remembered a story that Gerhard had told her when they had left the snow tunnels in the woods near the Château de Froid Coeur to walk toward the American lines. Charlotte had brought him to her—she had taken him from the hospital where he was recovering from his burns—promising to return for them both. She hadn't come back, and they had found out for themselves, of course, after they set out on their own, that the Americans had stopped their advance to let the Russians arrive ahead of them.

The story was of a heroine, the early Siberian explorer Mariia Pronchishcheva. It was one of a number of stories told to Gerhard by Clara, Fika's grandmother. Mariia had been part of the Great Northern Expedition that had sailed in 1733. She had died a brief three years later in the region of the Olenek River estuary, but she had been one of the first European women to see the reindeer as they migrated southward to winter in the taiga. She had watched the blue hare as it was born above ground with its covering of hair and its eyes wide open to danger. And she had marveled at the lemmings swarming through the tundra grasses in the summer and attempting to cross ice floes, rivers, and lakes in their search for food, then building burrows of dead vegetation and remaining within them as the thick snow blanketed and warmed them. Mariia had been Clara's hero, a model for her own epic journey across the Arctic on her way to the New World. Mariia had lived her short life to the fullest, and in winter had blanketed herself in snow, like the animals, to keep warm. Which is what Gerhard told Fika to do, too, at night, when they were in hiding. He had liked her to put snow on his eyes—badly burned in a cockpit fire—to ease the pain.

Strengthened by the food and the injection, Fika went outside. It was no longer snowing, and the sky had cleared. The sun was due west. If the sextant reading was correct, it was about six p.m.

Thick clouds of steam rose from the ice. Despite her sleep that day (how long had it been?), she had skied and drifted about twenty-five kilometers since the last sighting. She was right on track, right where she should be.

Now she could hear the ice rumbling. There were new leads opening, larger areas of open water and more wide fields of broken ice to be crossed. But she had to go on.

How far from land was she now? One hundred and sixty kilometers? Only that? The distance, on the map, was scarcely a child's hand-span.

The cold child had become a splinter of ice in her heart. She had felt it all night. Great, cold distances. Nameless longings. The universe inside the child was the well of space in which she was falling. She tumbled and tumbled until she landed, as she always did, on the plank boards of the labor camp bed. Gerhard lay there with his breath rattling. Suddenly, he sat up and asked her to fetch a pan so he could move his bowels. By the time she came back, he was dead, and somebody was gathering up the rags with which they had tried to stanch the sudden flood of blood from his mouth.

Fika got up and lit the stove, then crawled back into the sleeping bag to wait for the water to boil. She lay watching the slowly moving cracks in the frost on the tent ceiling, its beautiful changing abstract patterns shrinking into droplets in the rising warmth of her breath.

10

IMMEDIATE
PROGRESS

We have settled nicely, like country mice, in the warm, dusty corners of our Winnipeg houses, when Nathanial Bone arrives, having driven north, across the border, in a dark blue Cadillac, to shake us up. His shoes are shined like a million dollars, his soft leather suitcases plump out with hand-tailored shirts and cashmere sweaters. He checks into the Fort Garry Hotel—reporters are waiting to interview him, ready to worship at the shrine. His salary is in five figures. He owns passing and punting records throughout the States. He has played for the Rams, the Redskins, and the Packers. He has filled out; he's as big as Bill Bone at six foot one and two hundred pounds. He's a famous football player now, and we're just ordinary folks. I work for the city as an engineer, and I'm married to Mary. He's the new star quarterback for the Winnipeg Strikers. I don't know which marriage he's on this year. He hasn't been in touch with me since returning to California after his release from the POW camp. We're the stay-at-homes—or, at least, I am. Mary works up north, near Churchill. He's the hometown boy who made good.

"Albrecht!" He phones after he's been in town for a week. "Son of a gun, how are you?"

"Hey, Nate! I'm fine. How's it feel to be back?"

"Great! Just great! Say, Albrecht, I've been thinking, why don't we get together, all of us, for a weekend, just for old times sake? Catch up on things?"

"Good idea, Nate. What did you have in mind?" I'm thinking that he sounds more or less the same, although we're naturally a little stiff with each other. Beneath the enthusiasm, he's shy. Maybe things aren't all that they seem. There are rumors (although the Strikers deny them) about troubles with his feet and a sore arm; that the NFL wanted to get rid of him. Had he meant to come back here? Did he have a choice? What's it like to be a prodigal son?

"What about the whole gang of us going up to the lake? We could rent a couple of cabins and do some fishing. Remember?"

"Sure, Nate, whatever you say. I've got plenty of time."

"Does your dad still have that old car?"

"The Model T? Hell, no!" I laugh. "He got rid of it during the war. He doesn't drive anymore. He walks. He says cars are bad for his magnetic energy." I hear Nate's bluff guffaw in return, and I can imagine those nice white American teeth—so attractive in newspaper photos—flashing in that wide brown face topped off with a brushcut like a square of black turf. A fine figure of a man, says Mary.

It is said Nate likes a drink, which might explain the marriages. Mary had shown me a newspaper write-up of the last divorce. "She didn't like my friends. She called me a dumb football player, and when she found out I wasn't wealthy, she made it clear she only wanted money and told me she didn't love me anymore." Poor Nate.

"Poor Nate!" Mary had commented as I read the the write-up. "As if things weren't bad enough."

"What's so bad? If he doesn't have money, that's his fault. He earns enough." You couldn't read a sports page without finding Nate's name on it. Mostly the reports are about his brilliant play, his flair and talent, but there are other things: he tackles hard, and once he broke a man's leg in three places.

"He gives his money away."

"Nate? He's as cheap as an army tin plate."

"That's not what I hear."

"Oh, what do *you* hear, Mary?" But she didn't say. We don't tell each other everything. Life's too short. There's enough pain in it anyway. We don't exactly keep secrets, but I know there is some holding back.

"Too bad!" says Nate. "I loved that old car. Well, look. We can go in mine. Talk to Charlie and Pru. And Mary. She can come, can't she? We'll catch some jackfish and cook them over a fire. Drink some beer."

"Mary's up north. Her postings keep her away. I'm not sure when she'll be back. What about Bella? Is Bella coming?"

"Bella?" he says, as if this is the first time he's remembered that he's got a mother. Would Bella want to come?

He walks tall, his spine is straight as a board, and he's immaculate. You won't see stubble on that face, even at five o'clock. Bella sits up front with him in the Cadillac. Charlie, Prudence, and I squeeze together in the back. Charlie has his arm around Pru and is laughing. We've got the windows open, and the radio on. Even the dust is like golden sunlight. Wildflowers are sprayed along the roadsides—handfuls, scatterings, thick carpets of them in yellow and red and purple. Nate is singing lustily, and banging his fist on the steering wheel. His hands are small, and surprisingly delicate for a football player. Even Bella, usually rigid and silent, slowly unwinds. She hums, and removes her cardigan. I can see, from the set of her shoulders in the dark sleeveless dress, and the long, fine line of her arms, how she *could* have been beautiful, rising in the spotlight to touch the white plumes of her headdress with those white arms as she rode, standing bareback on a shining white circus horse. I can almost believe the magic.

Charlie and Pru keep laughing. Nate hands back, over the seat, an opened bottle of beer. We take turns drinking from it. I get to finish, holding the last mouthful of warm, heavy gold liquid in my mouth.

It is dark, and we've fallen quiet by the time we arrive at the lake.

We have dinner together, just as we'd planned, on the beach, cooking over a campfire. We've brought corn and potatoes to roast. Pru makes hamburgers, and Charlie cooks them on a grill over the coals.

Nate says Prudence makes the best hamburgers after his mother. Bella is so pleased that she pulls off her shoes and stockings and kneads her toes in the cold red sand. We sit and talk and smoke cigarettes, and watch the stars ride the sky. The lake picks up every sound and reflection, and holds them close to its surface: our voices, the drift of smoke, the glitter of the heavens are magnified by every breeze-lifted ripple. It's a huge, flat mirror with a surface of black, undulating glass. Nothing breaks it, not even the fish that, when they rise, simply push up into the air a perfectly shaped obsidian spear.

It is midnight when we go to the cabins, and a couple of hours later when, after reading for a while by lamplight, I go outside for a walk. I've been waiting for Mary. I haven't said anything to the others, in case they may be disappointed, but she'd said she'd try to come down on the late train from Churchill, and then drive up. My friend, Pietor, had said he'd lend her his car. She wants to see Nate. "Who knows when there'll be another chance for us all to be together," she'd said.

They've never been out of touch. I'd seen a number of letters, with his looping handwriting on the envelopes, slip through the mailbox onto the mat at the front door. She'd never opened them when I was there, and I'd never asked what was in them. My Mary makes her own rules, and the ones she doesn't make, the government, for which she continues to work, makes for her.

I'm standing on the headland looking down at the lake when she comes. Her scent of myrrh, dark and musky, mingling with the pine arrives with her touch on my arm.

"I didn't hear the car."

"I left it down the road and walked. I didn't want to wake anyone up. It's so peaceful, isn't it?"

She sits beside me, and we lean against each other, warm where we touch. The lake still looks like an antique mirror, but now it has a glow as if its depths have been stirred, and all the radioactive energy from the meteor that made the crater, thousands of years ago, has been disturbed from its ancient rest. "It's supposed to be bottomless," I say, and I tell her about my father and his magnetic measurements, and how we used to set out on those strange missions, my father and I, with his devices and notebooks, and me rowing the boat in lines up and down and across the lake's surface.

"You were a funny little boy," she says.

"I was?"

"What's that?" she says, pointing. Not far from shore, something moves through the water. It hardly splashes, and is too large for a fish.

"It's somebody swimming!" we both say at once. Whoever it is pulls up out of the water and onto a raft that is anchored about a hundred yards from the beach and almost directly below us. A second shape pulls up beside it. Mary starts to laugh.

"They're skinny-dipping! It's Pru and Nate!" She stands up. She's about to shout and wave, but something stops her. She crouches back down again. "Didn't Charlie come with you?"

You cannot always help where you are and what you see. You cannot be responsible for every shadow navigating waterscapes and pulling itself onto dry land. We are stuck where we are, hunched on the clifftop, near enough to see them and to hear their whispers as they reach out for each other. You cannot always help what you want. You reach for it, and touch a cool surface of glass and mirror. Your fingers follow the movements. They are fish swimming in an aquarium, they are the craft in which Nate and I rowed across West Hawk Lake toward a fallen meteor, overturned, our child bodies sinking endlessly toward the bottom.

"Albrecht? I'm afraid."

"Afraid? Why?" But Mary won't say. She leans back against me and I hold her close. "It's nobody else's business. Maybe Pru has her reasons." I don't want to look any longer, but I can't tear my eyes away. They are images, that's all. Moving pictures. "Pru wants a child, Mary, she's said so a hundred times. Charlie can't give her one. Maybe this is the way she wants it. Maybe Charlie knows." I turn her face to kiss her and my lips taste tears. "You're crying! Why? It has nothing to do with us. Come on, they won't see us now, let's go back to the cabin."

"She doesn't know! She doesn't understand!" says Mary. There is pain here that I don't fathom.

"It doesn't matter."

"You *know* what they did to Charlie in the camp."

"Charlie's not here. Nate's here. It's all right. He wouldn't hurt her. Charlie knows, I'm sure of it. Nate's doing them a favor. They're not children."

Mary looks at me, her eyes black with horror. Although I push the thought quickly away, I can't help but think about the letters Nate wrote to her, and what might have been in them.

11

PHYSICAL
LOSSES

The most active ice zones were to the east and west of the seventy-fifth meridian, and so Fika's route lay right along it. Here, in a zone of convergence, where two global spiral currents met, the ice sloped away on either side, and the most stable ice lay in the center. This line of longitude also entered and passed through the middle of what would be Fika's landfall, Ellesmere Island. Now that she had entered the shear zone, where moving pack ice from the ocean lay heaped and wrenched against the continental shelf in a band from eight to eighty kilometers wide, compacted and crushed against the more stable land-anchored ice, and thrust upward by the shallows, the idea of land, so long like a half-remembered story, had become almost palpable. She could imagine mountains, streams, and valleys, a definitive change of seasons, a tapestry of blue hills and golden skies.

Gold: that was the word that came into all her grandmother Clara's descriptions of what she had found in the New World. There were prospectors with gold pans, and picks and shovels, making fortunes in real gold after a few hard months in the mountains; and there were farmers with thousands of rich acres on which to run thousands of head of golden cattle.

But the ice that surrounded Fika was blue, and rose in towers and blocks as large as ships and as strung out as bridges. It formed impassable gardens and cities. There were mountains of ice to climb, gods of ice to worship. She was encased in loneliness, in the uncertainties, illnesses, and vagaries of her body and mind. Encased in ice herself, so it seemed, drifting somewhere between water and earth, earth and sky, life and death.

Summer was approaching—a northern summer of white nights and pale twilight. A season of mist and cloud as the ice melted and the waters warmed. It was the most dangerous time of the year to be on the ice. In the mist, pushing herself tiredly forward on skis, scrambling over heaps of ice rubble, she found herself accompanied, almost always, by the dead. She had grown used to them, and no longer tried to send them away. She was accustomed to the quiet scuffing of their feet at her sides, to the whispered advice of Marina and Ekaterina warning her of leads opening up, of pack ice about to break apart, of a dropped pole or glove that she hadn't noticed. They were so familiar that they were like parts of herself. But there were others, including a teacher who recited a passage on the liberation of Yakutia: *The Whites were sleeping, unaware until the last minute of the approach of the Red detachment of Vostretsov;* and there was her friend, Anna, an engineer, who described the design of a hydroelectric dam and kept offering her tea; and, of course, there was Gerhard, always Gerhard. Sometimes he just walked beside her, and at other times he had something to say— such as telling her about the first time he'd flown in a glider, a wooden SG38, launched from a hill like a slingshot; of his sudden sense of completeness as the world swirled slowly and silently below him. There were too many voices, all clamoring for her attention while she struggled to concentrate on making sure that her skis didn't break, that she kept to the route despite many neces- sary detours, that she fed and rested this body on which she relied, but which she scarcely seemed to inhabit.

And now the voice of her grandmother was speaking to her of the possibilities of the New World, and pleading the case for forgiveness of her abandonment of her infant daughter and husband, left behind in Siberia. It was not what Clara had intended to happen. She hadn't known, when she'd left, that she would never see them again. There had been plans for them to be together, once Nicholas acquired the right papers. But then came the First World War when Clara was scarcely on her feet in America, and after that the Bolshevik Revolution, which had once and for all closed the door on escape from the USSR. She had never stopped yearning for her child and for Nicholas, too, even as she had traveled to the miners' town of Deadwood looking for work, and had found a job as a cook in a boarding house, and had grown to love the miner, Frank Rivers, who boarded there.

They had married and decided to homestead; but Rivers had gone ahead to build the house, barn and corral and had never returned, leaving Clara alone and pregnant. Months went by, and the neighbors said that Rivers had been murdered. Clara found a job housekeeping for a widower, a sawyer at a mill in the mountains. It was there, in the mountains, that her son was born.

Clara had turned away from human companionship and had moved, with her child, deeper into the wilds, living in a cabin, surviving on venison and flour, struggling on by cooking in mill and mining camps until, eventually, she had met another man who wanted to marry her, and who would adopt and care for her child.

Clara slipped the black taffeta wedding dress, hand-embroidered with violets, over her head, and waited for the new husband to come, holding her little boy by the hand, feeling the small bones of his hand trembling like the heart of a bird. Trembling, herself, at this step into the future.

Fika felt that small hand in her hand, and then the child slipped free and vanished. She touched her fingertips, scabbed over from frostbite, to the sudden tears freezing on her face. She could feel the scraps of frost-burned dead skin that hung from her cheeks and nose and chin. She was half blind in the whiteness, but it seemed to her now that there was a fire a few feet ahead of her on the ground, and that she could make out dim shapes clustered around it. When she drew close, though, there was only Gerhard. He smiled, and she didn't notice, for once, the broken teeth, or the sallow color of his skin, or the shadows on his face. The smile went right through her so that she suddenly saw, as she warmed, that there was no fire, and none of the dead were with her. She looked around in terror, but found herself, at last, as if seen from a distance, skiing and climbing broken ice. She was alone, but she was still alive.

12

THE GREAT
TEST

MAY 1950

I have a dream the night before my child is born. I am standing
in a rocky field with Nathanial Bone. We are surveying the stars.
The place has a name, Field of Stars or Field of the Sky, something like that. As we watch, several of the stars grow brighter and
begin to fall toward us. I close my eyes for a second, and then I
feel the weight of a stone hanging around my neck. I open my
eyes and find that the meteor fragment Nate had found at West
Hawk Lake, when we were kids, is tied there on a string. I tear it
off, breaking the caribou leather thong, crying, "It isn't mine! I
hate it! Take it away!"

Then my father is with us. He is talking, explaining that the world's ills are caused by an overcharged electrical field. He gestures at the stars, which are getting closer. They are, to my eye, threatening, and I press close to his side for protection. He says he can sense the electrical anomalies in the middle of his ears, and on each side of his head, and at the center of the back of his head, and in the middle of his face. He is overcoming imbalances within himself, he asserts, and once this is done, he will be able to locate Gerhard.

Gerhard! The pain of hearing my brother's name, of remembering his absence, scores through me. I look around for him, but everywhere I search, there is only whiteness. I am a twin without his other half. I am less than myself.

By now, my father and I are walking across the field toward Nathanial Bone, who has gone ahead. Nate is standing with a group of Esquimaux. They show us a huge snowdrift, and as they do, I realize that we are now crossing ice pans. The pans have floated down from the Arctic into Hudson Bay, and through the river systems, to end up near our home. The Esquimaux tell us that beneath the snowdrift is a great iron stone that is called The Woman.

I awaken, my heart thumping. My father had once read a story to me and Gerhard about an iron stone like the one in my dream. This was the huge meteor shown to Robert Peary, the first man to reach the North Pole, by Greenland natives. The natives had used it to make spearheads for their weapons. My father read a great deal about the Arctic when we were small, and he was beginning his investigations into Personal Magnetism. He had been refused some expected advancement in the Odd Fellows—Grand Representative, I think it was—and had turned to Magnetism for solace. My father told us that over the Arctic there was an intense electromagnetic field—magnetic north, of course—and that most great cities, ancient and modern, and most other sites of significant human enterprise, were situated at strongly magnetic points on the earth. I try to remember more— there is something about the geometric shapes made when you draw lines between giant craters. He had mentioned Hudson Bay, Ungava Bay, the Gulf of St. Lawrence—all formed by meteors—and I attempt to imagine what figure that lines drawn joining them would make. We are all part of magnetism's great net, says my father, attracted and repelled to and from each other according to our inborn polarities.

I put my arms around Mary and snuggle in close to her back. Her skin is smooth and warm and damp, and I breathe in her smell and try to rid myself of the dregs of the dream. I do not often think of my brother. Gerhard is a pulled tooth. I get on just fine without him. Many people died or disappeared in the war. We have had to get used to our losses. This is normal. This is what life in the twentieth century is about. You bridge over pain. You carry on and stick by and stick to. But I had forgotten how much I have missed him, his presence, always to be relied on; his difference, helping me to outline myself, to know who and what I am. Gerhard was the star—distant, often cold, mysterious—around which the family oriented itself. He was my mother's particular star. I have forgiven him her preference for him—it wasn't his fault—and it left me free from her machinations. Gerhard simply did his best at what he was good at, and he was good at many things. I have even forgiven him for my never becoming the pilot

I wanted to be. In the end, certainly after the war, I could have taken the training, but I didn't use the opportunity. Why dream that my father could find him, now? I don't know how to ease this sudden ache.

My wife, Mary, groans in her sleep. It is early, not quite six, and I don't want to wake her. She sleeps badly these days, in the last weeks of her pregnancy. She has nightmares about our child being born hurt in some way. In many of the dreams, the baby drowns. The child falls out of a boat and she can't reach it, or she finds it facedown in a shallow pool of rainwater in the backyard. The doctor explains that many women have such dreams and their babies are born perfectly well. I try to reassure her. I tell her that her doctor has talked to the military scientists where she works. There is nothing for her to worry about. All safety precautions were taken, and there is no evidence, in any case, that an unborn child can be harmed by the mother's occupation. That's an old wives' tale. Mary replies that most women haven't worked, as she has, in biological and chemical warfare labs. There have been experimental projects outside the laboratory: the spraying of bacteriological agents at the mouth of the Strait of Juan de Fuca to see where wind patterns would carry them, and biological warfare trials with native populations during Operation Sweetbriar, a joint U.S. and Canadian defense exercise on the Yukon–Alaska border. And more that she doesn't mention. Mary presses her lips together, and salutes the flag. Sometimes, though, she wakes me in the middle of the night with her whispering. The Communists will approach through Alaska, or through the Arctic. The tests she undertakes are necessary to our survival. She will murmur restlessly like this for several minutes while I listen and nod, wrenched from my safe sleep, and try to make her feel as if nothing bad will ever happen to her, though the sweat springs forth in my armpits and runs down my sides. When she's done, she falls instantly back to sleep. I lie awake for hours, and stare into the darkness of the future.

"Albrecht?"

"Sorry, love. I didn't mean to wake you."

She eases herself onto her back, shifting with her hips, and following with her swollen belly. "It's all right. I wanted to get up early anyway. I've got things to do."

"You're staying in bed. You should rest."

"Should I?" She is laughing at me. "You'd have the baby for me if you could." I smile back at her. She's right. I would do anything to spare her pain. I want this child. I know it will knit us together. "Is it still raining?" She has closed her eyes again.

I sit up to take a look. There are streaks of water on the glass showing at the slit of open space between the drawn curtains. "'Fraid so."

She sighs. "I wish it would stop. I hate staying here. I wish we didn't have to."

I dislike it as well. We have moved into Pru and Charlie's house to wait for the birth. We have had to leave our own home in St. Boniface because of the flooding. The Red River has overflowed its banks, and several dikes have collapsed. Our house sits beside the Seine River, one of the Red's tributaries, and is in imminent danger from the rising waters. I'm the chief city engineer. I'm supposed to be able to get the catastrophe under control. On bad days, I imagine having a word with Pince-Jones, or with my father. Those two believe nothing is beyond them. God is a kite on a string they can pull. Maybe they can tell him to change the weather. We might have stayed in our house a little longer, but I didn't want to take the chance of anything happening, of becoming marooned there, not with Mary pregnant.

"I'd feel better at home," she says.

"I know you would. I would, too." I stroke the hair back from her forehead. Nothing has been said, not even to each other, but we both know Pru is carrying Nate's baby. Pru and Charlie can't know that we know—Mary and I had crept back to our cabin unobserved that night months ago at West Hawk Lake—but they must be aware that everybody understands Charlie isn't the father. My mother communicated her query with raised eyebrows; "Pru, expecting?" She had given me—the brother-in-law, after all—a considering look. Was I a candidate? Bella's glittery eyes had chased each other back and forth: "They've tried again?" She meant after the sad fate of Pru's first baby, so long ago. It joins a list of events—my parents' divorce, Bella's madness, Gerhard's disappearance, the terrible death of young Lily Bone—that is never spoken of because, I suppose, any item on the list could cause pain. But even in silence, the pain is still there, the truth is there, bridged over, walled in, capped, and waiting to erupt in dreams, if nowhere else.

It is fifteen years since the infant, born when Pru and Charlie were scarcely more than kids themselves, was snatched from under our noses; she evaporated into a summer's evening. What happened to her? Did she live? And if so, what kind of life did she fall into? I pray it has been a good one. I don't understand it, anymore than I understand why Charlie had to end up in that Mukden POW camp to be mutilated; I don't understand why things like this have to happen.

Charlie can't produce sperm; Charlie has had surgery, been subject to massive doses of X-rays, had injections of toxic substances in what was left of his genitals. Charlie, they say, was lucky to get out of that POW camp in China alive. So Charlie is lucky? How can there be an explanation?

"Wars are fought to be won. You don't win by holding back," was Mary's response when I had asked her opinion of the "why's" of that kind of experimentation.

"But what do you win by damaging other human beings, Mary? It's not a better world, of that I'm certain."

"Was anything learned?" she said, echoing one of my questions. "Would it make a difference to you if there *were* something learned from those terrible wartime experiments?"

"Yes. There'd be something salvageable, I guess, a tiny plus sign to put on the headstones of the dead."

"Well, Albrecht, they learned that people die when they're too hot or cold, or when you overload their bodies with pain or poison, or when they don't have the right antibodies to fight disease." We had stared at each other, instant antagonists. The "incident" of the mustard gas—soldiers crowded into a herd to be gassed by their own side—was another item on the list of events unmentioned. Even though I bear the scars, I can scarcely credit that it happened, or that she thought it was all right.

"It's just *us* or *them*, in the end, Albrecht. *Them* is who you do things to; *us* is the people who do them."

I looked at her in amazement. "You don't believe that."

"We used the atom bomb, didn't we? We won. Do you wish it had been the other way around?"

"That *we* didn't include me. I wasn't consulted."

"Didn't it? Would you really rather they had dropped the bomb on us?"

For a second I thought about saying "Yes." But it turned out I preferred not to be a victim.

"Why did it have to happen to Charlie, then? Why not somebody else?"

"Somebody more deserving?" Mary had turned away to sort baby clothes collected for her and Pru by Pru's mother-in-law, Clara Rivers. It was a clear signal that I should go away, shut up, and mind my own more urgent business. But I didn't go away. So finally she straightened up, peered straight into my back-of-a-shovel face, and asked, again, "Who did you have in mind? Who would you pick, Albrecht? It's your call."

"How should I know? It's not my job to choose."

"Is it God's job? Is that what you mean?"

"If there is a god, I suppose so." I shrugged my shoulders.

"No," she said, "that's not what you meant. You meant that you thought Charlie was a bad choice, and you have a list as long as your arm of others you'd have put in his place. Don't ever wish to play God, Albrecht. You wouldn't like it. Ask Nate, if you want to know how playing God can turn out; it doesn't solve any problems."

Ask Nate? What is Nate's problem? I didn't ask her what she meant. Altruism is Nate's second name, isn't it? He has solved Charlie and Pru's insoluble difficulty for them. They will have a baby, after all. They are both over the moon because of it. Why shouldn't they be?

Our Nate's a big star. He's teaching big-time football skills to Canadian boys just out of high school. He rides around in that Cadillac wearing handmade shirts and handmade shoes while the Canadian kids ride to practices on their bikes. There's Nate on the golf course, in the off-season, signing autographs, and here's Nate raising money for charity. Say, you want a ticket to a game? Just ask you-know-who. In his first game with the Strikers, he led his club to a 29–20 triumph by throwing a pair of touchdown passes, intercepting two passes, kicking for a forty-nine yard average, and scoring one touchdown himself. He's a one-man band, no kidding. He'll do it right, or if he can't do it right himself, he'll see that it's done right. Hands on. That's our Nate; he has a hand in everything. They say he punched one of the kids who stood up to him. But the Strikers are headed for the Grey Cup this year for the first time since 1941, or my name's not Albrecht Storr.

Mary and Prudence are due to deliver their babies on more or less the same date. There are endless jokes about sisters doing everything together. It's a wise child who knows its own father, I'd say.

"Do you think the water level is going down?" asks Mary.

I get up and pull back the curtains. It is raining heavily. Even here, in the Heights, water is pooling in the streets. "I doubt it. The rain will melt more snow. I should get going. Pietor is all alone in the office." Mary sits up and grimaces. Her face is round and puffy, its pointed features smoothed by the extra weight. I like the way she looks. She looks like a mother. She looks as if she might stay in one place for a while.

"Why don't you stay home with me?" she asks, putting a twist on my thoughts. "Let Pietor handle it. You could keep me company. I'm bored to tears." She hates not working. She hates having other people do things for her. She hates the way she looks.

I go over and kiss her. "I've got a job to do. I have to stick my finger in a dike." I stroke my hand down her beautiful big belly.

"I can't knit bloody baby socks all day."

"Get Charlie to take you out somewhere. He's got nothing to do." Charlie's mother, Clara, won't have him in the hardware store with the baby's arrival so near. The old lady is adamant. None of her husbands stuck around—for one reason or another—so Charlie has to be Mr. Father's Day, dancing attendance on Prudence, the mother-to-be.

"Charlie won't be here. He'll be lugging sandbags." She's right. All able-bodied individuals have been asked to volunteer their labor in the flooded areas.

"There's always Pru."

"Pru! She won't have time. She'll be at the Church Hall playing Lady Bountiful to the flood refugees."

"There'll be kids in those church basements, won't there? You should go too. They'll need mothering. You could use the practice."

She throws a pillow at me. I close the door behind me before she can find something heavier.

I still have ingredients from the dream stirring in my mind when I arrive at the airport. During the same period when my father read to us about the Arctic, Clara Rivers, Charlie's mother, used to come over to help out in the house. This was long before she had her own hardware store. My mother taught music in those days, going into the schools to give lessons in the afternoons and staying on at night to give lessons to adults. I don't know what happened, exactly, but at some point her methods were thought to be old-fashioned, and when someone else with better qualifications turned up, she was let go. She came home in a rage, I remember that. "They know nothing in this country, nothing! There is no future for us here!" That was when Gerhard's music preparation began in earnest, first with her at home, and later on with the best teachers my parents could afford. The aim always was to send him away.

In any case, when my mother was teaching music, there was Clara. She'd arrive, with Charlie, when my mother was at work. I'd forgotten about Clara, but she'd been a daily presence for several years. There was no question, not in those days, of my father cooking dinner, or helping with housework and homework and putting us to bed. My father put in his full day at the slaughterhouse. After that, he had a right to his evening leisure and the important studies he was pursuing. So my parents paid Clara, who was very hard up, a little money to do those things. With what my mother earned giving lessons, I guess they could just afford the help.

Clara liked to tell us stories about her early life. She had emigrated from Czarist Russia when she was a young woman. She had many stories about traveling in the north, way up in the Siberian Arctic. I liked the stories well enough, but not as much as did Gerhard, who had stuck to Clara like a burr. He'd even help her with the dishes, while Charlie and I wrestled on the floor, so he could hear one or two more.

When everything was cleaned up, and if there was time once our homework was done, we'd watch my father go through his paces. He would ask for a full wineglass of water. It was my job to get the glass out of the china cabinet, and Gerhard's to carry it—he had steadier hands—without spilling any. My father would then take the glass and hold it by the stem, just above the base, by his thumb and first finger only. He'd hold it that way for a good thirty seconds or so on a level with his chin, trying to keep it still enough that the water in the glass wouldn't tremble. "There, boys," he'd say when he'd done, "see what the power of the mind can do?" We'd all try it, with little success, endangering my mother's good glass. Then my father would hold the glass with his thumb and second finger, thumb and third finger, thumb and little finger. "I have stopped," he would crow in triumph, "all magnetic leakage."

One evening, he added a rose petal to the glass of water and tried to keep the petal still. I remember how shocked I was to see him tear the petal from the flower—where had the bloom come from? We did not have roses to spare in those days. Worst of all, considering the sacrifice, he failed to keep the petal still. It rose and fell on the swell of its miniature sea. "Restlessness, loss of vital force, erratic nerves," murmured my father sadly. "It is worth every effort to overcome them."

I climb into the LWD Junak 3, start the Junak's engine, put the carburetor de-icer on, and go through the cockpit drill. It always feels good to be here, to test the brakes and feel them strain against the engine, to go over the flight plan. When I'm waiting to take off, all life's possibilities are ahead of me. No door has been shut, no opportunities lost.

A heavy smear of ice and slush spreads across the windscreen, is cleared by the wipers, and smears again. I'm glad to see the ice. If the temperature keeps dropping, it will ease the snow-melt and stop the rain. I stand off the brakes and start down the runway, turning into the slight crosswind to straighten the plane. The slush thins and streams in narrow lines that flatten to points at the windscreen edges. I am glad to be alive, to be out of the office, to be away from what passes, just now, for home.

Pietor had flown the Junak out of Poland in late 1948 when he defected from the Soviet occupation. Pietor was with the Free Polish Air Force during the war. He is now my colleague in the city engineering department. Pietor, who is unequaled at getting what he wants, managed to keep the plane. The Junak 3 is essentially the same as the Junak 2, he'd explained, and since it was used only for primary training, it was of no military importance. He'd had it shipped from Copenhagen by sea. People do things for Pietor. I'd be surprised if the shipping had cost him a dime. He had offered me a half-interest in the machine when he'd joined the department, and I'd taken him up on it. I considered myself lucky. Most of the time, I can fly when I like. "Just think, Albrecht," he'd said to me when I'd signed the papers, "when the Commies come, you can get away. Everyone else will be stuck in their cars on the highway." We often talked about the coming Soviet invasion and what people will do. Pietor thinks that the Civil Defense instructions—to get in your car and drive out of town when you know the bomb is on its way—are amusing.

"Where should I fly?" I'd asked him, curious as to what he would say.

"North. They'll come from there, of course, but they won't stay. It's too cold. They want the cities, the industries, the mines and resources, and houses with running water and central heating. I know— they took mine. They'll want all the Hollywood movies in the cinemas and the fruit and vegetables in the grocery stores. Above the tree line is of no real interest to them."

"The dean of Canterbury says the Russians want peace. It's us who want war. He claims that at the Last Judgment, the Russians will come out ahead."

Pietor snorted. "What does your Madame Pince-Jones say to that? I'd trust her over him. His collar is too tight—you can see it in his face. It chokes off his thinking. I'll take my chances with the Americans. I've been in Communist hell already." I never know when Pietor is kidding.

I am flying in snow cloud. I pull back on the stick and the Junak climbs smoothly. Within a few minutes, we are in clear sunshine. I'd been up several weeks earlier, with some American engineers. They were worried, like we were, about conditions in the Red River valley. We'd seen a solid sheet of ice and snow covering the valley and the tributary streams north of Grand Forks, with only a short stretch of open water on Red Lake. Since then, we'd had warm weather, which started the ice moving between Emerson and Winnipeg. There was flooding in both cities. Then the temperature dropped again, retarding the flooding, but putting us in great flood danger if the return of warmer temperatures— melting snow and ice—coincided with the onset of spring rains. Which is exactly what has happened.

I check my watch, calculate my position, dive through the cloud, level out, and start looking for Emerson, or what is left of it. It is a town just north of the American border, about sixty-five miles south of Winnipeg. I find the swath of water lying along the river basin, and a few islands of buildings, roads, and railway tracks, and smaller islands of high ground to which cattle from the surrounding farms have retreated. It appears that the road north has been cut.

I follow the railway line. It is a narrow sand-banked ribbon, with water lapping at the rails. Telegraph poles, sticking up out of the lake, give the line a neat border. Water swirls through the fields, looking for an exit. In several of the small towns I identify along the way—Letellier, St. Jean Baptiste, and Morris—there are boats cruising through the flooded streets picking up evacuees. More rain and snow are forecast. Soldiers from Camp Shilo have been brought in to stand by in the city of Winnipeg itself.

I think about what I'm seeing below. Once the river has risen past a certain stage, it will not only overflow its banks, as it already has, but will spread until it joins with its tributaries, making one lake a hundred and fifty miles in length. What will we do then? How long can the city dikes hold under that kind of pressure?

I contact the control tower and am patched through to my office. "Pietor? Can you do me a favor? Could you check on Mary? I just want to be sure she's stayed put." What she'd said this morning, about wanting to be at home, is bothering me. In St. Boniface, the district where we have our house, water is seeping through sandbags at sewer openings. We've sent in men, equipment, and loads of earth to reinforce the dikes, but the possibility of a public health disaster looms.

"Sorry, Albrecht. Not possible. We've lost more dikes. I'm on my way to East Kildonan now. I hope you're on your way back. We need you."

I consider for a moment. I can't shake this sense of unease. My mother has told me that women develop a nesting instinct just before giving birth: they want to be in secure, familiar surroundings. ("I would have had my Charlotte in the woods at the farm if my mother had let me," she told me, surprising me more than she could have imagined—this from a fastidious woman who has run her finger along more windowsills, checking for dust, than you can shake a stick at. "My old dog went out and dug a pit for me under a bush."

"Why in the woods?" I'd managed to ask, hoping I hid my shock.

"I loved nature, when I was young. Nature was where I belonged." Not for the first time, I was shaken by the image of a very different woman than the one I knew, a woman who had vanished long before I was born.

"What about me and Gerhard, when you had us?"

"That was different. There was your father by then. Where he was, was where I wanted to be." That woman, too, is only a dim memory.)

"Albrecht?" says Pietor. "What do you want me to do?"

"Look, Pietor, can you find Nathanial Bone? Can you ask him to go and see Mary?"

"The football player?"

"He's an old friend. Nate won't mind doing me a favor. He's almost one of the family, and he likes Mary."

"Okay, whatever you say. I'd better go. Oh"—he stops for a second and I can hear him moving papers on the desk—"there's a message here for you to call Madame Pince-Jones. She says it's urgent."

Electricity scouts for a route to the ground, sparks crackle in the white void of the heavy cloud I fly into, and the patch frizzles out in static. My father says that there are invisible wires, magnetic pathways, fibers of force. He used to come into our room during thunderstorms and, standing in the darkness between flashes of lightning bolts, squeeze on a broomstick to increase the nervous flow to his muscles, neutralizing imbalances by placing ice between his feet and grounding the static. He made us feel safe. He was doing something about the weather, about the state of the world.

By the time I'm back at the office, many of the telephone lines are down. I try calling Charlie's house, but can't get through. I call Pince-Jones, but she is out. I get somebody else on the line, who tells me that it does not matter whether I look upon the world materially or spiritually, I am in eternity anyway, and then the line goes dead.

Bill Bone manages to get through on an out-of-town line. He and Mildred Lark have wintered over in a wild animal park outside the city. They've been homesick for Winnipeg, but have not yet officially moved back from the States. California still beckons and Mildred continues to rake it in from films. "What the fuck do you plan to do with us?" roars Bill. "You can't put four lions and six tigers in a school gymnasium."

"You don't have to move, Bill. We've got duckboats going out to the farms with supplies for the animals."

"I'm not on a fucking farm," he yells. "I don't need fucking oats. I don't need your fucking duckboats. My problem is, I can't keep the animals dry. The Russkies are sending planes, warships, and men to Red China, the Nationalists are out on a limb, backs to the sea, and the Canadian Army is screwing around out here in toy boats in three feet of water. What's going on? Do you know what it says on those yellow rubber-ducky-boats? 'Insurance for fucking Peace'!" He hangs up on me.

By now, it is nighttime. The water is up to the headlights of my '49 Chevy workhorse, but I get through to the dikes that the Royal Engineers are maintaining along Mayfair Street and parallel to Main Street, between the Red and Assiniboine rivers, to keep the rivers from joining. Pietor has radioed through that he has found Nate, and that Nate has promised to look after Mary, so I'm feeling better about things and thinking that, if I can, I'll go over to our house later on and see how it is standing up to the flood. In the meantime, I go out with a boat crew to talk to the patrols that are moving up and down the river trying to discourage looting. The current swirls its purloined junk in eddies and side-currents, and we pass islands of exhausted workers waiting for the river to make its next move.

At the Shriners' hospital, near the Assiniboine River, there are scores of workers and troops buttressing the dike that protects the hospital. Flood workers have flashlights strapped to their heads like miners. They trudge in long lines along the top row of the dikes, and I can hear a thin banshee wail of music from where, along the Wellington Crescent dike, a man paces up and down, playing the bagpipes, moving behind the workers as they pass in their endless procession with sandbags. I can see, in the floodlights, the sway of his kilt, and I wonder what the children in the hospital, awake or dreaming, make of the melancholy, stirring sound that since ancient times has sent men into battle.

From a hospital window, I watch the city spread wide in flickers of candlelight and flashlight. There is no power. In the near light provided by the army's generator-powered floodlights, I see rooftops and copses of trees on high ground. Beyond, farther than I can penetrate into the gloom, are the lines and spokes of railways, roadways, and bridges, all cut, at key points, by water. I step into the hallway and find my way by flashlight down the stairs. As I come out into the lobby, I see two people entering from outside. Bill Bone and Mildred Lark! They do not see me. They must have hitched a ride in one of the army's "toy" boats. Mildred leads a lion cub and two tiger kittens on leashes. She is in full regalia—purple satin trousers and red velvet jacket festooned with gold braid. Bill Bone is laughing. He bends down and scratches the lion cub behind its ears, then they head down the hallway to surprise the children.

I return to the office to finish my paperwork. The mayor needs my report right away. It can't wait; there are newspaper deadlines to meet. I write about dike-testing and water levels, and make notes on storage reservoirs, floodways, and possible diversion projects. When I close my eyes to rest them, I see people shoveling sand into potato sacks, hour after hour, working to extend the dikes against the unrestrained water, oblivious to the debris and sewage swirling in the currents, making heroic efforts. Behind them are the toy-top roofs and chimneys, pitches, eaves, attic windows, shadowed and doubled in the stirred mirror of rust-brown river water.

I finish my notes in the early morning hours, check by radio to see if I'm needed anywhere else, and when I find that I'm not, decide that this is a good time to go out to the St. Boniface house. Before things get worse, and while there's a chance of returning with a few more of our belongings. I try to phone Mary, but the lines are still out. Water has backed into manholes all over the city, and there are cable breakages under the Main Street bridge caused by debris in the river. But I have nothing to worry about, have I—my friend Nate is on the job.

I cross the river on a ramp laid over the Provencher bridge and then pick my way through the few still unflooded streets. A line of people is standing, in the dawn, at the edge of dry roadway, waiting for boats to come. Rescue and salvage boats and every other kind of craft from canoes to rafts ply the river. In some, people are helplessly rowing or poling wherever the current takes them. Power boats, overloaded with furniture and boxes of china, tip and slew along, creating panic among the rowers. In the distance are the dark outlines of the flat-bottomed duckboats—Bill Bone's "yellow rubber-ducky-boats"—for which we wait. These nose up to the windows of drowning houses. We can hear the shouts of people in houses that the rescue boats haven't yet reached, crying out their terror of being forgotten and left behind.

The dark river laps at the earth where we stand. "Better get out of here, mister," says a soldier who is shooing away spectators. I show him my identification and tell him my plans. He shakes his head. "It's your funeral." He continues down the line, urging everyone to leave, warning of failing dikes and the risk of disease from contaminated waters.

The streets behind the dikes are stopped-up with traffic. Evacuees stumble alongside cars in long, winding queues toward the remaining open bridges. Children cry, their voices echoing without interruption back and forth over the flooding. Children, boat engines, the calling of people trapped in houses—these are all the sounds. There are no birds or barking dogs, no noises whatever of normal daily life. Many of the watchers near me have left at the soldier's request, but a stubborn knot of us remains. We are a bedraggled group in boots and raincoats, the women with kerchiefs tied over their hair, the men wearing sodden hats, all of us with tired, red-rimmed eyes, as we wait our turn in the boats.

A man and woman are ahead of me. As they board the boat, a cat swims by with a dead kitten in its mouth. "For God's sake, won't somebody do something?" the woman cries. I pick up a stick and step into the water, but there is no way I can reach far enough. The current tugs at my footing. The cat slips under, but emerges a moment later, still swimming.

We had moved the furniture upstairs before we left, so the ground floor of the house is empty except for debris washed in by the river. Flotsam rides the indoor tide, slopping toward the mud-blackened corners of the rooms. I recognize odds and ends that have floated up from the basement—paint cans, a rubber boot, dirty rags. I make my way to the stairs, holding my nose against the stench of backed-up sewage and dead rats, of sodden, rotting food left in the cupboards. I am going to the attic to retrieve some of our belongings—Mary's wedding dress and photograph albums, my model airplanes (in case it's a boy), a pram and a cot we have stored for Pru. I haul myself up out of the foul odors onto the landing, and as I do I hear a noise like the thin mewling of a cat, and wonder, absurdly, if the cat I saw swimming in the

floodwaters has somehow followed me. I look up. I see the baby
cot smashed on the stairs, and above it a trembling light. And I
think I am back in my dream, although it is nothing like my
dream: all is darkness, not snow and ice, and I am gazing at a
candle that Nathanial Bone holds in his hand.

"Thank God you're here," he says. He looks shell-shocked, like
the men in pictures my father has shown me, men standing in
trenches, waist-deep in water. His face is smeared with sweat and
dirt. There is blood on his clothing.

"Nate! What are you doing here? What's happened?"

"Come and see, please come."

The mewling sound continues. I follow the broad, dark slab of
his back up the stairs. Shadows jump across the ceiling. I go into
the bedroom, where a woman lies on the bed in the dark. "Mary!"
I go to her and lean down. She cradles an infant on her breast. I
touch her face and only then realize it is not Mary. It is Prudence
lying there, quietly with her baby while light from Nate's candle
sends copper snakes through her hair. Pru smiles.

"Look, Albrecht! He's perfect." So he is. The baby's body is
long, his legs are curled up. He has a mass of black hair.

"Pru, he's beautiful." Tears come to my eyes. I kiss her cheek.
It is cool, smooth as sandalwood. Then I hear the mewling sound
again, from behind me, and there's a hot, sharp smell in the room.
I turn toward it. Mary stands in the doorway, leaning against the
frame. She holds a stained sheet around herself. Even in the dim
light from the candle, I can see that she is shivering. "Mary!" I
carry her back down the hallway to the smaller bedroom and ease
her onto the rumpled bed. Her face is blurred with tears.

"Don't let him do this, Al, please don't let him." Her hands
knot around my neck; she won't let go.

"Shush. It's all right, my love, I'm here, I'm here, it's all right."
I keep her close, and try to undo her hands so that she can lie
down, but she only holds onto me more tightly and starts to cry
out loud.

Nate looms in the doorway. His face glistens. His shoulders
square the darkness. He scrubs his hands up and down the front
of his thighs. Those long thin legs—bird legs, we called them—
on which he can run faster down the field, skipping past line
backers, than anybody. "There was an accident," he says. "They
were carrying the cot downstairs. They'd come by themselves and
had fallen, both of them. When I found them—I was looking for
Mary, as you'd asked—it was almost over. It wasn't so bad,
Albrecht. I've delivered babies before, in China, at the prison
camp. The women who worked in the factory used to come and
ask for me. They said I was good at it. It's okay, Albrecht, I've
worked with animals, too, I knew what to do."

"You were here? You delivered Pru's child?" Mary, who has
released me at last, is too weak to rise now, but her fingers pluck
at my shirt. I turn to her. "What is it, Mary?"

"Don't listen to him." Her voice is a dry croak that sends shivers through me. "Whatever he says, he's lying."

I am bewildered. I don't really understand what Nate is telling
me, or why Mary is so distressed, but all the fear that has lain
inside me, idling like seawater at slack tide, is rising. I feel it rise
and rise, covering my eyes.

"I saw him!" she cries out suddenly. "There was nothing wrong
with him!"

"Mary?"

"Albrecht, please listen to me. He took my baby. I think I
know why. Please, Al, oh please, just get him back for me."

Nate just stands there. Like my father, all those years ago, when he would come home from the slaughterhouse and pause in the porch before stripping off his blood-stained clothing, and wait for my mother to let him in.

"Mary hit her head when she fell," he says with an apologetic smile. "She doesn't really remember."

"You said you'd take care of her!"

"I did my best," he says, shaking his head in wonder at my anger. "I did everything I could."

"Yeah, sure, Nate. Just the way you did for Lily, all those years ago. You weren't there for her, either, and she died! Thank God nothing happened this time. No thanks to you." I know what I'm saying isn't fair, but I don't trust him. Not now. I don't trust that smile, those hands. I'm remembering Nate with his hands on Prudence, doing favors.

"No, Albrecht, no," he says, still smiling, placating me, "it's not like Lily. Come and see, come here and look so you'll understand." He walks over to the dresser, carrying the burned-down candle with him. Its liquid light wavers over a small bundle wrapped in a pillowcase. "See, Albrecht, Mary's baby is here." He picks it up. For a confused moment—I am so dumbfounded—I think it is some kind of present. He holds it out to me; I take it.

"No," sobs Mary, pleading. "I saw my baby when he was born. There was nothing wrong with him. You don't understand, I held him." Her voice is thick with fatigue and despair.

My head pounds. It is difficult to concentrate, hard to understand what it is I have in my hands. I keep thinking about the flooding, channels to be cut, data to enter, insurance, recommendations, things I can do.

"You see," Nate tells me calmly, "I've had to do this before. The POWs worked in the factory with the women. I smuggled parts for a radio to a man who gave me food and medicines in return. He was part of the Chinese resistance to the Japanese. He showed me a picture of himself, in Shanghai, with British officers. I kept nothing for myself; I gave the food and other medicines to the other prisoners. Some of the Chinese women captives were pregnant. When they had their babies, they asked for me, and I helped them. They knew they could count on me."

I have no idea why he is saying all this. I have no idea what he means.

"You've got to believe me! Please, Albrecht." Mary's scalp is so wet with sweat that her hair clings to her skull. My nostrils can't get used to the odors of blood and sweat and death. She is still shivering. I look at Nate, and think of my father, working in the slaughterhouse and then purifying himself of the blood through magnetic realignment every day, after washing, by standing on ice.

"Open it," says Nate, "go ahead. You'll see."

I lay the bundle on the bed and unwrap it. There's a little girl. Her hands grow straight from her shoulders like wings, and she has feet but almost no legs. She is like a little bird. And her head. There is a deep cavity in the top of her skull. I know that if I touched there, I'd feel her brain beneath the membrane of skin. Thin wisps of red hair. Oh, Mary. All our dreams. What have we done?

"Please," says Mary.

"It's all right," I whisper, so that only she can hear me. "It's not your fault."

But I am remembering Suffield, and standing under the flight-path of an airplane that sprays mustard gas on me, and Mary whispering into my ear, while I lie helpless, afterward, in a hospital bed, all those terrible words: diseases, and toxins, and spores secreting themselves in the ventilation system of the laboratory. I lift the child to me. I hold and rock the poor dead thing. Mary weeps and does not answer when I ask if we can name the baby Charlotte, after my mother's daughter who was killed in the bombing at the end of the war.

I look out of the hospital window at the rain. Mary has been drugged into sleep. The bones of an unborn child are soft, my father has told me. When the child is born, the bones become more solid, the magnetic patterns are fixed. They are specific to the magnetic energies at that point on earth. If we can find the exact point of magnetic origin we can, in theory, bring her back to life. This is the secret of Magnetism. It is what my father believes, and what I want to believe, for I can still feel the tiny weight of my child in my hands. Pince-Jones has given me a poem. She tells me it was dictated by my sister Charlotte's spirit (the spirit had come to her just before the children were born.) I read it over and over, and try to hear somebody singing.

> *You are too young*
> *to think of the dead.*
> *There is no right or wrong*
> *inside the cellar of fear*
> *while the bombs fall.*
>
> *Someone is singing to you*
> *of white flowers in the mountains,*
> *of blue flowers like drops of water,*

of stars bright as ice
beyond the searchlights
and the curtain of lights
that pin airplanes
to the paper night.

A star is silver—
it is a million children,
their spirits alight
as they fall, burning their shapes
into the snow.

They are ice and smoke,
frost on birches.
Everything is silver,
even my tears
as I sing for you,
even the shadows in the cave.

13

THE TRUTH
TELLER

MAY 26, 1960

Fika lay in the tent, shivering in her damp sleeping bag, waiting
for the melting ice to turn to water and come to a boil on the stove
so that she could make tea. She had already been outside to examine the day. It was gray, with whiteness in every direction, a period
to be lived through with a compass, checking direction at every
stop, although traveling, in general, was easier now. There were
large areas of flat ice where the skis seemed to move by themselves:
the days of clambering over daunting rubble heaps and blocks of
ice were past. The principal danger was of open water, but there
had always been a way across, always, so far, a bridge of ice.

Carefully folding the sleeping bag to make a pad on which to sit, Fika prepared tea. While she waited for it to steep, she poured some of the boiling water into a cup, and added a handful of meal to it. She mixed in salt, powdered milk, and a sprinkle of sugar. She ate quickly, then melted another few ounces of water for washing. There was no soap left, but wiping the small square of warm moistened cloth over her face, neck, and hands made her feel human. She did not look in the scrap of mirror she carried in the pack.

Mechanically, Fika broke camp. Every day, there was less to carry, and every day, as her proximity to possible safety grew, the margin of survival, both in terms of food supplies and her strength, became slimmer. She made a cache of discarded objects, including Ekaterina's and Marina's extra clothing. It was difficult to remember why she had carried these things as long as she had, but in the end she saved a scrap of towel that had been Marina's, and a sock that had belonged to Ekaterina, and held both pieces of cloth against her face for a moment before she started out.

Once she began skiing, Fika returned, in her mind, to her grandmother waiting in the taffeta dress embroidered with violets. Clara's little boy stood at her side as she was married to the man named Dorrity. Afterward, Clara climbed into a wagon and began the journey to Dorrity's ranch in the Black Hills between Lead and Rochford. The river that the wagon road followed was broad and placid, and flowed through a lush, humid valley. The fields were rich with thick grass. There were cattle grazing, and sheep pulling out thick tufts, browsing their way up the green hillsides from the valley floor.

At the ranch, Clara spoke with Dorrity's uncle and learned what Dorrity hadn't told her—that he already had a family, left behind in New York when he had fled the city after killing a man in a boxing match. Despite her anguish over the news, Clara decided to stay: she did not think she could pull up roots and be on her own with the child again. She stood listening to the distant tapping noise of someone cutting timber as Dorrity stumbled out of the house and down the steps to the pump, where he splashed himself with water. Then he mounted a horse and rode away. His figure faded into sunlight so bright that it was only whiteness. The cold, hot light burned her face.

One night, when Dorrity came home drunk, he chased Clara, who wore nothing but her nightgown, out of the house into the snow. She would have frozen to death if the boy, hearing Dorrity's snores at last, hadn't opened a window to let her in.

The day Clara left Dorrity, she first took Charlie to his music lesson in Rochford, then the two of them walked from Rochford to Hill City, a distance of twenty miles. Clara got a job working in the kitchen of a hotel. When Dorrity found out where she was, he came to bring her back, but Clara stayed put. When Clara fell ill, however, and could not look after her child, someone at the hotel, perhaps meaning well, sent for the husband. He came, waited for her to recover, shipped the boy to Winnipeg, Canada, where there were other Russian- and German-speaking immigrants, and had Clara committed to the state mental institution in Yankton, South Dakota, as a runaway wife. They strapped Clara, hand and foot, to a pole and beat her until she was weak from loss of blood. They dragged her by her long hair the length of the hundred-foot hall, and threw her into a dark room without ventilation or water. Clara prayed to die, but instead she stayed awake, and listened to the cries of the insane around her.

Clara was never sent before a board or a court of any kind, and she was entirely without friends. No one came to see her. When she had the chance, she took it, and jumped from an open window.

Fika pushed on, came to a lead, and followed it. The lead narrowed. At its narrowest, it looked solid with drifted snow. Fika began to cross, but when she put her poles down, they went right through to water. She threw herself forward, caught a ledge of solid ice, and dragged herself out.

No sun and no shadows. Only flat light that took away all sensation of height and depth. It was a light that evened the landscape, a light that was as heavy and dense as an old-fashioned iron, a millstone rolling over the ice. Fika kept bracing for it to hit.

She skied in a dream. She and Clara were traveling together in sight of a river that curled away and then returned to cascade down a series of terraces in a rocky gorge. They caught fish with a hook and line dropped through a hole in the river ice. They built fires of moss scratched from beneath the snow. They milked the reindeer when they came upon them.

The animals grazed over land where, at its thinnest, the snow was over a foot deep. They broke through the crust with their hooves and pawed up moss to eat. Although the snow stayed on the ground and did not melt, and the nights were cold, sometimes, during the day, mist and cloud would dissolve, revealing a golden world beneath clear skies. Fika and Clara followed the reindeer until there was sunlight and, just ahead, a group of dark, cone-shaped tents.

As she continued to negotiate thin ice, open water, wet ice, and the shadowless surfaces that made her fall repeatedly, Fika was drawn forward by the sound of voices and laughter. She felt that she and her grandmother were expected, and looked forward to meeting the people inside the tents, but when she entered the first one, the atmosphere of smoke, fish, and rancid oil repelled her and made her sick.

She came out of the dream retching. She had fallen again, striking her head on a chunk of jagged ice. When she had finished vomiting, she wiped a thin stream of bloody liquid from her mouth. She found the medical kit in the pack, and gave herself the last remaining injection of vitamins, and then another one for pain. There were two ampoules of morphine left. Not enough to do much harm or good either way.

With terrible slowness, she struggled to her feet, pointed her skis southward, and began to move once more across the ice shelf in the direction of Ellesmere Island.

14

THE TWO
MINDS

SUMMER-WINTER 1950

I am in some darkness of my own making, an icy, bottomless lake so black and cold that I feel nothing. It is a world of water and cold and emptiness. *Nothing.* From time to time I imagine stars, high above, in that other world I partly recall, but mostly there is nothing.

I float in my lake of numbness and listen to the music of nothing. The music is played by my brother, Gerhard. It runs backward, and is made of the energy of cold stars, and the scream of Lily Bone as she lay dying, and my wife's voice as she begged me, against all hope and reason, to believe her and not Nathanial Bone on the night our child was born. These are the limits of my thinking as I sit in the living room of our cleaned-up St. Boniface house, speaking to no one and listening only to the ticking of the clock, insistent as a Geiger counter, on the mantel.

When Mary comes home from the hospital, I hand her the oranges I meant to bring to her and never did, as well as the chocolates, the get-well cards, and the bedjacket I must have purchased on St. Mary's Road. She sits on the couch surrounded by these objects, and by baskets of fruit still covered in colored cellophane. I don't remember buying any of these things.

She sits, bravely smiling, and I come blinking out of my hibernation to see that we are surrounded by well-wishers. My father and mother are here, as is Madame Pince-Jones, who has made for us a plate of my father's favorite magnetic snack—raw steer meat, scraped, salted, and spread on hot toast. "Eat, children, eat. It will make you strong."

And will it remove sorrow? And will it stop the music that boils like white water, erasing my brain and all my feelings?

I've just come home from work. It's nearly a hundred degrees outside and I've walked all the way from the bus. I'm tired. I'm always tired. I want to pour a cold drink and sit outside in the backyard under a tree and look at the river. But there are dozens of sandbags piled up against the outer walls of the house all the way to the top of the windows. The place looks like a bunker. Inside the house, it is dark.

She's not in the kitchen. I walk through to the living room and straight into a post that wasn't there this morning. "Mary? Where are you? What's going on?" There is no answer, but once my eyes adjust to the dimness, I see not only the post, but an entire framework of posts, beams, and braces that has been erected in the middle of the living room. On the floor in the center of this construction, seated in a nest of pillows and blankets, is my wife.

I crouch down beside her. "Sweetheart, what is this?"

"Albrecht! I'm so glad you're home." She holds out a booklet she's been examining. "Here, I want you to read this." Its title is *Make Your Home Your Bomb Shelter*.

I take it from her. "What do you want me to read, love?"

"Page ten, please. It explains everything better than I can, I know you'll have questions." She touches her index finger to my mouth, as if she can feel those questions already forming.

So I read aloud: "*Shelter at Home. It is better, as a rule, not to use the basement for shelter purposes, but to select a Refuge Room in that part of the ground floor that has no basement underneath. The reason for this is that the extra protection afforded by the basement is more than offset by the risk of the occupants being trapped in the building without means of exit should it collapse.* Is that what you've done, Mary? You've built a Refuge Room?"

She nods. "As you can see, this is the best place for it." She takes the book back, flips ahead a few pages, and touches her finger to another place in the text. "Read this now, Albrecht."

So I read: "*It is essential that you should consider all factors and carefully weigh the possible disadvantages against the advantages.*"

Mary says, "I've done that, Albrecht. I've spent all day on it."

"And this is the result?"

"Yes, of course. As you see." Her eyes are as deep as twin lakes, and they are muddy with drugs and pain. "Do you like it?"

"Like it?" I lie back and pull her down beside me onto the cushions. We gaze up at the forest of four-by-fours and four-by-sixes overhead. "It looks pretty strong."

"Pietor says, even if the bomb falls, we'll probably be fine. The beams will support the ceiling. We can stretch a layer of chicken wire over the top of the framework and fix it to the walls. Then we won't be hurt by falling plaster."

Oh, Mary, I think, it's not falling plaster that will hurt us, and we have been hurt so much already. Then she turns to me to ask, as she does every day, "Where's Nate, Albrecht? He can straighten this out, you know. You must talk to him. There has been a mistake. It could have been an accident, although I don't see how."

"Nate's not here, Mary. You know that. Nate has gone away."

"He always runs away when he's in trouble, doesn't he?" she says, smiling. "Remember the other times? Remember?" She is insistent, demanding that I recall exactly what Nate is like. "Even when he was a boy, he wouldn't face up to things. You know how he is. Nobody knows him better than you."

"He hasn't run away," I say as gently as I can.

"Hasn't he? Then where did he go? Why hasn't he come to see me and give my baby back?"

I explain for the hundredth time about his elbow injury in an exhibition football game, and how he had to drop out of training for the coming season. I tell her, again, about the farm in Oklahoma, owned by relatives of Bill Bone's, on his mother's side, where Nate went to recuperate. "He sent us a letter, remember? He was staying in a shack beside the river. Every morning, he got up early, went out in a little boat, and caught a fish for breakfast." It sounds more like a fairy tale each time I tell it. I'm trying to keep it simple because she forgets anyway, and because I don't want to go into the rest. Nate had helped me out a lot in the past few months. He'd seen me through the funeral when Mary wouldn't have a thing to do with it. We'd buried my poor mite next to Lily Bone in the Brookside cemetery. It seemed to Nate and me—Mary wouldn't even discuss the arrangements— that it was nicer for the two little girls to be together. Nate has been a good friend.

But no matter how many other wires are crossed, there is nothing wrong with Mary's instincts. "You haven't told me everything; You never do," she says. "Tell me the rest, please. I'm asking you."

"How many pills did you take today, Mary? Did my mother come over to help you count them out?"

"Somebody came, but I didn't let them in. I was too busy." Yes. Busy constructing a Refuge Room, and ordering sandbags, and roping whomever she could into her madness.

"Was Pietor here today?"

"Don't put me off, Albrecht. I want to know about Nate." She licks her lips, her mouth dry from the pills. We aren't sitting close together now; she has moved away.

"You've seen the newspapers, Mary. You know there's a war on. Nate's joined up." I haven't wanted to mention the war. The subject raises ghosts I want left undisturbed: the ghost of the effects of handling weapons of war, for instance, or the ghost of untimely death.

"Nate's gone to war? But you told me he was resting."

"He was. I told you the truth. I always tell you the truth. He got better, and when the war in Korea started, he joined up."

Old soldiers never die, they dream of past glory; and if there's a chance of basking in more, of course they'll take it. So it is no surprise to me that Nate has gone back to the military. I would, too, if I could.

"Do you think he wants to die, Albrecht?"

"I don't think anyone wants to die."

"He might want to, Albrecht. He deserves to be killed, I think." They tell me it isn't really my Mary when she talks like this: it is the medicine. But if it isn't my Mary, who is it, and where has Mary gone?

"Are you going to go to war, too, Albrecht? It might not be a bad idea." Mary says sweetly. "It's what you always wanted, isn't it? You could find Nate and talk to him. I bet you never asked him straight out, did you?"

"Asked him what, Mary? What are you talking about?"

"Asked him why he tells those lies."

Pietor is Mary's advisor on preparing for World War III. He tells her that she's right to be frightened, that it's only sensible to be afraid. He tells me that I make things worse when I argue with her. "It's something she *can* get ready for," he says. "It's real, she doesn't have to make anything up. Mary needs things she can do something about." He doesn't have to remind me that what she wasn't able to do anything about, what she couldn't prepare for—the death of her child—has devastated her. "She should go back to work," he says.

"No, not yet. It's too soon."

"Too soon? Why? It would be good for her."

"You don't understand."

"What's to understand? You've lost a child. This is terrible, but you and she must pretend to yourselves that life is normal."

"Life isn't normal."

"You're telling me, an East European, that life isn't normal? I have East European teeth. Do you know how people treat me once they've seen my steel molars?"

"Stop joking, Pietor."

"Who's joking? I am a person who has lost everything, many times. I'm still here because, you know what? When you pretend long enough, it gets better. So, life is more normal for you now—anybody can see that. Tell me why it can't be the same for her."

"Mary's not fit."

"There's nothing wrong with Mary."

"Goddamn it, Pietor. You know the problem. She's ill. The doctors know she's ill. They give her pills. She thinks Nate took our baby. She's nuts—that's the truth. It didn't happen that way. Our baby died because she could never have lived. She was born deformed. She had no chance. For Christ's sake, Pietor."

"You know this for a fact, do you?"

"I was there!"

"I see," he says, and I think about the conversations he must have had with Mary.

"I'm told there are women who never accept the death of a child, and she feels guilty, of course," I say.

"Guilty? Why?"

"Fuck you, Pietor. You know!"

"I'm not as certain about everything as you are, Albrecht. I stick to things that are obvious. Such as"—he pauses to light a coffin-nail—"it's obvious that getting Mary off those pills and back to work will cure most of what's wrong with her. It's also obvious, by the way, that if North Korea and the Chinese Communists win the war, we'll be sunbathing in our bare bones beneath a mushroom cloud."

"Maybe."

"Okay, maybe. Maybe they'll keep us as slaves, instead. But

leave Mary alone, my friend. Let her do what she thinks she can do, what she wants to do, even if it leaves you behind."

What is it that Mary can do? Well, now that there is a new war and it looks as if we may be losing it, apparently almost anything. At least so say the military, if not the civilian, doctors. They want her back at work. They don't care that she may be crazy. I suppose, in these circumstances, it's crazy not to be crazy. What does being crazy matter if the world is coming to an end? Anyway, I don't have a say in it. She flushes her pills down the toilet and packs her bags and goes; and just as Pietor predicted, she gets better. So much better that it looks as if I'm on my own permanently, saddled with a home half converted to a bomb shelter. She's way up in the Arctic, on the DEW line, doing God knows what for God knows whom. I wouldn't dream of asking what it is, exactly, that she's involved in—not that she would tell me. I'm out of the picture, I guess, I'm a page of history. But hasn't she—haven't we—already paid a heavy price for Mary's career? Isn't one baby with wings enough?

"They'll take anyone!" cries Pietor excitedly, kicking open my office door. "I couldn't believe it." He switches off the fan so that I have to listen to him.

He sits down on the edge of my desk, disrupting a week's worth of carefully sorted papers.

"I went down there. They didn't give me a physical, they didn't look at my teeth." He sticks a finger in his mouth, pointing out the shining molars. "If they think you're between sixteen and sixty, they'll let you in. Christ, Albrecht, they didn't even ask if I'm a citizen! With an accent like mine!"

"But you are a citizen."

"Don't you see? It doesn't matter! Nobody cares. We're off to fight the Communists in Korea. It's a Holy War! I'm a soldier!"

He is pleased—obviously. I've never seen him so happy. "I'm glad for you."

"There was this guy next to me in the lineup. I said to him, 'What a beautiful day.' He didn't hear me. I said it louder. He still didn't hear me. He was deaf! They let him in. And this kid ahead of me, I heard him talking to the doctor, and he's saying that when he was on the farm, he'd get up in the middle of the night and strangle a sheep! They let him in!"

"He should be useful."

"You should join up, too, Albrecht. Go over there and kill as many Commie bastards as you can."

"I've heard it's a beautiful country."

"Who cares? It's full of Commies, Albrecht."

"The South Koreans are our allies."

"Sure. South Koreans—okay. North Koreans—not okay. Their allies are the Chinese. Do you know how many Chinese Communists there are?" He closes his eyes as the adding machine inside his brain scrolls through. The eyes flip open. "There are millions of them. They'll dispose of your 'allies' in five minutes. Yes, sir," he continues, "it's a chance to get rid of them." He lifts his arms and imitates operating a burp gun—*da-da-da-da-da-da-da*. "Come on, Albrecht, come with me."

"I'm not as bloodthirsty as you."

"You're an innocent, that's why."

"I have to stay. I have obligations."

"Obligations? What obligations? Who depends on you anymore? No one. Everyone is going. They've signed up, shipped out. Who's left? Nobody!"

"They didn't want me before," I say bitterly. "My brother flew for the Luftwaffe."

"You think that counts? Not now. That was then, Albrecht. Hitler's dead. Now we've got Stalin. Stalin's a butcher, his hands are bloody, and he's standing right behind the Chinese. Who cares about the Luftwaffe these days? It's the Commies or us."

It is mid-November when I see Pietor off at the station. There's a whole trainload of soldiers heading west to train with the Americans in Washington State, at Fort Lewis, where they'll find better weather, warmer climes, and maybe a dose or two of propaganda to tell them why they're going to Korea. Nobody seems to know—except for Pietor. They're as excited as schoolchildren on an outing. Some are running away from wives, or they're out of work or in debt, or they just want a crack at a good time overseas with their friends. They've heard that Korean women age quickly, so they're in a hurry. I hear it all in the buzz around me. This is the last train in the Canadian contingent.

Pietor embraces me and kisses me on both sides. Red spots of excitement stain his cheeks. His hair, jet black, is combed straight back from his forehead. He looks younger than I've ever seen him.

He stuffs himself on board with the others and fights his way to a window just as the train is pulling out. "Hey, Albrecht!" he shouts. "I'll see you over there."

"Sure thing, Pietor!" I answer, although I haven't made up my mind. I only say it because he's going.

"Great! We'll track down Nate Bone together. For Mary. We'll do it for Mary!"

"What? What's that?" There are women holding their lovers' hands as the train starts moving. Babies cry, and somebody, somewhere, plays "The Blue Canadian Rockies" on the harmonica. It is a strange, melancholy tune, clear as a church bell in all that uproar.

"Never mind, Albrecht! You can keep the plane!"

"What's that? What's that?" But Pietor is gone, and the train is just a hunk of thinning metal far down the line.

They were three hundred and twelve miles west of Edmonton, east of Canoe River in British Columbia, when the train started up a long, uphill curve. They were high in the mountains, and had just crossed a long trestle over a five-hundred-foot mountain gorge. They would have been wide awake at 10:35 in the morning, digesting breakfast, writing letters, reading a book, or just shooting the breeze. A transcontinental express entered the same curve from the opposite direction, and seconds later, without any warning, they crashed into each other. Pietor was riding in the third coach from the front. The car ahead of his telescoped and landed on the front of the one in which he rode. The coaches were wooden; they splintered into scrap wood in a pile about fifty feet high. I felt sick when I saw the pictures. Twenty-one men died, and over seventy were injured, many of them burned by the scalding steam from the engine. Pietor's body was never found.

There is no nightmare or dream, but there are voices, and they won't leave me alone: "Why don't you go, Albrecht? Maybe you should go and be killed, too."

When I arrive at the office in the morning, there's an envelope waiting on my desk. It's a letter from the Canadian government and the United Nations inviting Canadian engineers, particularly those with water and sanitation experience, to go to Korea. We are needed over there, it seems, to save lives.

Just before I go to Korea, I call Mary on the radio-telephone, but she's in the field and can't be contacted. In the field, in the Arctic, in November? I'd wanted to tell her I was going to Korea as she'd suggested, and that I'd try to do what she'd asked and look up Nate. I'd wanted her to hear in my voice the willingness to listen to whatever she had to say. I don't blame her for anything, and I hope she doesn't blame me. Life works its way through. It has to be digested, tonic or poison. I'd wanted to tell her that I'd be working in general public health—in waste and water supplies—and that I'm returning to fundamentals. I'd like to quiz her on arrangements in the north—you can let human waste freeze and then burn it with fuel oil. Does she know?

I hang up the radio-phone, worrying. If she's in the field, she'll be living in a temporary shelter. It'll be colder there than a witch's tit. There'll be a paraffin heater and poor ventilation, and constant danger from carbon monoxide poisoning.

I hope she's looking after herself. I hope she's found a reason to stay alive.

I'm dressed in a U.S. Army officer's uniform although I'm a U.N. employee, part of the Civilian Assistance Command. The chef de mission is an Englishman, a medical officer in the Indian Army.

There are six officers altogether, and two civilians. The Danish doctor and I hold the temporary rank of colonel. We fly from New York in a strato-cruiser to Minneapolis, then to Anchorage, and to the Aleutians. Not long after we take off from there, we cross the International Dateline. My father has given me a map of lines of magnetic variation so that I can plot our route and know exactly when today becomes tomorrow. At the right moment, Dr. Meyer and I share a drink from his flask to celebrate.

"No looking back now, Storr!"

"Here's to you."

From Japan, we take a military transport plane, land at Pusan, in Korea, refuel, and make our way to Seoul.

We wait a long time at cold Kimpo airport for the next stage of our flight. We are headed for Hamhŭng, the capital of Hankyng Namdo, about a hundred and sixty miles northeast of Seoul near the east coast, following in the wake of a great U.S. and U.N. advance. It is thought that the troops, in some sectors of the far northeast, may soon cross the Yalu River into China.

We leave while it is still dark, and fly northward over the Sea of Japan. From time to time, I think I spot a Korean junk or warship, but mostly there is nothing but the flat dark of the sea. Eventually, daylight leaks into the somber November sky, and there are islands and fishing boats near the coastline, then rice-fields, pine-clad hills, and patch after patch of tilled and terraced land on hills and valleys alike, all outlined with a dusting of snow.

As the plane taxis between frosty fields, we rumble alongside an irrigation ditch on which soldiers have made a skating rink. Straw matting, propped by two-by-fours, marks off the ends for hockey. A few players skate back and forth, passing the puck. "That's Yanpo Gardens," somebody jokes.

There is snow on the ground and the rooftops of the houses. Smoke rises from wood and straw chimneys. Every rice paddy looks, to me, like a potential skating rink. "Hey, Storr! You're from Winnipeg," says the soldier opposite me. "The hockey scouts will be waiting at the airport."

There's no hockey scout, but Nate is there, as promised. He's wearing heavy, warm clothing and heavy boots, and he looks bigger and taller than ever. "Albrecht! Over here!" I push through the crowd toward him. There are masses of soldiers and civilians. Our cargo plane is already unloading its belly full of goods and jeeps.

"Hey, Nate!" It is good to see him.

He claps me hard on the back in greeting. "Come on, let's go. We'd better get on the road ahead of this crowd. Bring your pals." He jumps into a jeep waiting outside, and Dr. Meyer and I and our interpreter follow, with me taking a last look, as we leave the airport, at the hockey players.

Gerhard and I used to make our own rink. We'd clear the backyard, then haul barrels of water by sleigh—every drop pumped from the standpipe in the street—to flood the ground. It took two or three winter evenings to do the first flooding. Then we'd give it the second flooding, which would smooth the surface out a little. After the third flooding, we'd let the smaller kids skate on it to knock off some of the lumps. The fourth flooding would make it perfect for playing hockey.

———

The Communists have left everything in ruins. Broken masonry and other debris block the streets, and there are burnt-out, gutted buildings everywhere. It makes the aftermath of the flood at home seem inconsequential. All along the road, we pass knocked-out Russian-made tanks. At some places, five or six are all smashed up together. Huge areas of industrial plants have been rendered useless. Beside the railway tracks, you see burnt-out and wrecked freight cars. These were destroyed by our aircraft when this part of the country was in Communist hands. It is impossible to look at them and not think of Pietor and to pray that he died instantly. "Kill the Commie bastards," Pietor said, but I have not come here to kill Communists. I don't want to be one of the death-dealers. I don't care now that I missed the real war last time. I'm needed here. There has been no advanced education for Koreans during the nearly forty-five years of the Japanese occupation, which only ended after the Second World War: Koreans were made to speak Japanese and to occupy menial positions. There are no professionals, no architects or engineers.

"You'll have your work cut out for you," says Nate.

"What do you mean?"

He points to fires burning in the distance. "Hamhŭng's a city of about a hundred thousand. There's almost no water, and there's no firefighting equipment. Everybody who ran the government has either been killed by the Communists or has gone off with them. They pilfered all the trucks and equipment. When a fire starts, you can't put it out."

There are people—refugees, Nate tells us—everywhere. Women carry babies on their backs, and bundles of cordwood or bags of rice on their heads. Small children carry smaller children, and old men and women step out right in front of us, offering to sell a vase or painting or a family tea service in exchange for K rations or rice. We stop at an abandoned hospital to pick up medical supplies. These are for the civilian field hospital that Dr. Meyer is to open. The only medical facilities currently available are for soldiers.

By the time we arrive at our billet, Dr. Meyer has his first patient, a boy who was lying in the street. He has a cracked skull, a broken jaw, a broken right arm, and his face is all burned and crushed. The interpreter, who questions the boy, tells us that he was playing in some ruins and touched off a mine or hand grenade. I have trouble looking at the child. His eyelids are gone and he cannot protect his eyes. Dr. Meyer puts his hat over the boy's face.

"You will get used to it, " says the interpreter, watching me. "You will see worse."

"Worse?" I ask. He smiles, but says no more for the time being. When we arrive at the lodging and have done our best to make the boy comfortable, the interpreter says, "What will you do with him?"

"Do? I don't know. What should we do? Isn't there some government place for orphaned children?"

He shrugs. "We have had to lie low for years. We have learned to wait until things change by themselves." He is slightly apologetic. "We don't have much zip. We will get our zip back, but it will take some time." He smiles gently and suggests that he begin teaching me the language. Nouns with twelve cases, word use that depends on whom you are talking to. Verbs that have six or seven degrees of politeness.

I set to, immediately, studying the problem of repairing the water-works system. The city gets its water from a series of wells. Many of these have been destroyed. Without enough water, people will die, if not directly from thirst, then from typhus engendered by poor sanitation. I get my hair crewcut and dust the team with DDT. I visit Dr. Meyer's new field hospital and the new Civilian Assistance orphanage, already full of children, and dust them all with DDT. The children live in large rooms with blankets spread on the floor for their beds. I make sure their drinking water is clean and that there are clean buckets for latrines. Nate comes to help out when he can, too, and we cut stars out of empty tin cans to hang from the ceiling for decoration, and then we teach the children a few simple English and French songs.

There is an epidemic of typhus in the POW camp. I sit with the dying North Korean soldiers in the huts where they are left more or less to fend for themselves. There is no one to look after them, no one to hear them or to bring them water to slake their terrible thirst. My father says that human beings are simply higher forms of vegetation, but it is not vegetation that I watch die, nor is it simply magnetic force fading that I feel when I hold these dying men in my arms.

On one visit to the camp, I find a small boy among arriving prisoners. He has no mother or father, and his only clothing is a sack he wears over his shoulders. His toes and some of his fingers are frostbitten. We take him back with us to the mess, where the mess sergeant dresses him in soldier's clothes. The boy eats in the mess and is given a place to sleep in the enlisted men's quarters. He is about eleven years old. The housemaid who cleans for us asks me what we will do with the child "when the Communists return." She has told me that more than seven thousand Korean Christians—she is a Christian, too—were murdered during the Communist occupation. When the Communists come back—she is sure that they will—she expects to die, too. I speak to Nate, and he says that he will see what he can do about getting the boy sent south to the orphanage on Cheju-do Island.

"Maybe we can send him on to my mother and Bella at their orphanage?"

"Maybe." He is one boy, and there are thousands of such children.

The worst days are when there is nothing I can do, when I am out of DDT, and there is no milk to give the babies who are brought to me to feed. Korean children nurse from their mothers until the age of three or four. If the mother dies, the child generally dies, too. The worst nights are those I spend wondering how many of the infants I've seen that day will still be alive in the morning. Those nights it is not emptiness I fear, but the presence of a small ghostly child who sits on my cot in silence. I close my eyes so that I do not see her. I swallow another of Dr. Meyer's pills and put my pillow over my head so that I will not have to hear her when she starts screaming.

Nate and I are in the mess one night, drinking. "We're like an old married couple, eh, Albrecht? Where you go, I go."

"It makes you think," I say. "Where should we go next?" I'm on my sixth beer.

"Out there," he says, sweeping his hand to encompass everything north and west. "Out there in the real Korea. You don't want to miss the real Korea, do you, Albrecht?"

"That's what I've wanted all along, Nate. The real thing."

"Good, then. You can come with me next time."

"Come with you where?"

"Shush." He brings his finger clumsily to his lips. "Shush. I can't say, but you can come along with me next time and see."

What he does is illegal—excursions, forays, raids—whatever you want to call them—but is unofficially sanctioned as action behind the lines. He blows up explosives depots and railway lines, and tries with his band of loyal Koreans to establish links with guerrillas in the hills. But since, as he knows, anyone in opposition in North Korea has been murdered or has headed south already, he doesn't have much chance of getting anything substantial going. Still, it's worth a try, Nate thinks. Any foothold or handhold in the impenetrable interior is worth pursuing if it will help put a stop to the killing. People still seep down from the hills occasionally, as the weather gets colder, and when they do, they bring rumors of possibilities.

The jeep slogs along a track that meanders between sopping larches, then crosses half-frozen marshland and rough meadowland. A harrier hawk cruises above us, then dives toward the ground beyond the trees.

"You know what we're doing over here, don't you?" Nate asks me, above the whine of the engine. "You've had a look at some of the civilians in the field hospital."

"I'm not a doctor. What do you mean?"

"Where does hemorrhagic smallpox come from?"

"I don't know."

"It's so rare, it almost doesn't exist. Do you know how many cases we've had?"

"What are you saying, Nate?"

"You've been around, Albrecht. You know what Mary does for a living."

"Biological warfare? Here? Being used here? You're nuts."

He says nothing more for a few minutes, then he turns onto another track. "I want to show you something."

We drive into the hills, gearing up and down, rounding blind corners and crossing makeshift bridges over gorges. The wind picks up and blows snow, so sometimes the visibility drops to almost nothing. Finally, Nate stops the jeep and we get out and walk uphill and downhill, hacking through scrub brush and brambles and half falling down slippery rock. Then, suddenly, there's nothing in front of us. It's as if a blowtorch has swept across the landscape, removing everything in sight and leaving behind a black crust that even the snow can't hide. I say this to Nate.

"A blowtorch? You're not far off. We dropped napalm here. It's made of gasoline thickened with coconut fat and naphthenate. It's carried beneath the wings of aircraft. A single canister can smother about a half acre of ground. It burns at three thousand degrees Fahrenheit. What can survive three thousand degrees, Albrecht? It terrifies the Chinese more than any other weapon."

"I've never heard of it."

"It's brand-new. Ask Mary, she'll know about it." He kicks a hole in the blackened earth, then looks up. "Has your father made you into a vegetarian yet, Albrecht?"

I shake my head.

"You would be, if you'd seen this. You know what a napalmed human being smells like? Like roast pork. I can't eat meat anymore.

What should I think about napalm? What side should I be on?"

We have nothing to say to each other on the walk back or on the rest of the drive to the hawk-hunter's hut.

We set out at dawn the next morning with the hawk-hunter, who is to be our guide. His bird is a wild goshawk, about three years old and trained for hunting. The hunter tells us the bird took three hundred pheasant last season. It rides on its owner's gloved fist. A bell, attached to its back just above the tailfeathers, tinkles constantly as the bird swivels its head in perusal of the environs. The air is clear and cold and loaded with white sunshine. The rocks and fields are outlined with frost. Higher up, on the hill slopes, there are shrubs and some bushes flagging a few dry, yellow leaves: these, too, are decorated, laced with frost.

We hike for an hour or so, climbing several steep hills that give us views of mountain ranges lapping into the distance. Their peaks stand stiffly in place, but the roots are shrouded in veils of cloud that shimmer and fold like thin muslin sheets. We cross tilled fields and descend into a valley speckled with huts, and climb the far side. At the top of this hill, we stop to catch our breath. The restless hawk shifts back and forth, pulling at its jesses. "I think this is it," says Nate. He has a word with the hunter, then we descend and split apart, taking parallel courses down the length of the valley. Nate and I swing sticks from side to side, striking the bushes. A pheasant flies up in front of us, but it plummets almost immediately into a heavily wooded ravine. Within less than a minute, the nervous pheasant starts up again, and the hunter lets the hawk go. The bird streaks down the valley on the unlucky pheasant's tail, and flies it into the ground. When we come up, the hawk is pecking out the bird's eyes. We walk a little farther. Nate speaks again to the hunter, and the hawk is let fly once more. He gives the man money, and we part company.

It is a walk of about two miles from there to the grotto. The last stretch of the path wanders up the face of a hill. Nate has been told that the series of caves, whose existence is little known even in the district, is being used as a hideout by North Korean anti-Communists. In our wanderings with the hawk-hunter, we have passed behind the lines—or at least where we think the lines are. There is no current military activity in the area. Nate carries a map drawn for him by his informant; even so, I am surprised when, about halfway to the top, he pushes aside some rocks to reveal a hole in the hillside.

"Are we going inside?"

"That's why we're here."

"Won't somebody see us?"

"Whoever's out there, if there is anyone in this godforsaken landscape, will be concentrating on our guide down there." He points to where the hawk circles high over the now distant valley. "They'll be wondering what he's doing. He's picked up two friends to take our places. They shouldn't notice the difference unless they've been watching the whole time through glasses."

He turns on the flashlight as we enter. There's a small cavity that drops almost straight down, but at the bottom of this, about twelve feet below, there are steep, rough steps.

"*Somebody's* been here," I say.

"A Korean chieftain hid himself and his people here for a generation, but after that the entrance was lost. Our friends stumbled on it by accident when they were running from a patrol.

"Stumbled?"

"One of them moved some rocks to make a shelter, and found the opening."

We grope for footholds and handholds, and at length slither and tumble into a huge cavern with stalactite formations on the walls. The limestone shapes are pink and glistening, like the inner workings of a human body. From here, there are passages leading out in all directions.

"I sure hope you know where you're going."

We pick a direction, marking out turnings as we come to them—dozens of them—with piles of rock, and eventually issue into a huge cavern maybe ninety feet high. Fantastic stalactite formations cover the walls and roof with landscapes of miniature upside-down mountain ranges, and seascapes of rising waves. There are pillars and standing stones that bulge like mushrooms or thrust up like phalli. A small opening at the cavern's far end leads into a narrow, low passage. I'm not happy that we have to crawl through it, and Nate's body blocks the light, but at the end of it, after perhaps thirty yards of wriggling, we pass through into another large and deep opening. Here, there are several fireplaces made of stone or clay. Smoke from fires has blackened the otherwise shining white walls. I'm relieved to see this evidence of recent human occupation.

"Albrecht, come here," says Nate who has moved away to explore. As I join him, he plays the light over a heap of skeletons, all crumbled together, huddled against the darkness. Rags of clothing wind among the bones.

"How long have they been here?"

He shakes his head. "I don't know, but for a long time."

"Well, they're not your anti-Communists. Maybe we took a wrong turn."

"Maybe, but those fires were recent." He flashes the light around, but there is nothing else of interest in the cave, and we decide to go on. Now we find small pools of water. We continue, splashing through the maze, until we come to a large cavity where two wooden boats lie on dry ground. We examine them carefully. They look usable.

"The cave probably fills up with water in the spring. I wonder where those boats would go?"

I gaze around, searching for a likely passage out, but there are too many shadows, too many ledges and folds and stalactite formations. One looks like the pipes of an organ. I go over to it and flick the stones with my fingers; they give off ringing notes that hit the walls and die.

"Let's sit down," Nate says. It is cold, so we sit on the boats and take turns searching the walls with the light. One stretch of wall, high up, glistens as if it is set with countless diamonds.

"Mary would love this."

"How is she doing? I often think about her." It is the first time he's asked about her. I haven't mentioned her; I've been waiting for the right time, or, perhaps, I've been afraid.

"She's back at work. She's all right."

"I hope so, Al, I do. You know I owe her a lot."

"Oh, yeah?" I can sense something coming. I don't know what it is, and I'm not sure I want to hear it. I don't like confessions, especially if they involve my wife.

"She helped me through a bad time, you know. I don't know what I would have done without her."

"That's what friends are for, Nate." It's my turn with the light. I find I'm making a cross-hatch pattern and putting in the X's and O's.

"I wrote to her when I couldn't talk to anybody. Did she show you the letters?" I shake my head.

"I didn't think she would, somehow," he says. He pauses, rubs at his eyes, and then goes on. "At the end of the war, people didn't want to hear about what had happened, they just wanted it all to go away. Even though you knew it wasn't your fault, you felt bad about it, as if you'd done something wrong, and whatever else they said, a lot of people felt the same way. A lot of POWs came back with problems."

"I didn't know, Nate. You didn't say anything."

"I wouldn't have told anybody, not even Mary, but she was there at the debriefing when we came home. You know what went on in that camp."

"I know what they did to Charlie, the bastards."

"What happened to me wasn't the same, but the doctors said I might never be able to have kids, and if I did have kids, there'd be a risk. They said I shouldn't have survived the camp. But, you see, I've proved them wrong. I'm still here, alive and kicking."

I've turned the light out. There is nothing to look at, so my hearing is heightened. I can hear water drops collect on the ceiling and make their slow way down each inch of limestone tubing.

"You've always been there for me, Albrecht, through thick and thin. I appreciate the way you've stood by, right from the beginning."

"What kind of risk are you talking about, Nate?"

"What kind? Some sort of mutations. They put me through hundreds of X-rays, and there were experiments with radiation."

"Mary knew this?"

"She was there at the debriefing. I didn't have to ask her not to say anything to anyone."

"She'd have been sworn to secrecy."

"I guess so. But I knew I could trust her."

"Why are you telling me this now?"

"You're my friend. I just wanted you to know. I wanted it in the open, to help put it behind me."

I don't realize that I'm crying until tears wash into my mouth. "You selfish bastard, we saw you fucking Prudence at the lake. We knew you were the father of that baby—Charlie couldn't have been." I don't realize that I'm standing, either, until I feel my foot jam hard against the boat. "Why didn't you say something? If not to anybody else, at least to Pru? Why didn't you tell the truth for once in your goddamn life? Oh, my sweet Christ, Nate, don't you see? Mary knew that poor sad baby wasn't hers—she knew it was yours and that you'd taken hers away. The dead baby was yours, Nate. And I didn't listen to her, I believed you."

The words feel sodden, ineffectual as sponge. I know I want to smash his face in, but my body has lost all will and feeling. I can scarcely move. It's all too late.

"Mary knew?" He is incredulous.

"You didn't think of that? You thought you'd get away with it? Do you know what you've done to her?"

"Mary's strong, she's always been strong. You and she will have more children." In his voice, I can hear the whine of a child who has never considered the possibility that what he's done could be wrong.

"You stole my baby, you broke my wife's heart, you ruined my life."

"But there were reasons! You don't understand. I had to make it right for Pru. She'd already lost a baby and I had to make it up to her. It was my fault in the first place; I had to fix it."

"So you had your finger in that one, too? Oh, Jesus, Nate, I don't even want to know. You're not God—didn't that occur to you? You're not even close."

"But where's the harm? You and Mary, you're the lucky ones. You've got each other!"

"There is no Mary and me anymore. That's gone."

I turn the light on and I walk away and I shine it upward on the wall of diamonds so that the last thing he'll see will be a dazzling. I want him blind when I go. "May you rot in hell, Nate," I say, and it's over.

It doesn't take long to find my way back. At each turn, I demolish the markers we made.

I meet up with the hawk-hunter as planned, and return to Hamhŭng in the jeep alone. I go straight to headquarters and tell my story. About Nate's complaints about the use of napalm and biological warfare, and how when we came across a North Korean patrol, he deserted.

"It takes some of them like that. It's the strangest thing, people you've known all your life, who you'd never think," Dr. Meyer consoles me. Only the interpreter looks at me strangely. I know he doesn't believe me, and I don't fucking care.

15

THE
MAGNETIC
MIND

WINTER 1950-51

He waits in the darkness for the dazzle to fade from his eyes. When it does, he heads straight for the opening, about a third of the way up the wall, that he had spied when Albrecht shone the lantern on it. He is crying. The tears are not for anything he has done—he had only done what he had to—but for the pain he has caused his friends.

It is not his fault. Ever since the arrival of the meteor, when he was a boy—the trail of lights across the heavens leading him to the iron stone—it has not been his fault. The stone was given to him so that he could learn how to use it to make things right. The way things used to be, as in Bill Bone's story, when the Indian Nations prospered, and there was healing of all wounds. With the new stone found, the flow of misfortune would be reversed: there would be an end to sadness, and disease, and death. It does not matter that others don't understand. Everything he has done will be understood, in the end.

He is not alone. He has not been alone since Lily entered his mind and became Explanata. He can feel her small hand in his, and she whispers, "This way, put your hand there, on the wall, lift yourself up." He climbs slowly, the cold texture of the limestone, its scrawled record of fossil life, under his palms; always waiting for guidance, knowing, beyond the shadow of a doubt, that she will take him where he needs to go, as she always has. The pain in his hands does not matter; if there is blood, it does not matter.

Explanata. The name is a current running through him. He understands that this current is the same thing as life. When it began, so did his life; when it ends, he will die. Everything that has happened has had a purpose. Everything will become clear. All he has to do is carry on.

His hands reach for and find the runnels of the wall opening. The entrance is smooth, worn by falling water, and dry now in the season between monsoons. He lifts himself up and balances on the edge. He is not blind in the darkness. He is safe, he is being led. He sits in the opening, trying to focus on the small white face partly inside and partly outside his mind, his legs dangling into the nothing on the other side of the wall. Riffles of moist, cold air touch his face. It will be all right—let go. He slips from the edge, adrenaline shocking flintlike sparks into his eyes. He has splashed through a skin of icy water and smashed his knees on the rocks before he knows what has happened, but he is already moving forward toward the glow of the outlet, half swimming, half wading, trying to keep some sort of equilibrium as his heavy feet numbly strike the stream bed. Then he is through, into a large cavern where the darkness has faded to a greenish glow. A stronger light at the far end draws him onward. He pulls himself out of the water. He is in a tunnel about six feet high and three feet wide. Every so often, along its length, there is a small space carved out of the rock, just large enough to house a sleeping man. Blankets, a pile of Chinese soldiers' clothing, the remnants of a fire indicate that the tunnel is in use. He has stumbled into an underground tunnel system being used by the Chinese. As he walks along, he looks around curiously. He has heard of these systems—housing for thousands. Still, he is unprepared when the tunnel suddenly drops and empties into a room roughly ten feet square. When he falls, he cannot get his hands out in front quickly enough to protect himself; he is simply too cold. The soldiers leap up from the table at which they are sitting. One runs forward and raises his rifle butt. Nate hears the sound of it smashing into his skull before he feels the pain. Three, four more times he is beaten, and then the gun goes off. He hears that, too, and the smack of the bullet into the wall.

When he regains consciousness, he is in another place altogether, lying, roughly bandaged, on an earthen floor. He is kicked into full wakefulness, and dragged to his feet. He looks around in confusion. Soldiers. He had learned enough Chinese at the prison camp in Mukden, during the war, to understand them. They push him into a chair, and one of them holds out a paper on which are drawn several flags: American, Canadian, Australian, British. . . . Which one? He points to the Canadian flag. A soldier takes out his bayonet and stabs it again and again into the Stars and Stripes.

Once upon a time, the story goes, in the book that Pietor kept with his belongings, which were all left to me, a Chinese emperor went to Korea in search of the elixir of life. He visited teachers and healers, but none of them could help him. One day, walking in the mountains, he found a small yellow plant that was new to him. He tasted a leaf, and he was still chewing it when he wandered into a cave. Deeper and deeper into the labyrinth he went, until he was lost and could not find his way out. He waited for death, but death would not come. Months went by before he accepted the bitter truth. The plant was the one for which he had searched. He had found eternal life and youth.

Sometimes he is heard. You can hear him singing and crying beneath the earth. His triumph and pain are in the earth you walk.

Nate is screaming. He is in a dark hole just large enough for him to crouch in. Water drips onto his naked back from some source above. The water is cold. He cannot move or stretch. Waiting for the drops to fall, he screams. He does not know that he is screaming.

"Why did you come to Korea?"

"To help Korea."

"Why did you come to Korea?"

"To fight for democracy."

"Why did you come to Korea?"

"To stop Communism."

"Why did you come to Korea?"

"I don't know!"

"You are here as cannon fodder for the Americans. You don't even know why you are fighting."

On the march north, they walk only by night. His head hurts all the time. He is given no medical treatment. After about a week, when he can no longer walk, he is moved across the Chinese border by truck. At the camp, he is put in a house that is being used as a hospital to die, but he does not die. When he is a little better, he is placed in solitary confinement in a hutch made from a dug trench thatched over with grass. It is so small that he cannot lie down. He huddles in the darkness and listens to his heart regulating the flow of his blood.

"You must sign a confession of war crimes."

"I have committed no crimes."

"When you sign, things will get better."

"I will not sign."

At night, his hands and feet are shackled. One morning, they drag him out of the hutch and he is placed in front of a firing squad. The soldiers are ordered to load. They take aim. "Confess your crimes!"

"I have committed no war crimes." He is too tired to lift his head to see his executioners. They do not shoot.

The singing in the cave grows louder. He feels it jolt through his body. The worn truck tires, grinding down to metal, scratch the rough road surface and wail like the rubbed strings of a violin over miles and miles of rock and dirt road. When the blindfold is removed, he blinks. There are mud huts; then a wooden barracks, barbed wire, and sandbags. The all-pervading stink of human excrement. He knows enough now to have some idea of where he is—this place across the Manchurian border. He has been here before during the Second World War; it is not far from Mukden.

He is taken to a room where he is fed soup with fish in it, and then he is left to sleep through several nights in peace. He sleeps, but when he awakens, there is always the noise in his ears—from the head injury, he thinks. Not the singing now, not the strings of a violin, but something deeper and sadder. A humming, as if somebody deep inside him wants to remember what it is like to be human. Explanata? Why am I here?

He looks up as the new interrogator enters the room. He sees a face more or less like the others, of smooth skin between a peaked cap and padded jacket. But it isn't like the others because it is a face that he knows. At Mukden, during the war, when he had been in the POW camp, he had smuggled radio parts from the factory where the POWs worked to a young Chinese. To do this, he had risked death. In return for the parts, the man had given Nate medicine for the POWs and for the women when they had their babies. As his bona fides, the young man had shown Nate a photograph of himself taken with British officers in a Hong Kong mess. He had belonged to the Chinese resistance to the Japanese occupation.

The officer motions the guard away.

"You are a foreign espionage agent. You have attacked an Army of Liberation. Are you ready to talk?"

Nate shakes his head.

"You are wrong and politically ignorant. Here is a confession for you to sign."

"I won't sign it."

"Read it." He hands the paper to Nate. As Nate looks at it, he weeps. He cries frequently. He cries from fear and hunger and confusion. The officer leans near, as if to read over his shoulder, and whispers, "I have not forgotten you, but I can do little for you here. If you stay here, you will probably die of starvation or pneumonia like so many others, but I can have you sent to a work camp in the USSR, in Siberia, where there are still many Second World War prisoners. There is an American consul in Vladivostok. I will get word to him about you. Some of the Americans in the Soviet Union are being released; but you must sign something first."

The humming stops. In the silence, he listens hard for Explanata's guidance. But he knows, he knows! Even before the little voice whispers the words and the scraped violin strings swell into music, a surge of joy rushes through him. Siberia! The prisoners! So that is why he is here! Albrecht had told him how the German POWs were gathered up and taken to Moscow at the end of the war. . . . They were marched back and forth through the streets for two and a half days. At the end of it, those who could still walk, and who had not been too badly injured by the crowds, were moved by train, then by sledge and foot to the farthest reaches of Siberia. They were taken as far east as possible, so far, it was said, that they could see the American flag dancing red, white, and blue on American ships at sea, and smell the American odor of fat beef and chewing gum. . . .

"Yes," whispers Explanata, "you are going to find Gerhard and make everything right. All will turn out well, in the end."

Nate's smiling face is on a Christmas card. He is holding a bottle of beer. Behind him, there is a tree all rigged up with paper chains and ornaments. Stars cut out of tin cans. "Plenty of Food, A Healthy Mind in a Healthy Body, POWs and Families Thank the China Peace Committee." The card is in my pocket when I hear his confession, with the others, on the newsreel. I am holding Mary's hand, squeezing it like a boxer with a ping-pong ball, clinging to it like a life ring in the darkened theater. "I have had a hostile attitude," he says. "I lied about my activities as a foreign espionage agent. I violated the territory of free Korea. I have participated in atomic, biological, and chemical warfare. I am disgusted by the ferocity with which we were hounded on to slaughter the civilian population. The types of warfare I participated in have brought about a revulsion of feeling in me after my capture, when I was treated in a friendly way by the Koreans and the Chinese. I was coward enough to do as I was told. Why are we using barbarous weapons when peace talks go on? When I think of my future, how can I tell my family that I am a criminal? A shower may clean my body, but my soul will never be clean." Nathanial Bone, who I had hoped was safely dead with the other ancients in that Korean cave, faces the camera, his face as bland as a watch or a dish of melting snow.

Back home, I shower and scrub. Mary knocks at the door. "Aren't you ever coming out?" When I do, I hold her because she has come back to me, because I have told her what I know of the truth. I put my tongue deep into her mouth, swallowing my sobs. "It will be all right," she says, at last, "he is being punished."

At Vladivostok, he is taken from the train in shackles and marched to the waterfront. He can only pray that his Chinese friend has kept his word and notified the American consul. He had asked him to mention Gerhard, too—he is so sure of finding him—so that when it is time, they can be freed together. He knows that others have been freed before: during the war, there were the fliers on combat missions against enemy targets in Japan, Manchuria, and the Kurile Islands who landed or crashlanded in Siberia and Kamchatka. They were interned, but were eventually smuggled out through Iran. And there are the priests, swept up at the end of the war accidentally—priests working in Eastern Europe—and sent to the camps, and who have since been released onto American ships sailing from Murmansk and Vladivostok. He is worth an exchange, he thinks. He will not be forgotten. They will want to know what he has seen and why he has done what he has. Explanata has promised him.

Almost happily, he steps on board the four-engined Soviet flying boat that will take him to Magadan on the Sea of Okhotsk. It is only natural that he is paraded with other shackled prisoners to the stockade there. From there, he is taken to an airbase for the long flight west to Yakutsk. Once more, he is put onto a train.

He could, with his dark hair and skin and high flat cheekbones, be from the Soviet East—a Tartar, some descendant of Genghis Khan, instead of a part-Cree from the Canadian prairies. The boxcar is filled with homeless men on their way to lumber camps and mines. The men smoke, drink tea, or vodka if they have it.

They steal from each other and protect their friends. Nate, who has no friends, who is nobody, loses everything within a few hours, even the warm boots and jacket with which he started out. There is straw on the floor, an oil drum for a stove, a bucket for a toilet, and two rows, upper and lower, of plank bunks. He pretends, for his own protection, knowing no Soviet language, to be mute.

From the windows, he can see white and gray forest soil, occasional limestone outcrops, and foothills and valleys virtually buried in the snow-covered ocean of the taiga forest. His hips and back ache from the hard wooden bench. There is ice on the windows and he is always cold. The stench from the frozen toilet makes it almost impossible to eat the mess of potatoes and black bread that is his ration, but by now he has learned to fend for himself. When the train stops, he dashes out with the others to fill a kettle he has devised from a can, and he uses the hot water for washing and for making tea.

They stop to work for a few days at a lumber camp, hauling logs from a partially frozen river, and stacking them. One night, as they bivouac in tents beside the river, they are awakened by a red light illuminating the northern heavens. A fireball is falling toward them down a long rib of sky. It disappears suddenly, right overhead, as if swallowed up by their own open mouths. The sensation of light burning inside him does not go away.

It is dark when they are driven in trucks from the train to the camp. The tundra stretches away on all sides. To the east is a mountain range, to the west is a silhouette of low snowy hills, transparent as settled smoke. The camp has been set up where a copper factory has been built. Once through the main gate, they are left to stand in the freezing cold while officials go through the routine of assigning the laborers to barracks; then they are lined up in the swirling snow and marched away to their quarters. "Almost there," says Explanata. "Have faith." And Nathanial Bone believes.

He sits on the plank bed, arranging his mattress, pillow, and blanket, and putting away the wadded winter clothing he has just been given. It is late, and most of the barrack's inhabitants are sleeping. He is too tired and too excited to sleep. The humming and singing in his head have started up with his fatigue. This is the end of the road; there is nowhere else to go. His last glimpse of the world as a relatively free man, a few hours before, was of barren land dissected by rivers, and stony waves of moraine, frozen by the retreat of a glacier, from which the wind blew a topspray of ice crystals over the tundra. He holds to this vision, although he knows that remembering alone will not take him back to that point of no return.

A fug of sweat, dampness, stale gas, and bad dreams has thickened the air, and the room is trafficked with the half-voiced cries of the dreamers. On the bed across from him, a young woman tends to a dying man, sponging his face and hands with water, sopping up the blood that seeps from his nose as he talks to her, and that gushes with each fresh spasm of his coughing.

Nathanial Bone stands up. It is the girl he recognizes first. Her features, even though changed by the years, are unmistakable. He had sat with her so many times when she was small, watching over her as she slept, listening to her breathe, examining the lines of her face for what it might become. The shock weakens him. There had been no warning of this. Elizabeth! Gerhard must have found her, as Nate had begged him to, watched over her during the war, and taken her with him! Waves of grief and loss and sadness overwhelm him. He sits down again and holds his head in his hands. It isn't until the man on the bed whispers something to the girl, and she gets up and moves far away into the body of the cavernous room, that Nathanial wipes his face dry and permits himself to fully accept that the dying man is Gerhard.

Gerhard's face is so white that it glows, bluish beneath the skin, in the light that is always kept burning low in the barracks. His blond hair has whitened. He is terribly thin. When Nate bends down to him, Gerhard lifts a hand to touch Nate's features. "I knew you would come. I've been waiting. I kept my promise, Nate. I did what you asked. I looked after her. Now it's your turn."

SPRING 1956

The move had taken place with no warning. First they were, as always, in the factory camp. Then—one morning—they were taken by train, and after that by sledge, east and north through the mountains and toward the coal mines near Providenija on the east coast. There were rumors, then, that some of them were to be released and relocated elsewhere. The government in the far-away Kremlin had changed. Nathanial Bone was taken away for an interview, and then Fika was separated from the others, put into an office, and asked where she would like to resettle. She didn't know what to say, so she said somewhere in Yakutia, where her grandmother had come from, and that she would like to study to be a doctor. Nathanial Bone has told her that he is going to be sent home, and that she will go with him in Gerhard's place. He has told her the whole story, filling in the blanks left at Gerhard's death. But she does not believe him. None of the Germans ever leave, and even though she knows she is not German, she had spent her childhood in Germany and she had lived with Gerhard, a German POW, as his daughter.

Nate simply smiles at her. He has belief enough for both of them.

It will all work out.

It is early summer. There are low clouds, and occasional sleet. The temperature hovers around freezing point. The ground is covered with a dense layer of mosses and lichens. When the sun breaks through, as it does frequently, a thick net of mosquitoes ripples up from the tundra and envelops the workers. From where they stoop, picking berries to supplement their diet, they can see the silver line of the sea along the horizon. Every now and then, if they squint, they can just about discern the silhouettes of ships that ply the Bering Strait, following the invisible line of the border between the USSR and Alaska, and calling at friendly ports. The nearest American landfall is on St. Lawrence Island. It is marked on the map that Gerhard had made before he died.

It is evening when the wind picks up. They build small fires against the cold, and shiver in the thin rags of clothing that had seemed thick enough earlier in the day. The wind drops as suddenly as it had risen, and fog rolls across the land from the sea until they can almost hear it singing and sighing as it billows over them. "The trucks will never come now," someone says. "They won't care if we freeze out here. They won't come for us in this." They sit on whatever they can find that is dry, and endure bursts of sleet that nail down hard through windy rents in the fog.

Hours later, after she has shivered herself into sleep, Fika opens her eyes on brilliance. The fog has cleared, and the stars have exploded inwards inside the dome of the sky. They are so near that without thinking, she reaches out a hand to touch them. Light crackles along her skin, sparks dance in the hairs of her forearms and send her heart into a quick ecstasy. She turns her head, and sparks fly from her hair. Light dances all around them, color oscillates from horizon to horizon, a full spectrum of color, shimmering over the heads of everyone sleeping. She watches until the veils fold away, and there is only the solid outer wall of Arctic night.

The trucks come at dawn. Fika and Nathanial Bone are loaded into one on their own. They are driven, not toward the camp with the others, but to the Providenija docks, unloaded there, and left to stand in the rain. Fika's stomach, shriveled with hunger, is a hard knot. There is little to see except the tied-up fishing boats. They are rusted, most of them, with dirty decks and clouded portholes, and surrounded by pools of oily water where they rock. There is no one around. Her fear increases when she catches sight, through the mist, of several larger vessels, slumped at anchor, not far away. It is the kind of place where anything might happen. The engine of a trawler starts up. Nate holds onto her arm as a man emerges from the trawler's hold and jumps down from the deck; he advances across the dock toward them. "Where's the other man?" he asks Nate. He speaks with an American accent.

"She's the one. I told them to tell you it would be a girl. They know all about it."

The man looks upset. "I was told about two men. No one said anything about a girl."

"What does it matter? She was born in Canada. She can't stay here. She has to go home."

The man speaks to the armed Russian who has been standing, all along, behind them. Fika is so used to the presence of a guard that she has forgotten him. "Well," the American asks the Russian, "who is she? Where does she come from?"

"She is German. She came with the German POWs. She has lived in the camps for many years."

"But this man," answers the American, indicating Nate, "says that he knows her."

The Russian shrugs. "Ask him for his proof."

"Ask her!" says Nate. "She'll tell you who she is."

The American looks at Fika suspiciously. "Why are the Russians willing to let you go?" he asks in Russian.

"I have no idea."

"Did you come with the German POWs?" This question is in German.

"Yes, everyone knows that. I was in Germany during the war."

"What do you know about your home in Canada?"

"I know what I've been told about my family. I know the street where my father and mother live. I know where I was born. I have a map."

The American listens to this last answer, given in Fika's accented English. "Where are your other papers? Don't you have anything else? A birth certificate, a memento?" She lifts, from round her neck, a fragment of rock attached to a leather thong.

"There is this."

"What is it?"

"I don't know. I have always had it."

"I gave it to her myself, when she was a baby," says Nate.

The American turns it over. "There is nothing on it. No name, no initials. It's just a piece of stone. It's not evidence." His face hardens. He turns to Nate. "She cannot come. There is no proof that she is who you say she is."

"But she has to come! I made a promise."

"I will not risk the security of the Western world for the sake of your promise. You have caused enough trouble already. You can come, but the girl stays."

Nate turns away. As he does, Fika sees on his face a look of despair and indecision; and she understands, at once, that whatever chance there was for her has been lost. It does not matter. She has never believed. Gerhard has taught her not to believe in anyone but herself.

It takes only a minute. Nate and the American board the trawler, on the deck of which are suddenly other men, taking photographs. The engine races, and they pull away, smashing snub-nosed into the choppy seas, forcing a passage into the other world that must be beyond, through mist and rain.

16

MAGNETIC MARGINS

JUNE 3, 1960

Ancient mountains, with sharp points thrusting above the ice. Cone-shaped mountains, with the same profile as the tents of the Yakuts. Mountains born a hundred thousand years ago and still covered in ice thousands of meters thick from the last ice age. Ice that was the final resting place of mastodons, musk-oxen, and the migrating tribes that hunted whales. Fika did not need to open her eyes to see these mountains. They were always there, whether she slept or was awake, as evident as the hand in front of her face, which she now raised to wipe the mist from her eyes.

There was no middle distance. There was the hand with its

map of lines, and there were miles of ice fields swirling through colors from ivory to deep blue, scattering light like dust in the dustless air. Around the edges, where the dark swam, rising and falling with the pitch of her skiing and each gasp for air, the light flashed in quick spurts of flame, forming a corona at the rim of her vision. She blinked to regain her sight and saw ice again, a dizzying blend of diamond white and blue like a bruise. She closed her eyes, and let the skis run quickly over the flat. . . .

A bitter southwest wind gusted, blowing loose snow and sharp particles of ice into Fika's eyes. She blinked through the snow. She was skiing into a shadow. She could feel its weight on her face. She looked up, and squinted hard against the whiteness that whirled round her. There. It came, and went. Then it stayed. She blinked a dozen times to be sure that it was staying for good, and then knelt down to feel with her hands where the ice turned to gravel.

The shadow crossing the lip edge of ice was made by a mountain on Ellesmere Island. She had reached land.

DEATH AND LIFE: OR THE VANISHING ILLUSION

JULY 1, 1960

It is summertime. Today is Dominion Day, the day we have picnics and set off fireworks; the day of Nathanial Bone's funeral. The ground is still wet from last night's rain and electrical storm. My father stands on the porch next door in his blue and white striped pajamas, running through his repertoire of exercises, neutralizing to counteract the overcharged electric field initiated by the electrical storm, stimulating his receptors by tapping them with the end of a ballpoint pen—brain, thyroid, heart, pelvis, spine, legs, feet—channeling to his personal magnetic pole by turning slowly clockwise, and then counterclockwise, through the four directions. This is a sight I have seen regularly since moving back to the Ross Street house.

Madame Pince-Jones comes out, yawning, to join him. She is dressed in a loose, flowing, red, white, and blue garment, decorated with tiny mirrors. Her hair is wrapped in a turban made from the Red Ensign. She is nothing if not patriotic, although I do not know how her costume will be received by the Rebekahs, with whom she is meant to march in the funeral parade. She waves to me as I set out. When I glance back, they have both assumed the standing, dead-still posture meant to turn every disturbing influence into an idle wave battering hopelessly against a strong wave of calm.

By the time I reach the station, the Churchill train is just drawing in. From habit—Mary is already here—I scan the faces pressed to the windows of the sleeping car, but I do not know any of them. Mary is helping Bella with the flowers. I do not know when she will be returning north. It is not something we have had time to talk about.

I hurry onward to the siding where the circus is gathered, ready to be loaded and to move off right after the service. The hands are busy with the loops and hooks that stabilize the wagons on the flatcars. The waiting elephants and the big cats trumpet and scream their dislike of close confinement. I spot Bill Bone, red-eyed, weary, scratching the armpit under his stump, but dressed, in deference to the occasion, in a blue suit. He and Mildred Lark, who wears a tuxedo, supervise the set-up for the disposition of the cats onto the train. They will run the animals through a cloth tunnel strung over a steel plank bridge between the transport trucks and the railcars.

Mary comes up behind me and puts her hand on my shoulder. "We finished early," she says. We both watch the boy helping to place the tunnel frame. He is Pru and Charlie's ten-year-old son, Gerry, named after my twin brother, Gerhard. "He's beautiful," says Mary. The boy glances up and catches sight of "Aunty Mary and Uncle Albrecht." He waves, and we wave back. We watch for another minute, cold and fire squeezing our vitals, until Bill sends Gerry away to work in the feed car.

Mildred Lark calls out to us. "Don't wait for us, you folks go on ahead. We'll be right along." She makes a small hexing sign—the one she uses to render wild animals safe—and we back off. It is clear that Bill has taken Nate's death hard. "I'm a shell of myself, I'm a fuckin' old engine with no spare parts," he'd said in the night when he'd phoned. "I should have been there, I could have done something." Bill was, and is, drunk as a skunk. It makes no difference to how he handles the cats—he can do that in his sleep— but if he had a rifle, he'd be waiting to see the whites of our eyes. He throws a baleful glance our way, and I can feel the raw meanness in it. *Who's responsible? Is it you? Is it your fault my son's dead? It's somebody's fault, you fuckers.*

Mildred edges nearer, leaving Bill to urge the first of the tigers into the tunnel. "Don't worry. I'll get him there, there's plenty of time." I hold a thin yellow paper out to her.

"What is it?" She takes it from my hand. "Oh." It is the "good luck" telegram I had found on Nate's body. I don't know what I can say. "Didn't do him much good, did it?" she says with a sigh.

She takes the gum from her mouth and rolls it in a handy slip of waxed paper from her pocket. "I don't believe in luck, myself. When your number's up, it's up. I don't think I'll mind dying— I've come close enough times—but I hate to see suffering." She looks Bill over as if he is a small arithmetical problem. Mildred Lark is at the end of her tether. I wouldn't want her in charge of my old folks home.

"Give it to him later, Mildred. Tell him it meant a lot. Nate had it in his boot when he died."

Low rays of sunlight skitter along the main railway line, skipping hot metal coins as a lava-black engine pushes coal cars by. We walk through the cool blocks of shadow cast by the cars, and into and through the station. Mary is holding my hand.

In the street, the procession is already forming up. There are Shriners on tricycles, sounding rubber-bulbed horns, pedaling furiously, harem trousers billowing, fez tassels swinging, shunting people into line: the Winnipeg Strikers, led by Sweets Christmas; the rest of the Blue and Red All-Stars; reporters and photographers; the mayor of the city, once the boy Nate had saved from the charging elephant, Queenie; the Ban the Bomb organization to which I belong; Mary's Technocracy friends. The Odd Fellows and Rebekahs, grouped in their local branches, all of them wearing ceremonial chains and jewels in Nate's honor, gather behind a banner showing the three links of 'Friendship, Love, and Truth.'

"We could tell them a thing or two, eh, Mary?"

"He's dead, Albrecht. What does it matter?"

I glimpse my father being steered into place by Madame Pince-Jones. A small knot of Magnetists, who regularly attend his lectures in Pince-Jones's salon, stand close to him. He aligns them carefully, according to their energy patterns, struggling to keep aloft the sign he carries:

> *Personal Magnetism*
> *It Takes a Brain that is Wrong*
> *and*
> *Makes It Right*

I feel tears pricking my eyes. "Don't speak ill of the dead, is that it? But I forget, you and he were such good friends, despite everything."

"You were, too, Albrecht," she admonishes gently. "You loved him, too." And she quotes, "*And we were mutual Elements to us. And made of one another.*" Mary astonishing me.

"Albrecht!" calls my mother. I turn away, not wanting her to know I've been crying. "Someone is here to see you! She has something to tell us!" My mother is excited, red spots sting her dry, pale cheeks. A tail of orphans strings out behind her, winding and curling, with Bella Bone at one edge, trying to straighten them out. Madame Pince-Jones suddenly pushes in front of my mother—I wonder if the Rebekahs have turned her away—and thrusts a brochure into my hands—*Consultations in Absolute Confidence*—and then is gone. I bend my head, my hand shielding my wet eyes to read:

> *She whose eyes have felt the touch of spirit-land*
> *Looks through the door that has no key*
> *And in strong fingers takes the scroll*
> *Of your poor life and reads*
> *The secret symbols of your earth-bound soul,*
> *Finds wasted days, God's lilies with Life's weeds.*

A young woman, appearing frail and dreadfully tired, stands before me. "You are Gerhard's brother?" She speaks with an accent I can't place. "You must be, you are so like him." I look at her, knowing I have seen her, or someone like her, before, and I have a feeling of something about to happen, pins and needles of the brain, and at the same time I know it doesn't matter, there is no forever.

Mary squeezes my hand to dust. She knows there is no forever, too.

ACKNOWLEDGMENTS

EPIGRAPHS

Appleyard, Bryan. In a review (*The Sunday Times*, October, 1991) of *Powers of Darkness, Powers of Light* by John Cornwell. London: Viking, 1991.

Gray, Alasdair. *Lanark*. Edinburgh: Canongate Publishing, 1981.

Plato. Speaking of Socrates, as found in *The Collected Dialogues*. Edited by Edith Hamilton and Huntington Cairns. Bollingen Series LXXI. Princeton, New Jersey: Princeton University Press, 1980.

Wilde, Oscar. From *The Picture of Dorian Gray*, but as found in *Confessions: Memoirs of a Modern Seer* by "Cheiro." London: Jarrolds, 1934.

Yourcenar, Marguerite. *The Abyss*. London: Black Swan Press, 1985.

QUOTATIONS
WITHIN CHAPTERS

Chapter One: "Let him at least note/ That my heart was bloody young/ That strong, like fear, was my will to live/ Strong and crazed/ Like my final day." (Leyb Kvitko) Found in *Russia: A History of the Soviet Period* by Woodford McClellan, Prentice Hall, New Jersey, 1986.

Chapter Three: "You will never be alive again/ Never rise from the snow." (Anna Akhmatova) Found in *A History of Russia* by Nicholas Riasanovsky, Oxford University Press, Oxford/New York, 1993.

Chapter Five: "Enough of living by the law/ Given by Adam and Eve/ The jade of history we will ride to death/ Left! Left! Left!" (Maiakovsky) Found in *A History of Russia* by Nicholas Riasanovsky, Oxford University Press, Oxford/New York, 1993.

Epilogue: "And we were mutual Elements" (John Donne). This is an incomplete quotation.
"A palmist if you will, yet lay your hand/ But for one moment in his own, and he/ Whose eyes have felt the touch of spirit-land/ Looks through the door that has no key." (Anonymous) Found in and adapted from *Confessions: Memoirs of a Modern Seer* by "Cheiro", Jarrolds, London, 1934.

I also wish to acknowledge contributions from *Korea: Canada's Forgotten War* by John Melady, Macmillan, Toronto, 1983; *Deadly Allies: Canada's Secret War 1937-1947* by John Bryden, McClelland & Stewart, Toronto, 1989; and from *Born to Be*

Magnetic by Frances Nixon, Magnetic Publishers, Chemainus, B.C., 1971.

Many friends, family members, professionals and kind strangers helped me in researching and forming the background to this book.

To Lorna Berg, Gilbert Comeau, Lois Howard, Gordie Hunter, Bud Korchak, Vince Leah, Jack Matheson, Kevin O'Donovan, Keith Pearce, Dr. C.B. Schoemperlen, and Bud and Hazel Tinsley, I offer my apologies for failing to write what I had planned, and my thanks for what you gave me of the time and place that animates *Visible Worlds*.

My love and thanks to Marian and Gordon Grist for their support in Winnipeg, and to Liz Lochhead for an enlightening conversation.

Roxana Argast, Thelma Bowering, Rick Bowering, and my mother, Elnora Bowering, gave me access to letters and materials important to the story. Uncle Mel, and my father, Herbert Bowering, kept on telling me *their* stories, and my brother, David, let me probe his memory. To all of you, my heartfelt thanks.

Other important information was generously made available to me by Elizabeth Woodworth and Dr. Tim Johnstone.

I would also like to acknowledge Marnie Swanson and the University of Victoria Library, Polar Books, and the English department of Memorial University of Newfoundland where I was writer-in-residence during a needed writing period: you gave me support at various times and in various ways, and contributed greatly to the completion of this book.

My agent, Jan Whitford, and editor, Ed Carson, were, as

ever, long-suffering and encouraging. Thanks to Ed, especially, for never being less than enthusiastic.

To Michael, with love: it was a long journey from Sooke to Seville and back.

To Xan: I promise that one day I will resurrect Mr. Boo.

And to all the writers on magnetism whose books gave me much pleasure: Perfect Health of the Body, Perfect Health of the Brain.